Originally from the West Midlands, Rhiannon Barnsley currently lives in London with her husband and her cat Salem. She's a corporate lawyer by day and writes after work and during weekends.

Rhiannon is a Faber Academy Writing a Novel graduate and loves to write dark and twisty thrillers with a particular focus on women. When she's not writing, she can often be found reading or training with her cheerleading team.

instagram.com/authorrhiannonbarnsley
x.com/RhiBarnsley
tiktok.com/@rhiannonbarnsley

Also by Rhiannon Barnsley

The Clique

SLANDER

RHIANNON BARNSLEY

One More Chapter
a division of HarperCollins*Publishers* Ltd
1 London Bridge Street
London SE1 9GF
www.harpercollins.co.uk
HarperCollins*Publishers*
Macken House, 39/40 Mayor Street Upper,
Dublin 1, D01 C9W8, Ireland

This paperback edition 2025
1
First published in Great Britain in ebook format
by HarperCollins*Publishers* 2025
Copyright © Rhiannon Barnsley 2025
Rhiannon Barnsley asserts the moral right to be identified
as the author of this work

A catalogue record of this book is available from the British Library

ISBN: 978-0-00-864617-2

Printed and bound in the UK using 100% Renewable Electricity
by CPI Group (UK) Ltd

For Tom, for being my biggest fan

'Stronger than lover's love is lover's hate. Incurable, in each, the wounds they make.'

Euripides

HotCelebGossip!

22 January 2024 by Daniella Swan

Ethan Simmons and Tori Scott: Everything you need to know about the wedding of the year!

Here at *HotCelebGossip!* we love a summer wedding, but especially when it includes two of our favourite celebrities. Ethan Simmons and Tori Scott are Hollywood's hottest couple at the moment. It's been a whirlwind romance for the two who met when Tori was over in America working on her new solo album. The lovebirds met at a party thrown by singer Alexx.a at her California mansion to celebrate her new single 'A Girl has Gotta Lie'. According to attendees, it was love at first sight for the pair. Alexx.a, who belongs to the same record label as Tori, introduced her to Ethan after she met the actor when she found out she would be singing the theme tune for the first movie in the *Aces & Diamonds* series (based on the popular books by young adult author Zara Ryan).

Hunk Ethan hadn't been pinned down to any one girl since his catapult to fame playing swoon-worthy male lead Leo Trax, after the books went viral on TikTok. When Ethan was cast, he became an overnight sensation.

But Ethan is said to have finally found his match and has fallen head over heels for Tori already. Apparently the two spent the entire night in each other's company and some say they were spotted smooching in the corner before leaving the party together.

We called it here first at *HotCelebGossip!* after they were spotted at brunch the next day. The two denied dating at first, but we knew these two lovers wouldn't be able to hide their affection for long.

A year after meeting, Ethan proposed to Tori during a romantic sun-soaked vacation to the paradise island of Mauritius. Ethan hired a string quartet to play by candlelight as he proposed on the beach during golden hour. It was the proposal of the century!

We've heard from sources that everybody is dying to attend the wedding of the year. Ethan and Tori have chosen to have a weekend of celebrations in Fiji. Tori is set to have an entire wardrobe of wedding looks designed exclusively by Dior and *HotCelebGossip!* has been granted exclusive access to the wedding. Look out for our June issue, where we will share exclusive photos and stories from the day. You won't find this anywhere else.

Ethan Simmons and Tori Scott: THE Wedding of the Year

Here at *HotCelebGossip!* we were lucky enough to be granted exclusive access to the beach wedding of Ethan and Tori Simmons. Inside this week's magazine you will find 28 pages of exclusive photographs from the event. If you head to our website, you'll find videos, including mini-interviews with some of the guests and even some words from the happy couple themselves!

You'll be able to spot more than a few famous faces in there! Ethan's co-stars from the *Aces & Diamonds* series were in attendance, including the very glamorous Nikki Feldman who wore a custom red Dior dress to the sandy affair. Singer Alexx.a, credited as the one who brought the duo together, was also in attendance in a two-piece with a low-cut pink blazer and matching trousers.

Tori's former bandmate from her 00s pop group days and long-time bestie Shelley Frank was by Tori's side all day as maid of honour. The couple went for a classic ocean-blue colour scheme to match their surroundings.

The entire weekend was sun-soaked and the couple had spent the two weeks leading up to their wedding on the paradise island topping up their tans and making sure everything was in order. It clearly paid off because the day went without a hitch and the couple looked like supermodels as they tied the knot on the beach.

Tori spoke about her pre-wedding diet and exercise regime to make sure she was in top shape for her wedding. She told us she was following a strict regime of no carbs after 2pm and reformer Pilates six days a week. We can certainly say it paid off as Tori displayed an enviable figure as she swayed down the aisle.

We asked the lucky couple about what's next and they revealed they are heading off on a month-long honeymoon. Following their honeymoon, the couple has a big decision about where to settle. Tori is a London girl whereas Ethan was born in Texas but currently lives in L.A when he's not filming for the *Aces & Diamonds* films. Ethan told us that after the honeymoon, he would soon start shooting for the second film in the series based on the smash hit books.

We asked if there were any plans for children but the two are keeping tight-lipped for now.

We wish the happy couple a world of happiness. We know true love when we see it!

HotCelebGossip!
30 August 2024 by Daniella Swan

Trouble in paradise for lovebirds Ethan and Tori

We are devastated to report that there is trouble in paradise for *HotCelebGossip!*'s favourite couple, Tori and Ethan Simmons. It was only a couple of months ago that the couple wed and we revealed our exclusive snaps from their wholesome day. However, the celeb world has been shaken, as an inside source tells us that the pair are having crisis talks as their relationship is in turmoil.

Someone close to the couple claims that Tori suspects Ethan of infidelity while he has been in Vancouver filming the second film in the *Aces & Diamonds franchise*. We've heard that Tori has given Ethan an ultimatum – that he has to move to London to be with her or she will call time on their marriage. Ethan is said to be trying to rearrange his filming schedule to save his marriage.

We wonder who the mystery girl could be. A source inside Ethan's camp has revealed he has been spending a lot of time with his glamorous co-star Nikki Feldman. The two have been spotted hanging out and the photos taken by our photographer (see page six) show that they look more than just friends to us.

Our hearts are breaking for Tori after they were so loved up. Fans have taken to social media to support the singer in this difficult time. Our love goes out to Tori.

An anonymous source close to Tori told us that she is struggling with the gossip around Nikki and Ethan. They say that Tori has always struggled with the fact that she and Ethan have often had a long-distance relationship due to their different work projects.

Apparently the topic of children is a sticky subject for the pair. We hear that Tori is ready to start a family and wants nothing more than to be a mum, whereas Ethan is said to want to delay having children for several years.

Whatever the issues are, we hope the couple can work past them.

HotCelebGossip!
6 April 2025 by Daniella Swan

Ethan v Tori: The hottest trial of the year!

We were so sad to bring you news recently that one of our favourite a-list couples has been feuding but we've just learnt that the couple's rocky relationship has taken a dramatic new turn. We are going to court! Get your formal wear ready.

Things seemed to go from bad to worse with Ethan and Tori after Ethan lost his role as male lead in the *Aces & Diamonds* series. He was replaced by hottie Shaun Henderson in what the director told press was a "change in direction" for the series. Many expressed outrage that Ethan was replaced after already starting to film the second instalment.

Sources said at the time that Ethan blamed Tori for him losing his job although Ethan never went on the record about it. However, Ethan's latest shock move, suing Tori for "loss of potential earnings and reputational damage", makes those sources' allegations even more credible.

Ethan is suing Tori for over £55 million for defamation. He alleges that Tori lied about his cheating which led to him losing the contract for the film series. Ethan has not filmed anything since and his acting career has dried up.

Meanwhile Tori is apparently counter-suing Ethan, claiming that his allegation that she is a liar has damaged *her* career. You couldn't make this stuff up. This is not the first celebrity defamation trial we've even seen this year, with more cropping up. A lesson for us all to be careful about what we say!

The trial is set for June 2025 and is scheduled to last for a week. It's not only going to be the temperature outside that will be hot. In a UK-first, the trial will be livestreamed as part of a trial run after the US has had public praise following its livestreamed trials, particularly celebrity defamation trials. We cannot think of a better subject to act as a guinea pig – we can't wait to hear all the saucy details of Ethan and Tori's relationship played out in court. We also know that the outfits of both parties will be to die for.

HotCelebGossip! will be watching the entire trial and publishing content every day. Our Instagram feed will have constant commentary, and on TikTok we will be collaborating with influencers to talk about their latest reactions to the events and scandals that emerge.

Whose side are you going to be on, Ethan or Tori's? Who do you believe? Do you believe Ethan is telling the truth #ExonerateEthan and Tori was lying when she said he was a cheater #ToriTellsTales?

Or do you think Ethan did cheat on his wife and is suing to cover that up "allegedly"? Are you team #TrustTori and #ExposeEthan?

Time will tell, but we can't wait to see this one unfold. Look out for our 1 June 2025 issue where we will tell you everything you need to know about the trial of the year.

Before The Trial

Chapter One

@THETRUTHISGREY

I hate this photograph of my dead sister. It sounds ridiculous how much it bothers me given everything else, but every time I see it, all I can think about is what happened to her, where she is now. I probably shouldn't use the word 'dead'; after all, my sister could still be alive. What is the proper term? Is it 'missing, presumed dead'? When is the line crossed between someone being missing and when everyone gives up hope and assumes they are gone for ever? I constantly flit between thinking she's gone forever and moments of hope. My brain tells me to give up, to stop searching, but my heart can't. It's only been a few months since she vanished, but whenever anybody talks to me about my sister, they look at me with pity if I suggest there's still a chance she could come home. They give me condescending renditions of 'oh, Riley' and purse their lips.

And those pitiful looks are one of the worst parts, but not as bad as this photo. Everyone uses it. The newspapers, the TikTokers who report on my sister's case. They all seem to use the same one, as if no other photos were ever taken of my sister, when I know there are hundreds on her social media – she loved the camera and it loved her back. There's probably hundreds on her old Myspace account although they aren't the type she'd want plastered everywhere – she'd be mortified if she came back and saw those grainy photographs all over the internet. But they always use this one. I don't know if it's pure laziness or if there's something about this photograph that they think will elicit some sort of emotional response. She does look beautiful here, but that's not unusual.

This photograph in particular doesn't look like Alice, which makes no sense if they are trying to encourage people to report sightings. It's taken at a weird angle and she's a brunette, which is odd because Alice had been getting her hair bleached every eight weeks for most of her adult life, although she somehow still had healthier and longer hair than anyone I've ever met. They must have found the one photo from the few weeks Alice decided to strip her hair back to her natural colour on a whim, before deeply regretting it and booking a salon appointment.

It's from when she was a student, so a good several years before she went missing. I think I took this when I went to visit her in Exeter. She was showing me around the town and we'd just stopped for some lunch. Alice made me go to a place called Nando's that she kept raving about. Apparently all the English kids go there regularly. I wish I'd visited her more in England. I was always worried about money but now I regret using that as a reason to stay away.

I flick through the articles on my phone recounting my sister's disappearance. It's a sadistic ritual but at least once a week I undertake an extensive search to uncover if anything new has been published since I last checked. When she first disappeared, there were new articles and videos all the time and I was addicted to reading each one. I had to devour every single bit of information relating to Alice's disappearance. Lately though, I don't find anything new when I look so instead I re-read everything over and over. I'm sure I could recite some of the articles. I worry that if I stop this routine, I'll miss something and only have myself to blame for her not coming home.

The cops in England still have no leads on what happened to Alice. I've never understood it – how can someone vanish in a city full of cameras and people? I've always thought something didn't add up. I've often suspected some sort of cover-up. According to the official story, Alice was last seen entering Mill Hill East underground station and never seen again.

The only theory the cops had was that she may have been the victim of a serial killer. Another woman of a similar age to Alice had gone missing two months prior. She also disappeared after entering the tube network. They thought perhaps somebody had found blind spots in CCTV networks and was ambushing these girls somehow and quickly luring them into a vehicle. I remember her name almost as well as Alice's: Matilda. She has also never been found. The trail went cold for both girls, and they both became a statistic, a number, another warning to women about the dangers of the world.

I stayed optimistic for the first month, but as the months have ticked by, it's been harder to keep that hope alive. Sometimes when people ask me if I have a sister, I struggle to answer. How do I explain that I have a sister but I don't know where she is? I have to have hope, it's all I have left. But I'm starting to wonder if I even have that anymore. Maybe all that's left is the emptiness and a gaping hole in my life that can never be filled.

Because Alice isn't just my sister. She's my twin. We aren't separate people but two halves of one person. One soul that happened to be divided between two bodies. With her no longer here, that half has disappeared and all that's left is the shards broken into so many unique fragments that they can never be put back together. There's not enough glue in the world to fix it.

In some ways, our family was lucky that the news loved her story. The world is obsessed with twins and the fact that one twin had disappeared without a trace was clickbait for the masses. It meant more attention on Alice's case. More people trying to find her. Everybody wanted to interview me and compare me to Alice but the comparisons were always unfavourable. Although we are identical twins, Alice is petite and striking. I cut my hair short, dye it bright colours and have piercings and tattoos. We don't look alike, not like when we were younger. I'm much better behind the camera than in front of it, so the media quickly grew tired of me.

One stand-out moment since her disappearance was when a psychic begged my family to go on her show because she was convinced I could use my twin 'telepathy' connection to find out where Alice was. I fell for the rhetoric and ended up feeling humiliated when it didn't work. But I think the part I struggle the most with is the conspiracy theories put forward by the armchair detectives that insist they know about Alice and know about me. There are people who genuinely believe I'm actually Alice and killed Riley to steal her life. If people knew anything about us they'd know that Alice was the one with the life to envy, not me. Nobody has ever wanted to be Riley Grey.

The disastrous investigation is why I became a true crime TikToker. I started by posting about Alice's disappearance, talking to people about leads I thought the police weren't following up. I included my own theories and evidence I'd uncovered. I did initially get a warning about interfering in the investigation but the cops quickly lost interest, especially when I moved back to the US.

I gained more followers than I predicted but things stalled after that first month. The day she was reported missing, she was all over the English news websites, on the homepage. One website had a live blog. Her disappearance didn't make the news in the US but as she went missing in England, I told myself that was what mattered. They weren't going to find her here. On the second day they were still covering the case. By the end of the week somebody else had gone missing and they'd moved on to posting about them. The sad reality is that people go missing in big cities like London all the time and so many are never found. My TikTok account was originally focused solely on Alice but viewers quickly tired of seeing the same content consistently especially as I had nothing new to report. So I started reporting on other disappearances. I started with Matilda's and noticed more engagement. Unfortunately, there was no shortage of missing people to report on so I was never lacking content. I started with disappearances in London, since that's where Alice was last seen but I started talking about US cases too to grow my audience.

I had a modest number of followers but not enough. All I cared about was getting more. Every new person was a new opportunity, a new chance that perhaps they would help me, that they knew something. I started posting every day to maximise engagement. I left my job as a video editor so I had the time to properly dedicate myself to this new pursuit. I started varying my content to include other crimes which helped, but the thing that really made the difference was when I started reporting on celebrity cases. It started with the usual – DUIs, assaults on photographers and now the flavour of the season seems to be defamation cases. People love a downfall. People began messaging with possible sightings of Alice and leads, drawn to my channel by the celeb lure. None of them have panned out, yet. And I'm sure most of them are just trolling but one day that might change.

There's no new content to consume about my sister, the macabre ritual complete once more. I have some content to post for TikTok anyway. I position my phone in the centre of my ring light and turn the front facing camera on so I can check my set-up looks okay. I take my videos in front of a green screen usually so I can post screenshots or photos over my background. It's hard to believe this is my life when Alice was the one who loved being in front of the camera. I wonder what she'd think if she could see me now.

The past week I've been reporting on a celebrity DUI court case. The model has been arrested twice before for driving while drunk – it's always after she's attended a party and is trying to take herself home. Luckily she's never hurt anyone but there's been speculation all week that they are going to make an example of her and give her jail time. The judgement is due out any minute now and I'm going live on TikTok to give my reaction to the news. People love it when you go 'live' – it makes the viewer feel like they are in the same room as you, having a conversation.

I refresh my other phone waiting for the news to come in. I have two phones – one for filming and another so I can check facts and figures while I'm on camera. I refresh the page, still nothing. I won't push the button to start until I have the judgement. I want to be the first to report on it. I refresh again and the news is there at the top of the page. She's been sentenced to 200 hours of community service and a six-month suspended sentence. I read the article as quickly as I can, trying to digest it all so I don't give out wrong information. People value facts on TikTok. You also have to be careful – you don't want your words being used against you.

'Hi everyone, so the news is just in, the model Emily Ross has received 200 hours of community service for her latest arrest for drunk driving and a six-month suspended sentence. Although I've heard rumours that it wasn't just alcohol in her system if you catch my drift.'

I have to be careful what I say. It's well known that Emily has a drug problem but I'd be straying into dangerous territory if I started calling her a drug user – I don't want to be sued.

'It's the third time Emily has been arrested for this crime in the last year. It's a miracle she hasn't hurt anybody. The sentence seems super lenient to me – if she wasn't a celebrity and the daughter of famous rapper Nate D.R. then she definitely would've been doing time. Maybe somebody has been pulling some strings, but one thing is for sure, she's going to have to be on her best behaviour for the next six months. I'm not sure our girl Emily would cope with being inside.'

I pause, reading the comments of the people watching so I can gauge which side they are leaning towards so I can agree with the majority. It's always good to have the odd controversial opinion but if you want to be successful on this platform you need to follow the masses.

'What do you all think? Do you agree with me?'

I pause for effect.

'Yes, I see lots of comments here about how the result is unexpected. One person says they think because the only harm was to the car that the judge didn't want to put her away. Another says three arrests clearly shows she doesn't care about consequences. I agree, Emily never seems to care about her arrests. Some celebs apparently see it as a rite of passage.'

I continue with the livestream for a few minutes, interacting with viewers and talking about the case. It isn't one of the most interesting cases I've covered but Emily is one of the 'it girls' of the moment so people crave news about her.

'Okay I'm going to end the livestream here but look out for my video later this evening with a summary of the case and the judgement. As always, if you have any ideas for celebrity court cases or even true crime that you think I should report on, do inbox me. Also please follow if you don't already and check out my pinned videos. And remember, the truth is always grey.'

I end the livestream and remove my phone from its placeholder, switching off the harsh ring light. 'The Truth is always Grey' became a slogan I always end my videos with because of my surname – Grey. I can't remember how or why I started using it but it stuck and it does well to have a memorable brand. The pinned videos on my account are some of my videos about Alice's disappearance. TikTok lets you choose videos to 'pin' to the top of your account page so they are the first thing any user sees when viewing your profile. I always direct people to them at the end of any video. It only takes one person to view those videos for everything to change.

I check my inbox. It's usual after any livestream to get a flurry of messages. I try to check each one but it can be time-consuming. Some are short messages from fans saying they love my content. Some have ideas for new cases they want me to report on. Sometimes I report on cold cases too. Usually if somebody requests something, I'll do it because I know there's at least one person who wants to see that type of content and variety is a good thing.

There's one message that is different in tone than any of the others.

@thetruthisblackandwhite2011
You need to report on the Ethan and Tori Simmons defamation trial. It's important that you do.

@thetruthisblackandwhite2011
It will be more enlightening than you
realise.

I was already planning to report on the Simmons trial as it's all anyone is talking about – a goldmine for content. Ethan used to be Hollywood's golden boy before the director of the *Aces & Diamonds* series dropped him. The series is one of BookTok's obsessions – people used to host masquerade balls based on the series and dream cast the characters. There's countless fan art based on the male lead and a multitude of fanfiction stories cropping up. I don't even read very much but the videos have infiltrated my 'For You' page.

Tori's music career hasn't really taken off in the US but her whirlwind romance with Ethan has always kept her in the magazines and relevant over here. She was in a semi-successful girl group in the early noughties and I know some of their songs even if they never managed to 'break' America. The trial is in England so I wasn't planning to fly over or anything. Usually with the US cases I try and go to court at least for some of the trial as nothing beats footage captured of the celebrities arriving and leaving, but England only brings up bad memories for me. I'd rather watch from the comfort of my couch.

@thetruthisgrey
Hey, thanks for your message. I will be
covering the trial.

@thetruthisblackandwhite2011
You need to go in person.

@thetruthisgrey
I wasn't planning to I'm afraid but I'll
have tons of content and will be
livestreaming every day!

@thetruthisblackandwhite2011
You need to go. It'll help you find out
what happened to your sister.

I pause. This is probably a cruel joke. There was a time where I would've dropped everything and gone to England based on a hunch but I've become hardened after constant crushing disappointment. Some people find it entertaining to give me false hope.

@thetruthisgrey
I'm sorry. I don't know if this is a joke or if
you mean well but I can't just drop
everything to go to London.

There's nothing for me in London. Not anymore.

@thetruthisblackandwhite2011
Don't you want to find out what
happened to Alice in Wonderland?

Alice in Wonderland. It's what I always called my sister when we were younger and it stuck. My special nickname for her. We'd seen the movie and I called her that because her name was Alice and she had long blonde hair. She used to call me Mad Hatter for no real reason other than she knew it annoyed me. I know that I've never used that nickname on this channel – it's one thing I always kept to myself. I never told anyone, except our parents who knew as they'd overhear us using the nicknames. How can this person know my nickname for Alice? Is it a lucky guess? It has to be a coincidence and it's not enough for me to fly out.

Before I close the app I get another message, as if the user of the account can sense my hesitation and knows they need a greater lure to get me to London.

It's a photograph. I click to enlarge. A selfie taken of my sister with none other than Ethan Simmons, she's kissing his cheek so her head is slightly turned to the camera but I can see enough of her face to tell it's her.

@thetruthisblackandwhite2011
Don't be late. It's a very important date.

APPEAL FOR MISSING LONDON WOMAN
AS CONCERN GROWS

22 November 2024 16:34
Editor: Jane Cunningham

An appeal has been made to find Alice Grey, 31, who has been reported missing by her flatmate after failing to come home.

Police have launched an urgent appeal to find her. Alice was last seen on CCTV entering Mill Hill East tube station, in the late hours of 20 November. The Met Police said, 'We are very worried about Alice's welfare. We understand she has not been in contact with her family or friends since 20 November and this is very out of character for her.'

Alice is described as five foot two with a small build and long blonde hair. She was last seen wearing a black dress with a black leather jacket and heeled ankle boots.

Anyone with any information is asked to call the police on 101 or Tweet @MetCC and quote MISSPER20241120. To report information anonymously, contact the independent charity Crimestoppers on 0800 555 111 or visit crimestoppers-uk.org.

Transcript of TikTok Video uploaded by user @thetruthisgrey on 24 November 2024 at 7.32pm:

Hi. This feels weird. I'm not used to this app but apparently since Covid this is where everybody is. I need help finding my sister. She's been missing since 20 November. She went missing in London and I'm really worried about her. Her name is Alice Grey and she has long blonde hair and is short and thin. She looks a bit like me if you imagined I had blonde hair and no nose piercing. We're identical twins. She lives in Mill Hill East and was apparently last seen going into the station. I don't live around London as you can probably tell from my accent. Can everyone please keep an eye out for her?

Comments:

@ellen_rose99
You should add photos of your sister to the video so we know what she looks like. Just a thought x

@Steven.Even112
London is a big place … you need to be more specific if you want people to help.

@lewis_mufc_2000
Harsh much.

@Steven.Ellen112
Didn't mean to be. Just trying to help.

@SashaaaSha
I agree. You should add photos. There are tutorials online.

Okay I'm trying this again. A few of you said I should add photos to my video about my missing sister because it would be more helpful. I had to watch a few video tutorials to work out how to do it, but I think I've managed it. I've put a few photos of my sister behind me. The one the media is using doesn't look like her anymore; it's quite old. I'm not sure why they are using it. These are all recent ones I took off Instagram and some which she sent me privately. One person commented that I needed to be more specific than Mill Hill East but that's the only information that I have. As soon as I know anything more I'll post another video. Thank you to everyone who followed me and is trying to help on this journey. I'm so lost.

Comments:

@startrightnow29
So sorry to hear about what is
happening. I hope you find her soon.

@Alex_ontrees
Not another missing person case 🙁
What is happening in London right now?
So many people going missing…

@truecrimepodcastOG
Hey, are you ok with me posting about
Alice on my account? I can try and get
some more attention for you.

Chapter Two

VICTORIA 'TORI' SIMMONS

It's the crowding that is the worst. Too many people swarming around me, sticking a camera in my face like I'm some sort of caged animal at a zoo just to get a photo that they can use to humiliate me, that people online will jeer at; they'll call me names and insult every aspect of my appearance to make themselves feel better. Too thin. Too short. Too fat. Too tall. How is it possible to be all those things at once? I've had the plastic surgery, the Botox and the fillers, thinking it would stop them finding flaws to dissect, but it's still not good enough.

I should be used to it after being in the public eye for so long but I've never experienced attention like this. This type of desperation, it's frightening as it feels like they'll do anything to get what they need. They shout my name like I'm a dog that will come when called. I may be a bitch but that's not the way to get my attention…

'Tori, Tori, over here. How do you feel about the trial?'

'Tori, do you think you'll win? What are your chances?'

'Are you and Ethan going to stay married? Are you getting a divorce?'

'Are you just doing this for attention? Is this trial just for publicity?'

'Tori, is your new single about Ethan?'

I'm drowning inside a sea of photographers and journalists and I can feel myself going under, sinking into the abyss as they chant my name over and over like the song of a siren luring me to my demise. I want – *need* – to scream to block them all out but I can't breathe properly as they're pressing against my chest. It tightens, and it feels like a fist is gripping my heart and squeezing hard, depriving me of oxygen. My thoughts are no longer my own and my feet seem to slip from underneath me. I brace myself for impact when a firm hand grips my own and tugs me into to a taxi. I escape, this time.

'Tori has no comment on either the trial or her relationship with Ethan at this time and would appreciate it if you could respect her privacy.'

My agent, Jessika, slams the door shut. The men outside don't stop shouting as if they have some sort of entitlement to poke and prod me. All I ever wanted to do was sing. I didn't sign up for this. At least now I have my own space. These people are vultures, hungry.

'Bloody journos. They get worse every time. There's no ethics these days. All willing to do whatever it takes just for a quick payday. Can you take us to Chancery Lane, please?' she asks the taxi driver.

Jessika tucks behind her ears the black strands of hair that have fallen out of her neat bun as she swipes across her iPad. She's obsessed with that thing.

'So, how do you think the interview went?' she asks.

Good Morning Britain invited me onto the show this morning in the primetime slot to discuss my new single – *Heartbroken* – which comes out tomorrow, just ahead of my album launch in two weeks. It's the first music I've had out in a while as my solo career hasn't been as smooth as I'd have liked. This is the last chance for me before my label drops me. The interview was going well and I was enjoying talking about my music and my upcoming album until the presenters started to steer the conversation towards the trial. I knew it was an inevitability.

People seem sceptical when I tell them it's a coincidence that the first single from my new album, *Cheater*, will be released on the first day of the defamation trial. It's not as if I have any decision-making power in that regard. It's all up to the label. Maybe they timed it deliberately, maybe they didn't, but I'm fed up with answering questions about a decision I was never involved in.

If it was up to me there would be no trial. Yes, it's true that my new album probably wouldn't have gotten as much hype if it wasn't for the trial, especially considering my last album failed to chart. Nobody wanted to interview me when my last album came out. None of the magazines came calling and none of the radio stations wanted me to appear. This time it's different, it's like how it used to be when I was in the girl group Lipstick Lasses. We were never chart-toppers but we at least clung onto spots in the UK top 40 and went on tour a couple of times. We even had a reality show called *Kisses from the Lasses* at one point that ran for two seasons. We had some hardcore fans but even they don't seem to want to buy my music, judging by my poor sales figures.

'It started well. They seemed interested in my music and the inspiration behind the album. And then it changed and all they wanted to know about was Ethan.'

'It's to be expected they asked about Ethan.' She's typing on her phone as she speaks to me. Jessika's acrylics tap against the phone screen: a sound I wish I could tune out. I used to think it was rude but now I know that the only way Jessika manages to get through her overwhelming to-do list is by constantly multitasking. She's probably negotiating some important contract over email while speaking to me.

'I know but I don't want to talk about the trial. And my solicitor said I need to be really careful what I say in case I jeopardise my defence. I want to talk about my music. It feels like all people care about is Ethan and the trial and not new songs.'

Jessika puts her phone down. 'Tori, we've talked about this. There's a lot of buzz around this trial and we need to capitalise on it to get some hype around the album. We couldn't get any media slots for your last album and you were almost dropped. I had to fight for your label to give you another chance. Yes, okay, most interviewers just want the juicy deets of the trial but that's going to have a positive effect on the album sales so just go along with it.'

'I know, but…'

'This is a good thing. Once the trial has ended there will be some attention depending on the outcome. Maybe you or Ethan will appeal. But once that's died down people are going to forget about Tori Simmons. They forgot about you when Lipstick Lasses split and you only became relevant again because you started dating Ethan. I know the trial is draining but think of it as a gift for not just your music career but your brand in general. I'm fielding so many exciting calls about you lately. More than I have in the past few years combined. There's so many avenues we can explore after the trial but if you clam up and refuse to talk about it then all the attention will just go to Ethan because he's more than happy to speak. Is that what you want?'

This isn't the first time she's had to say something like this to me and from her tone she getting fed up with my attitude.

She's right though, I don't want Ethan to be getting the attention.

Ethan is taking me to court because I happened to whisper in the ear of his film director at a party that he had been cheating on me and I'd walked in on him doing so. I was going through a tough time. Unfortunately for Ethan and unknown to me, because the *Aces & Diamonds* series is produced by a studio that makes films for children he had a morality clause in his contract. It's in all their contracts apparently. Must be an American thing because I've never heard of it. Soon after, Ethan lost his starring role and claimed it was directly related to my conversation with his director. I don't know how he found out what I said.

Supposedly I've ruined his career and he's lost out on earnings potential by losing his job. He's probably right there – they had another four films to produce as they are based on the book series of the same name. Ethan was the male lead but was fired while filming the second out of five. They've since replaced him. The first was a box-office heavy hitter, eclipsing all the other films that opened on the same weekend. It is the *Harry Potter* of the romantasy world. The rest in the franchise are tipped to do just as well and Ethan's replacement seems to be plastered on every billboard and in every advert. *Just like Ethan used to be.*

'I did mention Christian though,' I say, hoping to appease her.

Christian Yates, He's one of Jessika's other clients. A DJ that's 'up and coming'. His last single went viral on TikTok. I must admit it's catchy. Jessika has been asking me to hang around with him and get some paparazzi shots of us so that the press speculates we are dating. Apparently it's good for his brand to be linked to an established name. She says it helps my public profile to show I'm still desired by men. I think it's ridiculous personally but Jessika says she can't change how the world views women.

'That's good. I'm glad you got that in,' she says. 'Here's fine,' Jessika directs the driver, who pulls into a side road and comes to a stop. We're outside my barrister's chambers. I always imagined chambers to be a grand, imposing building with everyone inside wearing robes and those funny little wigs. In truth, the building doesn't stand out from any others on the street. The inside is nice but if anything the décor is slightly dated and has a stale smell. I much preferred my solicitor's modern City office that overlooked the Shard but we've stopped meeting there now the trial is imminent. I've been here so many times it almost feels like home, which is actually a fairly miserable thought when I think about it.

'I need to go run some errands. I'll see you later, okay?'

Jessika doesn't wait for my answer before speeding away. I didn't even know she wasn't coming with me. I take a deep breath and walk inside chambers, tottering up the stairways to the reception – these stairways are not made for heels. I'm greeted immediately by the perky receptionist.

'Tori, you must be here to see Faye. Take a seat and she'll be with you shortly.'

Faye Robertson KC. That's the name of my barrister. She was highly recommended to me by one of my former bandmates, Shelley. We all went our separate ways and tried solo careers that didn't work out very well for any of us. At least I wasn't the only one. Shelley is probably the most successful of us all as she's a regular celebrity judge on one of those music talent shows. She was the best singer but also the most charismatic, always the one fronting our interviews. She's just finished filming a new series of *Pop Group UK* which aims to find the UK's next big band.

Shelley got in trouble a couple of years ago after making

comments in *Hello!* about how one of our fellow band members was the reason for Lipstick Lasses breaking up, and she was taken to court for defamation. Faye helped Shelley win the case and even managed to successfully counterclaim. So I trust the recommendation.

I take a seat. There are no glossy magazines or even books in the waiting area so I scroll on my phone. I notice one of the news accounts I follow on Instagram has posted about the trial and I can't help but peek at the comments to see what people are saying.

@Celeb_News_Now
Ethan or Tori, whose side are you on? Is Ethan a cheater or is Tori a liar?

@LJ_MUFCX
Anyone else think this whole thing is a publicity stunt? Not sure who is worse, her or him!

@Sabrinnaaah99
Ethan clearly only took Tori to trial because he's annoyed she outed him for being a cheater. It's so obvious he's a f boy

@AdamSaunders
Funny how it's only lasses saying Tori is in the right. Ethan lost his job because of her. Can't just go around spreading lies

@the_govern0r_
Tori seems like a fame-hungry nasty piece of work. Her career was dead so she decided to bring Ethan down with her.

@erik8937

Hope when Ethan wins this trial that he can find another role. He was the perfect Leo.

@DBSpencerr

Definitely backing Ethan in this #SimmonsTrial. I've always thought Tori had no talent and leeched off him.

@TaraTweets

Anyone else so excited for the livestream starting tomorrow? Feel like it's going to be juicy.

I sigh. I'm not surprised to see how many pro-Ethan accounts there are. Jessika warned me that the public opinion definitely seems to be swaying towards him. It doesn't help that he's painted himself as the victim. He's done countless interviews about how I've ruined his whole career and claimed I made the whole thing up. Everyone loves Ethan because they love Leo Trax, the character he played, but they forget that he and his character are not the same person. There's an entire fandom on BookTok that seem convinced he is in fact the character in real life. Just because he has a six-pack does not mean he can do no wrong.

'Victoria, do you want to come on through?'

I don't know why Faye insists on using my full name when nobody else uses it – it makes me feel like she's my teacher, even though I'm sure we are close in age. I take a seat on the same brown leather armchair that I always sit on. My solicitor, Ava, is in the corner. She and Faye have obviously already had a debrief. Ava mostly sits in the background now that we have Faye working on my case, but in the beginning it was just me and her working a lot of late nights while I tried to deal with Ethan taking me to court. She's pleasant, if a little quiet.

'So, let's get to it. Trial starts tomorrow. How are you feeling?' Faye asks. She's immaculately dressed as usual, a black suit that fits her perfectly. Her brown hair is in a slicked back bun and there's not a single hair out of place. She crosses one leg over the other and clasps her hands together.

'Nervous. I wasn't until today. I don't think it's really hit me that we are going to be in a court tomorrow and that it's going to be livestreamed. Everybody is going to watch it and have an opinion. I was scrolling on social media earlier and I feel like everyone has already made up their minds about me.'

'I wouldn't get too wrapped up in social media. The only person who matters is the judge.'

I'm thankful every day that it's not a jury trial. Apparently those aren't the norm for defamation trials in the UK, at least that's what Faye said.

But having it livestreamed is just as bad. In this industry, reputation is everything. If the public hate me they'll never buy my music and my career will be over. I've seen what happens to celebrities the public turns on and it isn't pretty. They receive death threats, rape threats; their addresses and personal details revealed. One celebrity had her phone hacked and all her nudes were leaked. At the moment it's just hate on social media but I know how bad things can get. One wrong move and I'll be cancelled. I wish I had the confidence of Ethan, he has that type of personality that can charm anyone and he captivates a room. I suppose that's why he's an actor although personally I think his good looks have been a bigger factor in him getting roles.

'Shall we go through the case again?'

We've been through it so many times but I need to hear it again. The repetition is comforting.

'So Ethan is claiming defamation, in particular slander, based on comments you made to his director that he was cheating on you. You claimed you walked in on him having sex with another woman during your marriage. Ethan had a morality clause in his contract and the director fired Ethan from his role on the *Aces & Diamonds* franchise for breaching it.'

I remember the day I walked in on him. I should have known as there were rumours in the press but the media love to rile celebs up to get content and make up things. I thought it was all fabricated. We were living long-distance at the time so it was hard to spot the signs. Ethan was filming in Canada and I was in England caring for my mum as she's unwell. I'd gone out to visit him, to surprise him, hoping to also silence the gossipers, but the only surprise was my heart breaking.

I probably shouldn't have told the director about what was going on but I couldn't help myself. It was the Christmas party a few months later and I'd had a lot to drink. I've had media training before but Ava told me that slander is when the comments are spoken and not permanently recorded somewhere. Who knew I could be taken to court over something I said?

These defamation trials never used to be a thing. It seems like every other month somebody is in the courts because of what they've said or written. The punishment will be financial and if Ethan gets what he's asking for, I'll be bankrupt.

'I remember.'

'So Ethan's argument is that you making these comments ruined his reputation as he went from, according to the words he used in this claim form, "Hollywood Heartthrob" to a "Playboy Pauper". According to Ethan, the director specifically mentioned your conversation and that he didn't want a cheater playing his lead character and that he'd breached the morality clause in his contract. Ethan had played Leo Trax for one out of five scheduled films and was in the process of filming the second. Ethan claims he has lost out on earnings of potentially fifty-five million dollars and that is what he is claiming from you.'

I once asked Faye to explain how Ethan's legal team had arrived at the figure of fifty-five million and she said it was a complex calculation based on contract earnings and projected earnings from sponsor deals and endorsements and future work. I don't know how much truth there is to it anyway.

'So, as we've discussed before, the defence is that what you said about Ethan is true,' Faye reads from her notes, not bothering to make eye contact with me. This is all easy for her. Law is her career, her world. I'm not one of those celebrities constantly in the news for driving while drunk or assaulting photographers and the like, I try to keep myself grounded and out of trouble. I've never had any brushes with the law.

'Now ideally we'd have some photographic evidence of Ethan cheating on you as proof but you've said you don't have anything.'

She says this as if it's a failure on my part, but it's not like I paused to take a photograph of what I walked in on.

'I never thought we'd end up in court over something like this and like I said, the evidence was that I saw him cheating with my own eyes. I wish I'd taken a photograph or something but I was in shock and then I stormed out.'

Faye nods. When I first told her I had no evidence of Ethan cheating she didn't seem to believe me. She thought for sure I'd have hired a private investigator or something to catch Ethan in the act. I did hire one later on her suggestion but it was too late; I think once Ethan started the court case he cleaned up his act so he wouldn't get caught. Faye said what mattered was whether Ethan was cheating when I told the director he was cheating although apparently evidence of him cheating now could be an indicator of past behaviour. Once a cheater always a cheater, as they say.

'So that means it's all going to come down to you. It's hard because you need to convince the judge to believe you based on your words alone. He said, she said situation. It's not like Ethan can produce evidence that he *wasn't* cheating. It won't be easy though. You have an uphill battle for sure.'

'So it's all about who the judge believes, right?'

'Essentially yes. It's your word against his.'

Only one of us is telling the truth. Let's hope the judge can tell which one.

Chapter Three

ETHAN SIMMONS

'I'm not worried. Tori knows she has no evidence against me. That woman ruined my life.' I'd never been in love before I met Tori and if I'd known how badly it would mess up my life I would have stayed single. I'd take the texts asking 'what are we?' over this any day.

'You've got a good case. She doesn't have anything to back up her remarks. Are you sure you don't want to submit these photographs of her into evidence though? I'm telling you it would go a long way to undermining her character,' Thomas says. 'As your barrister, I have to recommend that we use these.'

Thomas Grantham KC leans back in his desk chair, his hands together with his fingertips pressed against his lips like he's deep in thought. He's slightly slumped and his right leg is crossed over his left and it shakes as he bounces his leg on the floor. On his knee, he rests a notebook which he occasionally writes in despite the hardwood desk in front of him. He doesn't appear at all stressed about the trial but I suppose tomorrow is another day at work for him.

The said photos of Tori are fanned out across the chestnut-brown table like a deck of cards. I can't help but think about how hot Tori looks in those photos, the arch of her back, her toned legs that I've always loved despite her insecurities that they aren't long enough. Tori was convinced all her problems would be solved if she was three inches taller. Her round brown eyes that I thought made her look like Bambi. That's what I used to call her when we first got together – Bambi, I thought it was cute. She is petite all over but her eyes are slightly too big for her small head which I've always found striking. The moniker wasn't just because of her eyes though; she wears these pencil-thin heels to fool everyone that she's taller than she is. Despite years of practice she can't properly walk in them, instead she hobbles around. I often had to catch her when she stumbled. I don't even know if deer walk like that but it was the first thing that came to mind.

'I'm not sure. I'm conflicted.' I mimic Thomas and lean back in the velvet armchair, stretching out my legs. I shift my back into the chair to get comfortable. When I first walked into this place I was intimidated by its grand interior but I quickly learnt that all this grandeur is just a British thing rather than anything to be in awe of. Places don't look the same as in America.

'If you submitted these as evidence, the case would be a slam-dunk although I still think there is a high likelihood of success already. I can't see how her team would find a way to answer these photos. They would destroy all her credibility. Tori's team will be trying to prove that she's telling the truth. The judge will definitely be swayed once she sees these, even if she tries hard not to let herself buy into stereotypes. Nobody trusts women that engage in this type of behaviour.'

'It won't just destroy her case though, it'll destroy her. If I use these there will be no going back for us. I'm still angry about what she said because she destroyed my career but I was in love with her for so long ... who knows, maybe I'm still in love with her. I just don't know if I can use these.'

It's difficult to explain that I both love and hate my wife simultaneously. Sometimes I don't know which emotion is stronger. Love lights a fire within me, pushes my feelings to places I never thought they'd go, but hate, hate burns inside me, unrelenting.

She's ruined everything I had but at the same time, she was my first love, my only love. Every time I think about her too much, I start to regret this entire thing, but leaving her financially ruined is easier to stomach than humiliating her.

Thomas sighs and shuffles the photos into a brown envelope, sealing it shut with a treasury tag and slipping it into his desk drawer. For him, this is a job. He wants to win the case and reap the rewards of the career boost he will no doubt get for being part of a trial with an unprecedented amount of attention. And then he'll go home to his family and sleep soundly – his life will remain unaffected. My doubts about using all the weapons in our arsenal because of a silly little thing like love are getting in the way of his strategy. I've lost count of the number of times I've watched his eyes roll when I've talked about my marriage.

'Well, it's your choice. As I have explained to you previously, I'm very discreet. Other barristers would have told you that you have no choice but to hand these over as part of the discovery process but my interpretation of the law is slightly different and I take a more contextual approach.' He smirks after he says it, his lips curled up at each end, his eyes narrowing in delight. I did a lot of research before choosing my barrister and everyone said the same thing about Thomas Grantham – he likes to operate in shades of grey. Well, grey just happens to be my favourite colour. He knows just how far to push things to avoid getting into any serious trouble and his clients all benefit from it.

It's why I hired Thomas. There are a fair few lawyers in London specialising in celebrity court cases but Thomas has a reputation as a bit of an oddball. Once I'd heard he didn't like to play by the rules I knew we would be kindred spirits. I also knew the press would love that I hired him, especially given that the whole trial is being livestreamed. There's no denying things won't be the same because of that.

Thomas said to think of barristers like actors on a stage, playing their part, trying to remember their lines and attempting to win favour. The difference between a good actor and a good barrister is that only one has to follow a script. The one person that really matters is the judge, but in this game of love and war, sometimes I wonder if any of us will really be winners.

'If you decide later on that you do want to submit your photos, then we might run into an issue with the judge. She might not allow the photographs into evidence so you can't use them at all. Tori's team will argue including them is unfair as they won't have time to consider and properly respond to them. Or the judge might allow the photographs but give them less weight. We can argue our case.'

I nod along.

'We can always get creative though. If we aren't allowed to submit the photographs into evidence that wouldn't mean they have no use ... One small message to the tabloids and these photographs can be everywhere.'

'You make good points. I need to think about it. I want to try and keep this trial as dignified as possible.'

'As you know this is the first time the UK courts have livestreamed a trial. I know you already had livestreaming in the US and I'm sure I don't need to tell you the impact it's had.

These trials, especially the ones with celebrities, are a new breed of reality TV shows. One couple even got a reality show series off the back of their trial.'

I don't mention that my agent is hoping to secure a similar television deal about this experience and following my life after the trial.

'Do you mind?' I reach into my jacket pocket and pull out a vape.

'Go ahead. I think we are due a comfort break anyway. You know where the smoking area is from last time, I assume?'

'On the terrace.'

Last time I came I tried to vape on the street outside and got an earful from the receptionist. Apparently they didn't want me getting papped outside and chambers ending up in some magazine. The snotty receptionist said the other clientele wouldn't want to be associated with that.

The terrace is breezy even though it's summer. I still haven't gotten used to the weather in England. I only ever came here because Tori told me I had to or she'd leave me. But I hate it here – I never realised it was possible to rain so much. These English people carry around an umbrella everyday 'just in case' it rains – and it always does. I don't want to live somewhere like that. We could've had a better life in the US – and none of this would have happened. Tori could've had a music career out there, maybe she would've done better. England is such a small market. I have contacts in LA that I could've introduced her to. Maybe then she wouldn't have been so jealous of my success.

I check my phone. I don't actually use social media that much. I have a couple of profiles that my agent, Owen, runs for me because I can't be bothered with the algorithms and the trolls. I just get Owen to send me details of whatever he wants to post so I can approve it. I have a few messages from him now. Lots of magazines are interested in hearing my story so he wants to know which, if any, I want to talk to. He's also messaged me about what time he'll be meeting me before court tomorrow. The final message is a link to a video he wants me to watch. Curiosity gets the better of me and I open it.

Nobody else is nearby so I turn the volume on my phone to full. Tori's face fills the screen. I recognise the studio she's in from the background; this must be the breakfast show that Owen was telling me about yesterday. He said Tori was going on the show to discuss her new single and upcoming album. The video just appears to be her discussing her music. Why has Owen sent me this?

'So, Tori, how are you feeling about the trial tomorrow? It's all anyone can talk about,' the female presenter asks.

'Oh. Well it's difficult as you might imagine. I find it hard to speak about.'

'I'm sure it must be upsetting to have your private life literally played out for the world to comment on and judge. This is the first time the UK has ever livestreamed a trial and it's a very controversial decision. How did you feel when you found out?'

She's fiddling with her wedding ring – which I've noticed she still wears – and I know that is her tell for when she's feeling uncomfortable.

'People have commented on our relationship from day one. People have said mean things about everything I do. I've been in the public eye since I was a teenager so usually it doesn't get to me but the attention has never been this extreme.'

'Have you spoken to Ethan lately? What is your relationship like now?' the male presenter asks.

'No. He moved out of our home at the same time all of this mess started. I've seen him for some pre-trial things we had to do but we didn't exactly speak.'

The female presenter leans in closer to Tori and places her hand on her shoulder.

'Do you miss him?'

'I miss what our relationship used to be. Things were so good, we were so in love. I've never felt as high as I did when I was with him.'

'Do you regret your actions? Do you wish you'd never told his director about his alleged cheating?'

'Yes. I wish it had never come out like that. It was unprofessional of me and I should never have aired our dirty laundry with other people, especially not someone he works with.'

'Did you know about the morality clause in his contract? Was it a calculated move to get him fired?'

'I … I can't remember. I don't think I should say anything else.'

It's hard to see from the small screen of my phone but Tori looks as if she's about to cry. She's right, before all of this started we worked well together. We had the type of passion that people write stories about, and make fan edits of on TikTok. I don't think either of us will be lucky enough to find that with someone else.

'Well things might be looking up for you, I've heard rumours you are dating Christian Yates. Is that true?'

Christian Yates? Who is that?

'We've been hanging out. It's still very early days and I don't want to rush anything but he's been really helpful during this difficult period.'

She's seeing someone? She's not even divorced. She's still wearing her wedding ring. I rush to find a photo of this Christian guy. He's good looking, annoyingly, and some sort of DJ, who are always the worst because they have an overinflated ego. There are several photographs of him and

Tori online as well as articles about their suspected romance. How have I not seen these before?

I type out a message to Owen my fingers striking the keys.

Ethan

I can't believe this. Who does she think she is dating someone else right now?

He replies almost instantly.

Owen

That wasn't why I sent it. She said she regrets what she said. And then she dodged that question about your contract. You're with your barrister, right? Show it to him and see if he thinks you can use that tomorrow?

Ethan

Oh yeah, I'll ask. But what about this Christian Yates, do you know him?

He doesn't answer and I'm too cold to stand outside waiting so I go back inside.

'That was a long break,' Thomas says. I can never tell when he's joking or being serious but that could be a British thing. Tori used to always tease me saying that I didn't understand sarcasm and needed to stop taking what everyone said at face value. Why can't people here just say what they mean instead of adding a second meaning to everything?

'Yeah sorry, Tori did an interview this morning so I was just watching it.'

'Anything interesting?'

'You tell me,' I say, opening the video and sliding my phone across the table. Thomas watches intently and I can tell by the wrinkling near his eyes that the cogs in his brain are turning.

I want to bring up the Christian point but I stop myself. Thomas won't care about it unless it helps with the trial strategy.

'Interesting indeed. I might use this in my opening statement. I'll send it to Roger too. He should see it.' Roger is my solicitor, but I never see him these days. Apparently I need both, I can't just have one 'lawyer' – another quirk of the English legal system I've had to get used to.

Thomas sorts through the papers on his desk, seemingly looking for something that he can't find. He gives up. 'I heard from reception that Jasper has landed in London. My clerk is making sure he gets to his hotel okay.'

Jasper, my former director and our star witness. I don't know how Thomas managed to convince him to come and testify at the trial but his testimony will be gold. He will tell the court exactly what Tori said to him: all the lies she told.

'I think we've spoken about strategy enough so you know how everything will work. Tomorrow will be the most important day for you because you need to give the performance of your life when you give your witness statement in court.'

'We've rehearsed the witness statement enough times. I'm ready.'

'You'd better hope the judge believes you. I don't need to tell you what will happen if they don't.'

Chapter Four

@THETRUTHISGREY

I almost didn't get on the plane. I bought the ticket after @thetruthisblackandwhite2011 messaged about Alice, but I had instant panic. Panic about being back in London when that place has been responsible for so much hurt. Panic about getting my hopes up about actually finding out what happened to my sister, only to have it lead nowhere once again and find myself feeling more lost than ever before. But there's also another type of panic which I think is the real reason I almost reconsidered going to London. When I find out what happened to my sister, that will be it. Maybe resolution will bring me peace, isn't that what they say? Or maybe knowing what happened to her will be much more horrific than not knowing. If I know she suffered, if she was in pain, I'll never be able to pretend otherwise.

It's almost like @thetruthisblackandwhite2011 was inside my head and knew what I was thinking because I got another message hours before I was supposed to be at the airport. I had decided not to go, hadn't packed my suitcase and had resigned myself to losing the money I spent on flights and the hotel.

@thetruthisblackandwhite2011
I hope you're not having second
thoughts. Look at my page if you're not
convinced.

I didn't respond but I did look at their TikTok page – I couldn't not. My parents tell me I have an unhealthy obsession with Alice's disappearance. According to them, there's a difference between wanting to know what happened to her and trying to find out every detail and run down every lead. When they first told me this, we argued, a blazing row which resulted in me not speaking to them for several weeks. It was my dad that finally convinced me to come home. I thought they didn't care enough about finding her because they had given up. They thought I needed to try to move on with my life. He said it was like they'd lost me too.

There was a single video on the account. I clicked on it. There was no picture, just a blank screen so I put my AirPods in and cranked the volume up to maximum so I could listen. It was Alice's voice speaking.

'What do you think your wife would do if she found out about us?'

And then, a male voice replied to her:

'She wouldn't care.'

'Doesn't she love you?'

'No. It's all for the cameras. We both know the deal, being part of a celebrity couple makes us easier to sell, we become a package. Tori has known that since the beginning. But it's you I care about, Alice. It's you I want to be with.'

That must be Ethan speaking. Tori isn't exactly a popular name. Victoria, sure, but most people go by Vicky or Vic.

'Do you think we could ever be together properly?'

'You know I want to be with you. It's just not easy to leave Tori. I

want to do it the kindest way I can. I didn't intend to break my marriage vows but I never expected to meet someone like you. One day I'll figure out how to tell her but I need time to work out how to do that.'

'It just doesn't feel right what we are doing.'

The sound stopped abruptly, as if someone had intentionally cut the video midway. There must have been more but this user is dangling the information in front of me, deliberately only giving me breadcrumbs hoping I'll follow to see where they lead. The witch to my Gretel. There's so many questions. How do they have this? Who recorded it? Why would somebody record a clearly private conversation? Perhaps to blackmail Ethan? He has money, after all. Or was my sister the target? I played the video on repeat listening for a clue or hint as to where it was taken. I messaged the account back, asking how they had the audio. Maybe Alice or Ethan made the recording. And now I think about it, Alice's phone was never found.

Whoever is behind the account didn't reveal their source but told me to catch the flight and so that is where I am now, about to land at London Heathrow airport. I had no idea my sister was in a relationship with Ethan Simmons until the account told me. I don't know why she didn't tell me, but it's hard to solve the jigsaw of the last few months of her life without all the pieces. Perhaps she was worried I couldn't keep her secret, or, more likely, she knew I'd tell her it was a bad idea and didn't want me to judge her. She said I did that sometimes, judged her decisions. Although looking at us you'd think I was the wild one with my appearance, that couldn't be further from the truth. Alice was the one always making bad decisions, acting like my younger sister instead of my twin.

Whoever is behind @thetruthisblackandwhite2011 knows

things about my sister's disappearance that I don't, things that nobody else knows including the detectives investigating. They certainly never mentioned Ethan so I doubt they knew. He was never questioned or a person of interest. They did ask if she had a boyfriend or partner but I told them she didn't.

The plane lands, interrupting my thoughts as the pilot welcomes us to London. My phone has been off since I left Chicago so I scan my notifications. Before I left, I posted updating people about coming to England. Lots of comments on my latest TikTok are about coming to London to cover the trial in person. A few people have commented that they don't understand why I need to fly all the way here when the trial is being livestreamed. They have a good point but of course they don't know that I have an ulterior motive – somebody wants me here in person to witness whatever secrets are about to be uncovered. Or maybe they want me here for a different reason. Could this person be dangerous? Could this person actually be responsible for what happened to Alice? It wasn't something I'd considered until now, and I wonder if I should've been so quick to come. What if this is a trap?

After passport control I scroll through TikTok while I wait for my taxi. There's a lot of videos about the Simmons trial. I consider it research to know what content other creators are producing on the trial but also I'm curious if anyone knows about the Alice connection. I make a quick video telling my followers that I've arrived in London and upload it to my story. I try to post at least three times a day but I'm low on content due to the flight.

@celebgossdesk has uploaded a new video. I hate Oskar, the man behind the account. He likes to dramatise things and bend the truth just for views. He likes to have controversy surrounding him – he'd tell you the sky was green just to get a reaction out of you. I wouldn't say we are rivals but our paths have crossed before online. Once or twice in person but he lives in Germany so rarely ventures to the US. I called him out once because he was misrepresenting a celebrity trial about a fight in a nightclub which ended with the celebrity charged with assault. Oskar made out the celebrity started the fight over a spilt drink when actually the celebrity was being harassed and didn't hit first. He didn't like being called out so we exchanged heated messages.. I click play on his recent video.

'Yo, so my celeb gossip lovers, your boy Oskar is going to England today to cover the Simmons trial. Trust me when I say this is going to be the most explosive trial of 2025. It's being livestreamed and I'm going to be reporting on every minute.'

Great. I didn't realise he was going to be here as well. I hope I don't run into him. He sweeps his dirty-blond hair out of his face. It's always slightly too long and gets in his eyes. I don't know why he doesn't just get it cut. From the uncomfortable-looking seats he's passing in the background, the numerous people wheeling suitcases behind them and the plane company logos plastered everywhere, I'd guess he filmed it at the airport. Maybe even this one.

'Anyway, I'm so excited to be in London to cover the trial. I saw a few other TikTokers heading over and couldn't miss out on all the fun. I will be outside of the Royal Courts of Justice aka the big RCJ to get footage of Tori and Ethan. You do not want to miss what is sure to be a fiery few days. Follow me to make sure you hear everything as it happens.'

I despise the way he makes everything feel like a big game when these are people's lives. I like to think I at least try to report on things delicately and I never mislead my audience. Maybe I'm wrong and the truth is I'm just as bad as Oskar – aren't we all profiting from somebody else's pain?

A couple more accounts have posted videos about the trial.

Quite a few of them English which makes sense as the trial is based here. I've read a few news articles about why Ethan chose to go through the courts here instead of the US. After all he is American, it is Tori who is English. The most common opinion seems to be that it's because he wanted to avoid a jury trial in the US. Apparently it's very rare for juries to be involved in slander trials in England. I guess Ethan wasn't confident enough that he could charm them.

My Uber arrives and I slide into the backseat while the driver sorts out my suitcases. I send a message to my parents to let them know that I've arrived safely. I didn't tell them why I was coming. They've already lost one daughter here.

The driver has the radio on in the background which I'm not really listening to – I can barely make out what they are saying with my headphones in – but then he turns it up and I can hear it over my music. I take out my headphones to ask him to turn it down but the content piques my interest.

'Police are still identifying the body found in a disused carpark in London this morning but it is believed to be female. Further enquiries are ongoing.'

'They found a body?' I ask.

'Yeah. So sad. It's morbid to think how many dead bodies there are lying around this city waiting to be found. You know, you wouldn't believe how many bodies there are in the river. People around here say there's hundreds that are buried so deep they will never wash up.'

'Do you know where?'

'Huh?'

'Where in London the body was found.'

'Oh, I'm not quite sure. I don't remember if they said. I tell you one thing, if you ever wanted to hide a body, chuck it in the Thames. They'd never find it.' The cab driver laughs as if he's told a funny joke, although he doesn't know quite how sick that joke has made me feel. His Cockney accent only adds to the brutality of his statement.

So many bodies in London, he said. Could one of those be my sister's? Is she somewhere waiting for me to find her?

The trial starts tomorrow and so does my search for answers.

Transcript of TikTok Video uploaded by user @thetruthisgrey on 1 June 2025 at 8:21pm

Hello everyone. I've arrived in London for the biggest trial of the century. That's right, I've flown all the way from America just to make sure I get the most exclusive content for you all. The trial starts tomorrow and I cannot wait. Ethan was one of the biggest stars in Hollywood and his romance with Tori was constantly on the front page of all the magazines. We all saw the incredible photographs from their idyllic summer wedding.

Sadly, that all came crashing down when Ethan was fired from the lead role of Leo Trax in the Aces & Diamonds series. Ethan claims Tori told his director that he was cheating on her, and that led to him being fired. We thought that was the end of it but then several months later we found out that Ethan was taking Tori to court in England!

I think this will be one to watch and it's a real 'he said, she said' story. I've never been a big fan of Ethan's but there are two sides to every story. Tell me in the comments below whose side you are on.

Remember to check out the pinned videos at the top of my profile and remember, the truth is always grey.

Comments:

@badgirl78
Definitely with Tori on this one. Ethan gives major player vibes. Bet he's been around a bit.

@Helen_truecrime

It almost doesn't feel real. I hope they turn the trial into a movie. I'd watch it.

@Promo_for_free

Hi, I love your channel. Do you want to earn more $$ from your content? Follow my page to find out how.

The Trial

Chapter Five

VICTORIA 'TORI' SIMMONS

'You look like you're going to a funeral, Tor,' Shelley teases as she checks her lipstick in the hallway mirror. She's agreed to accompany me to court every day as my emotional support. Luckily my barrister says that the trial will only last a week. I don't feel lucky, but apparently sometimes these trials can go on for ages. I'm glad I have Shelley to literally and emotionally hold my hand during this next week because I don't know how I would cope without her. I know I have Faye, and my solicitor Ava, but they will be preoccupied with doing their job, as they should be. Jessika will be there but she's not the most empathetic person I know – she's all business. Everything will be about how the trial is affecting my career rather than my mental state. Last night she sent over photographs of the expressions I should limit myself to during the trial; at one point in her message she told me to practise my sad expressions. She thinks that people will be watching my reactions so I need to be careful because the biggest newspapers will have body language experts analysing me.

'That's fitting. I feel like I'm going to the funeral of my

career.' I attempt a laugh to pass it off as a joke but I'm not fooling Shelley, it's an empty gesture. She knows how anxious I've been about this trial and I've not been able to hide that from anyone, especially someone who's known me as long as she has. I can't remember the last time I slept properly and my appetite is non-existent.

'Don't be like that. Faye thinks you have a good case, right? Anyway, these things are unpredictable.'

I shrug – I think it's the opposite – I think Faye thinks we are going to lose. 'I'm not so sure she thinks that. But I suppose we will see what happens.'

I check my appearance in the mirror. I'm wearing a fitted black dress that wouldn't look out of place in an office but I want to look smart today and not give the papers any reasons to criticise me. I don't want to be accused of turning court into a fashion show. It's slightly too baggy on me even though it fit when I bought it a few weeks ago. I have a blazer over the top, part of the same set that I got from Reiss just for the occasion. I already have all my court outfits planned out and organised in my wardrobe – that was another tip that Jessika gave me although I actually followed her advice. It sounds shallow but how I look is the one thing in this trial that I can control and I want to make sure I look like I have my shit together. If I look dishevelled or chaotic it will just give the media more fuel.

'Are the glasses too much?' I turn to Shelley, holding out a pair of black frames. She snatches them from me.

'A bit overkill. You look fine as you are, even if the whole ensemble is very … black.'

'Black is smart.' I should have asked Jessika to approve my outfit choice like I do for special occasions like awards ceremonies and TV appearances. I'm surprised she didn't insist on it.

'It's just not very you. You've always been so stylish, but

this is very modest and boring.' I take out my shoes from the box, a two-inch pair of black heels with a rounded toe. 'Jesus, if this is how you're going to be dressing all trial then I think the tabloids are going to be disappointed. I heard they are running a spread reporting on your court outfits each day. I guess they thought you'd wear something worth talking about.'

That's exactly the point. I don't want to give them a reason to talk about me because I'm fed up with seeing my name alongside a list of things I'm doing wrong. I saw an article last week where I'd been photographed grabbing coffee with Shelley, which said I looked 'unbothered' by the upcoming trial and so wasn't taking it seriously.

'Why am I not surprised?' I groan.

'You know what the mags are like. But I'm sure the newspapers will report on the actual trial. I'm so glad that when I was in this situation it was never livestreamed. Definitely adds extra pressure.'

I stay silent, constantly messing with myself, tugging at my dress, sweeping my hair out of my face. I'm trying to remain calm but I feel as if I'm about to spew all over the floor. I wipe the beads of sweat from my upper lip.

'Come here,' Shelley says, holding out her arms and cradling me in a hug. 'I know, it's a lot. People can be so quick to judge. Try to block everyone out.'

'I just hope that people can finally see Ethan for the man he really is.'

We arrive at the court to a crowd of photographers and journalists. I see them scream to get my attention but I can't hear them – Shelley offered me earplugs in the taxi on the way here and I can't thank her enough. I only wish I couldn't see the microphones and cameras being forced into my eyeline. I understand now why people often look like they are being led into court by other people, it's because they are blinded by the mass of lions hungry for their next kill. And right now, I'm on the menu as the catch of the day.

The Royal Courts of Justice is every bit of impressive as its regal moniker sounds. It's a cross between Hogwarts and Oxford University. It is adorned with white pillars with grey turrets on the top, like a castle sitting on the streets of London, somewhere full of history and secrets. Stained-glass windows only add to the allure of the enchanting building which wouldn't look out of place in a film about princes and dragons. Inside is a labyrinth of corridors and a mosaic floor that is so shiny I'm worried that one wrong move will see my heels skid across the floor, sending me crashing down.

'Oh god, Ethan is over there,' Shelley says, her nose scrunched up in disgust.

My stomach flips. Obviously I knew Ethan was going to be here but I haven't seen him in so long. I've seen his face plastered all over the internet but there's something different about being near him again.

'Don't fret. Don't let him see you anxious, you've got this. Faye should be around here somewhere, let's go find her. She will know what to say.'

Shelley pulls me into her, shielding me from Ethan's view as we scuttle around the corner away from him. I'm not sure if he saw us but the sound of our heels on the tiled floor probably gave us away, even if this pair is lower than what I'd usually wear.

'There's Faye and Jessika over there,' Shelley says, ushering me towards them. Jessika and Faye are exchanging heated words. I can tell when Jessika is unhappy as she's the sort of person that uses her hands to talk. When she's mad, her hands frantically wave. With her acrylic nails those flailing hands could easily cause serious injury.

'...I just don't think you've got her best interests at heart.'

'Yeah, well you know nothing ... there are things to think about ... Ethan isn't who you think ... and...'

'Why would he do that? Do you think he—'

I overhear parts of their hushed conversation as we approach until Jessika spots me and taps Faye on the shoulder to make sure she stops talking. I expected Faye to be dressed in her wig and gown already but she looks relatively normal standing here, especially next to Jessika who has chosen a hot pink suit for the occasion.

'Tori, what is with the dreary all black look? Did you not get my message about the style column? You look so ... *dull*.'

'No I—'

'It's too late to change it now. This'll have to do for today but I'll come to the house after court and we can pick out an outfit for tomorrow. You usually dress so well but this is so nine-to-five, office-worker plain.'

'Can we talk about the case instead of what we are wearing?' Faye interrupts. Faye never has any time for Jessika's obsession with image. As we've been speaking, my solicitor Ava has joined Faye and handed her some folders.

Jessika rolls her eyes and crosses one foot in front of another, flashing the red soles of her stilettos. She looks immaculate as ever; she always told me that how she looks is a reflection on her clients so she needs to look like she is in control. If she was to turn up with frizzy hair and un-ironed clothes, people would assume her clients were a mess like her.

'We have an issue. Ethan's barrister is trying to add a new witness to the witness list. It's very last-minute so there's every chance that the judge may not accept this witness but I think we need to be prepared for the fact that the judge may allow it,' Ava says. 'I've just been talking to Ethan's solicitor but they aren't backing down. It's completely in bad faith but his legal team are the type that never play fair.'

'I was just telling Jessika about it when you came over,' Faye says.

'Who is this new witness? Why would they add them so late? You said there were rules about when they could submit evidence.'

'There are but there will always be circumstances in which people try to file late evidence or add new witnesses. It might be that the person was previously unavailable to give evidence. There's lots of genuine reasons but it can also be a dirty tactic that Thomas employs often.'

'Honestly, trust Ethan to do this. He's probably trying to get under your skin,' Shelley says. I know she has good intentions but the idea that Ethan has done it to unsettle me makes me feel queasy.

'Does the name Blair Priest mean anything to you?' Ava says.

'I … Did you say Blair Priest?' It is the last name I expected to hear. Blair has nothing to do with this trial and the only reason Ethan would add her is because he wants to hurt me as much as possible and destroy my career. I thought everything with Blair was something he'd keep to himself. Married couples have secrets they take to their grave, at least that's what we always said.

'Yes, Blair Priest. I haven't had a chance to digest the documents yet but it seems they want to use her as a character witness,' Ava says.

'A character witness?'

'About your character. My best guess is they will try and show you have a history of making things up, of lying. They know that our defence is that you were telling the truth about

Ethan cheating so they will be trying to discredit you, make you look untrustworthy.'

Blair won't just discredit me, if they make her part of this trial I may as well give up now and accept my fate. I can't bear the thought that the things she knows about me might be livestreamed to the world. Intense rage burns within me and it takes all my willpower not to storm over to Ethan and slap him. The only reason I stay rooted to the spot is because I know causing a scene will give Ethan more ammo to use. I will not let him play the 'hysterical woman' card.

'Maybe we should try and settle again,' I whisper to myself but it wasn't as quiet as I thought.

'You want to settle? Who is this Blair person?' Shelley asks. 'You've never mentioned her to me.' The thing with Shelley is that she likes to know everybody's business. It makes her a great friend to confide in but at times like this I need her to understand that there are some things she can't know.

I glance at Jessika. She is the only other person here who knows who Blair is. I can tell by her furrowed brow that this development concerns her as much as it concerns me.

'Faye, trust me when I say you can't let Blair give evidence. We need to settle,' I say.

'I can try, but I'd say it's unlikely it would work. You offered money in the mediation talks but that didn't go down well. I don't think Ethan's motive in this is money – he wants this trial to go ahead. You'll have to significantly up the previous settlement offer for them to even consider it,' Faye says.

'You have to think about your reputation too. If you settle now then you may as well say you made the cheating scandal up. That won't go down well with the public, your producers or the brands you work with,' Jessika says.

'She's right. Look, we don't know if the judge will even

accept Blair as a witness given how late they've tried to add her. I'll appeal to the judge and try to get it disallowed. If it is, then we don't need to have this conversation, okay?'

I nod, knowing that they are both right and that settling probably isn't an option, but I can't let Blair become part of this trial. I knew this trial was going to be hard but I didn't think Ethan would play dirty; it seems like all bets are off. Well, two can play at that game.

'Wait, Ava, Faye, anything we tell you is confidential right?' Jessika asks.

'Privileged, yes. Why?'

'I'll tell you why we are so worried about Blair Priest so you know what you need to do to stop her.'

Chapter Six

ETHAN SIMMONS

'Honestly, Blair will be the nail in the coffin for Tori if the judge allows it. I already told you I thought you had a good chance of winning but this really seals it.'

I'm glad I managed to convince Blair. We tried at the start but she said she was unable to give evidence due to being in a fragile state. I think my incredibly generous donation to her daughter's college fund might have worked, not that it was in any way made to induce her to give evidence. At least, that's what I'll say if anyone ever finds out.

'That other thing we spoke about last night … did you put the wheels in motion?' I ask.

Thomas nods and continues speaking quickly, not pausing to check that I understand him or have anything to add. I used to think it was because he liked the sound of his voice but over the last few months I've realised it's because he's so smart and has so many things to say, like his brain just works on a faster level than us average humans. I can't help but tune out as he starts going into detail about how the case will work. I know I need to listen but I've never been the best at paying attention.

It's gotten me in trouble more than once in Hollywood. One of my ex-directors used to say it was because I was waiting for my turn to speak rather than listening to what was being said, whatever that means.

Thomas is still droning on. I hear heels scrape against the wooden floor and see Tori and her sidekick scurry away from me. Shelley is one of my least favourite people on this earth. She's so loud and brassy. I don't know how Tori puts up with her but every time I hear her voice it's like someone is drilling a nail into my skull.

Tori is pretending not to look at me, her head facing the floor, but I spot her sneaking a glance. Shelley on the other hand is giving me her best stare down. Nobody will ever be good enough for Tori in her eyes. I remember Tori hosted a dinner party once and Shelley picked apart everything I said. She made out like I'm some sort of shallow Hollywood robot, which I thought was rich considering how fake she is – I'm convinced half of her is plastic.

'...I just don't understand how you got her to change her mind. Ethan, are you listening?'

'Say that again?'

'Blair. We tried to months to get her to agree to give evidence but she said she wasn't in a fit state to do so due to ill health so then it seems out of the blue everything changed.'

'I guess she made a miraculous recovery.'

'I wouldn't be surprised if they make a Hail Mary attempt to settle at the last minute. If the judge allows this new evidence in it's sure to shake them.'

'I'm not going to settle.'

'I know. Anyway, I need to go and get ready. You know where to go, right? I've seen Roger this morning so I think he should be around somewhere. Probably getting a coffee, never known someone so addicted to caffeine.'

I actually have no idea where I'm supposed to be going but I'll figure it out. Coffee sounds like a good idea, although I'd prefer something much stronger.

'I'll see you in court.'

I stifle my laughter. I don't think Thomas meant it as a joke but it just makes me think of those legal sitcoms where everyone sues everyone. I auditioned for a part in one of those but I didn't get it. It was at the start of my career where I was grateful for any scrap of work, even playing Witness Number Three.

Courtroom thirteen is straight ahead through the winding corridor. Unlucky for some. The courtroom looks almost identical to the one in *Legal Affairs*, a British detective series I played a minor character for an episode on the filming break for *Aces & Diamonds* – after I was given an ultimatum by Tori, I spent all the time I wasn't filming in London. I was trying to dip my toe into the British acting scene to see if I'd be able to diversify and find some work here between US acting jobs, and it meant I could spend time with Tori as most of the filming studios are near London. I remember thinking that the job was beneath me, but now my name has been disgraced I'd be lucky to get anything better than that.

Everything is brown, oak coloured. Brown benches and desks but all different heights. The judge will be at the top, peering over all of us. I wonder if they'll have one of those tiny hammer things or maybe that's just in America. I can't remember what happened in *Legal Affairs;* I was concentrating on my own part. This courtroom even has antique-looking books filling bookcases as tall as the ceilings which seems pointless because it's not like anybody is going to be reading.

We take our seats. Tori is here with her solicitor, Ava. When I first brought the claim, we spent a lot of hours in a grey office around a circular table. Tori and I had to watch on while our solicitors argued between themselves trying to come to some sort of agreement. Obviously that exercise wasn't successful.

Her agent Jessika is here too. Living apart from Tori has meant not having to see Jessika daily which has been a great result. Jessika annoys me, she sighs all the time. More than a normal amount. I guess I don't like most of the people in Tori's life but she has bad taste in friends.

Owen is sat on my side of the benches. The media are here too. They've been following me around so much lately that I recognise some of them. Almost like those neighbours you don't like but seem to run into every time you leave the house. I see Fred from *The Sun,* he's easy to spot as he has full sleeve tattoos on both arms. I also spot Paul from the *Daily News.* He's bald but with an impressive moustache and beard combo. I give them a wave and Thomas duly enters and takes his space next to me, now donning his robes and wig.

'All rise,' a female voice echoes around the chamber. We all stand like we are puppets on strings being pulled upwards.

We go first. I remember Thomas saying that because I brought the claim we'd start the proceedings. At least I can get it over with.

The judge outlines the procedure of the case, gives the various introductions. She makes reference to the fact that the trial is being livestreamed and broadcast to the public. I expected the cameras to be obvious but I only spot them when she points them out explicitly. Knowing the cameras are on me makes me straighten my back, sit up taller and stick out my chin.

Thomas stands.

'My Lady, on 1 December 2024, Ethan Simmons attended a party at the house of Jasper C Morris, his film director on the *Aces & Diamonds* series, at his house in Vancouver. It was the annual Christmas party for actors and actresses working on all of Morris's films in the past few years. As was customary, Ethan's wife, Tori Simmons, was invited.'

Thomas pauses.

'It was at this party on 1 December 2024 that Tori Simmons had a conversation with Jasper Morris which led to the termination of Ethan Simmons as the lead role of Leo Trax on the multi-million-dollar film franchise. We will hear from Ethan's director that Tori Simmons told him that Ethan was having an affair. He will tell us how as a result of this information, Ethan was in breach of his contract due to a morality clause. Although becoming increasingly rare in Hollywood, the studio insisted on morality clauses in all their actors' contracts after one of Jasper's previous films tanked due to controversy in the media around the male lead.'

It sounds like a Shakespearean monologue and I understand now why Thomas compares barristers to actors. I should listen and pick up some tips for my next performance, if I ever get any new work, that is.

'Despite having started filming for the second film in the five-film series, Ethan was informed by Jasper that his contract was being terminated as a consequence of the breach and that he would no longer be part of the *Aces & Diamonds* cast with immediate effect. The following month, Ethan found out from the media that Shaun Henderson would be replacing him in the star role.'

I remember how sick I felt hearing that news. I know Shaun, I thought we were friends and I couldn't believe he never told me that he was going to play my role. He'd been one of the first people I'd rung for advice when I found out what had happened. I wonder if he fed that information to his agent and used it to swoop in and snatch my part. He didn't even have the balls to tell me himself. I had to find out from someone tagging me in a promotional post on Instagram. We haven't spoken since.

'Not only that, but Ethan was lined up to be the new face of a brand-new aftershave being launched by Givenchy. There was a huge campaign in place, a TV advert to be shown internationally. The contract was worth seven figures and was agreed in principle. However, on the same day as the announcement regarding Shaun Henderson came out, Ethan found out that Givenchy were refusing to sign the contract. We will put forward that this was directly caused by Ethan losing his role in *Aces & Diamonds*.'

The way Thomas is coming across, surely Tori and her team have no chance. It's almost magical watching him come alive as he tells this story.

'The key part of any slander claim is that the statements made were untrue and that they were made maliciously. It is our proposal that Tori told these lies to Jasper knowing that he would fire Ethan Simmons. We do not proclaim to know why Tori did this but we will show throughout these trials that Tori has a history of telling lies for her own gain. We will build up a character history of Tori which shows her to act impulsively and shows that what she did was entirely in character.'

Thomas pauses and I almost raise my hands to applaud him before catching myself and realising where we are.

The courtroom is silent, the only sound the odd cough. The type of silence that you can only usually experience wearing noise-cancelling headphones. I'm scared to move in case my chair creaks.

'My Lady, with the court's permission, I'd like to call my first witness, Mr Ethan Simmons.'

That's my cue. I stand and move to the chair at the front of the room. It feels odd to now be facing Thomas instead of looking behind him. I need to block out the audience – because they basically are an audience watching the show – and concentrate on Thomas. I can't look at Tori in case I lose my nerve.

'Mr Simmons, in your own words could you please describe what you do as a job?'

We've rehearsed this. Thomas said we would start with questions I'd find simple to answer to ease me in and help me get used to speaking in court. Although I'm used to acting in front of people, I'm not used to playing the hardest role of all – being myself.

'I'm an actor. I've acted ever since I was young, starting with playing small parts. I was always an extrovert, wanting to perform for all my parents' friends. I started taking acting lessons and auditioning. As I got older I got some bigger roles, some minor recurring characters, but it was only when I was cast as Leo Trax in the *Aces & Diamonds* fantasy series that things changed for me.'

'Changed in what way?'

'I became a household name almost overnight. I was offered a multi-million-dollar contract. The *Aces & Diamonds* series is based on a set of books which have won tons of awards, sold millions of copies. At the time I was given the contract there were five books and I was contracted for five films. After the success of the first film, the author started writing more books and my director said to me on numerous times that if the studio decided to develop those films I would continue my role as Leo Trax. It's set to be the biggest fantasy franchise since *Twilight*.'

'And you are no longer playing the role of Leo Trax even though not all of these films have been developed, correct?'

'Yes.'

'You were only Leo Trax in the first film, *Five of Spades*, is that correct?'

'Yes.'

'It is Shaun Henderson that is playing the role of Leo Trax in the second film, *Ten of Hearts*, isn't that right?'

'Yes.'

'But you did initially start shooting scenes for *Ten of Hearts*, didn't you?

'Yes. I learnt the script and we had started shooting some of the scenes. We always film scenes out of order – something I don't think people realise. But there's a big scene in the middle of the film where Leo and Asaskia are in the forest and we had filmed part of that.'

'And when did you learn you were being replaced?'

'I found out I was being dropped in December. Shaun was lined up just after the new year.'

'How did you find out?'

'My director, Jasper Morris, called me a couple of days after the Christmas party inviting me to a meeting. He said I'd breached my contract by being unfaithful. He said that *Aces & Diamonds* is primarily a young adult series and he couldn't have these stories leaked about me as it would damage the film's success. He was obsessed with me portraying Leo Trax as this dream fantasy boyfriend and apparently a cheating scandal would ruin that. Our production company mainly focused on kids' films so he said it wasn't a good look. I think he'd also been burnt by that actor in his last movie who was photographed doing cocaine and then there was a campaign to boycott his films as he was a bad influence.' I repeat the lines I have rehearsed word for word, giving Thomas all the ingredients he needs to make his argument. I look into one of the cameras as I make my point.

'And how did you work out that these allegations had come from Tori?'

'Jasper told me. He wouldn't at first but when I said that

those things weren't true, he said he'd been told by someone who knew me better than anyone and wouldn't lie because of how it would affect them. I asked him if it was Tori and he admitted it. And then I asked her and she confirmed it.'

'And you deny all allegations that she made?'

'Yes. I've never cheated on Tori.'

'It is your view that if Tori hadn't told those lies to your director, you would still be playing the role of Leo Trax?'

'Yes. And I'd still have my Givenchy contract too.'

'In your opinion, what made Mrs Simmons tell these lies?'

I remember I have to be careful here. Thomas says I can't sound spiteful or vengeful; I need to sound level-headed and reasonable. 'Honestly, I'm not sure why she did it. I'm not sure I'll ever know. I asked her, believe me, but she never told me. The only thing that springs to mind is that perhaps she was trying to distract from her own infidelity. Maybe she thought that if she pointed the finger at me, people would think if I accused her it would only be out of retaliation.'

'You're saying Mrs Simmons was unfaithful?'

'Yes. Multiple times. My wife … she has a high sex drive. And that's been great for obvious reasons.' I pause, not because I don't know what to say, but because Thomas told me that pausing every so often is a way of letting words sink in before moving onto the next thing. 'But I was never enough for her. I should've known when we got together, it was well known that my wife lived a certain lifestyle before she met me.'

'Can you be more explicit? What do you mean by a certain lifestyle?'

'She liked to sleep around. She said it was empowering.'

'My Lady, I would like to direct your attention to exhibit SIM005 in your bundle on page 35. You will see an article from

The Mirror newspaper penned by Mrs Simmons dated 18 June 2017.'

The judge turns the pages in the folder in front of her.

'In this interview, Mrs Simmons talks about how sleeping around makes her feel empowered. To quote Mrs Simmons: "If I ever did meet a person that I loved, I would want an open relationship. I personally think the only way to make a marriage last is by being able to satisfy your desires whether that's with each other or with other people." Is this the type of lifestyle you mean?'

'Yes. I knew her reputation before we got together but I hoped she'd change for me. She raised the idea of an open relationship fairly quickly after we got together but I told her I didn't want anything like that.'

'But your wife didn't stick to this agreement?'

'No. I wasn't enough for her. I found out about it by accident when a friend of mine mentioned he'd seen Tori check in to the hotel he was staying at, with a man. I hired a private investigator. He found out she was seeing multiple men.'

'How did that make you feel?'

'Betrayed. Hurt. I confronted her and she admitted everything. She even tried to get me involved, said she had some female friends who could join and it could be a group thing.'

The look on Tori's face is a picture. Just wait until she finds out what's next.

Chapter Seven

@THETRUTHISGREY

This trial doesn't seem to have anything to do with Alice's disappearance and I'm questioning why I'm here. What if this was all a big prank from a bored teenager who thought it would be funny to make me travel over here and relive everything? If I've learnt anything from my time on TikTok it's that people can be sick and twisted … but they knew things about my sister, about her and Ethan. Part of me expected to me ambushed by the anonymous account as soon as I got to the court today. Nothing happened but I stayed here just in case.

There's no doubt this is a juicy trial. I don't think any of us expected to learn that Tori had been the unfaithful one in the marriage as she always seemed so devoted to Ethan. I cringed when that lawyer brought up her past exploits as evidence of her cheating; it had nothing to do with their marriage but that's what they do, isn't it? They show that a woman likes sex and then it must mean she's sleeping around. I hope tomorrow when Tori gives her testimony that her lawyer does the same with Ethan. He used to have a different model on his arm every week when he first started making a name for himself – but that never seems to reflect badly on men.

The first day of the trial has finished, everyone is getting ready to leave, but then people start becoming more animated. Is it because Tori or Ethan is about to walk out? And then my phone explodes, message after message. And in the middle of all those notifications is a hit on my Google alert on Tori's name. Something has been published.

I wasn't prepared for the news. A magazine, *HotCelebGossip!*, has apparently received photographs of Tori showing her cheating on Ethan and in very compromising positions. According to the article she is wearing her wedding ring in the photographs so it must have been after she got married. This is a shocking turn of events. There's a rumour that some people are planning to put the unblurred photographs on unsavoury sites for everybody to see. Where did these photos come from and how did the magazine get hold of them? I need to make a video about this.

I find a space to set up. There are yells and shouts coming from all corners. There's camps of photographers stationed outside the entrance blocking the traffic so people are blasting their horns. There are official-looking people trying to sort out the chaos but they look defeated. The press looks up in my direction as I pass them, check who I am then quickly bow their heads when they realise I'm a nobody. In a circle around the courts are various presenters equipped with microphones and speaking into cameras.

Oskar, who goes by @celebgossdesk on TikTok, is stationed in the corner near some of the paned windows covered in greenery with his tripod and iPhone. He's already beaten me to it. I don't record many public videos; I prefer to make them at home in my bedroom rather than dealing with the awkwardness of everyone staring at me, but it's a twenty-minute tube journey to my hotel as everything close to the courts was fully booked. If I wait until then, Oskar and others will have already dominated TikTok with their opinions and thoughts and nobody will care what I have to say. The person with the earliest video will get the most hits. I haven't brought a standing tripod with me so it will have to be an old-school selfie style vlog. As I raise my phone to a flattering angle I hear a commotion behind me. Cameras clicking, flashes making my head spin and people shouting Tori's name.

I spin and switch to the rear camera to face the scene and press record. Tori emerges from the courts, a jacket over her head but she is clearly flanked by her agent, Shelley and her legal team. The paparazzi are screaming her name and I can't help but feel a sharp stab of guilt as I film her. I don't know how she feels but I can imagine she's upset.

I'm broadcasting live so I see the comments trickling in, lots of shocked emojis and people talking about how she is dressed. I tell myself that I'm doing this for Alice, that it may seem wrong to be using this woman's distress to get more views but I need the views to help me find my sister. It's a worthwhile price to pay.

Tori's car has left. The driver had to play chicken with the journalists and at one point I really thought he was going to run one of them over. With Tori gone, the atmosphere is already less charged; the journalists have put their cameras down, and some smoke while others chat amongst themselves or fiddle on their phones. I can hear people talking about the trial, about the photographs. Ethan is still inside so I'm sure people will be waiting for a shot of him as he leaves, although he won't be crucified in the same way as Tori was.

I calculate my route to the hotel. Once I'm back I'll upload some content with my thoughts about the first day – there's certainly a lot to say. And I got the prime content of Tori,

I think. Oskar was too busy filming himself to get any footage so at least that's a win.

A notification stops my train of thought.

@thetruthisblackandwhite2011 has sent me a message.

@thetruthisblackandwhite2011
Did you enjoy the first day of the trial?

@thetruthisgrey
It was … lively. I don't see what it has to do with Alice though??

@thetruthisblackandwhite2011
Wait until tomorrow. All will be revealed once Tori takes the stand.

@thetruthisblackandwhite2011
Nothing will ever be the same again once the truth comes out.

@thetruthisblackandwhite2011
There's right and wrong. No moral grey area.

@thetruthisblackandwhite2011
The truth is black and white.

@thetruthisgrey
I don't understand. What's going to happen tomorrow?

I don't understand the messages and they've almost become clichéd. Is it a play on my tag line 'the truth is always grey'? This account has been set up to target me. 2011 after all is the date that Alice went missing: 20 November. I didn't realise it at first because the dates are the wrong way round and I thought it was a reference to the year but then I remembered reading that in England the dates are reversed.

Whoever this is has an agenda, I just haven't worked out what that is yet or whether their intentions are good. And how do they know so much about what happened to my sister?

I've looked online to find out more about the profile but nothing exists. There is no account matching that handle on any other social media site. There are no articles or references.

After the journey back to my hotel room I still don't have a reply from the account so I message again.

@thetruthisgrey
Hello???

No response. If this continues I'm going to have to get some help finding out who this account belongs to because my searches have yielded nothing and I'm not going to wait around to find out. I don't like them being so in control of the whole situation. The messages sound so ominous and I can't help re-reading them looking for some sort of hidden meaning but the words start to blur into one and become nonsense. If they really do know something about my sister I wish they'd tell me instead of making me wait for the trial like it's some sort of Broadway show. Maybe I should go to the cops or something, because if they really know something about Alice's case and they aren't coming forward then surely they can track this person down for obstruction of justice?

But then the cops have never been particularly helpful when it comes to investigating Alice. I always thought they gave up too easily. If I take this to them I might jeopardize the entire thing and blow my only chance to find out the truth. I can wait one more day to see if what they are saying pans out.

I can't face filming any content for TikTok but I know I need to. The trouble with the algorithm is that it works best if you post consistently. The more you post, the more your posts are featured on the 'for you' page so you're able to reach strangers on their homepage. That's a thought; maybe somebody out there knows who this account belongs to. If tomorrow doesn't help me I can post the messages online and see if my followers can track the account owner down. You wouldn't believe the sleuthing skills of people on the internet. There was a case a few months ago where internet detectives managed to compile a dossier of evidence against a social media guru showing he'd faked his alibi on the day his neighbour was murdered. The guy ended up being arrested and found guilty of murder. It's cases like this that drive me, If I could only get the right kind of people to pay attention to what happened to Alice then I know they'd do a better job than the police.

I find a space to place my phone.

'Hi everyone, so if you've been watching my stories you'll know that I'm in London this week for the Tori and Ethan Simmons trial. And let me tell you, this trial has already been explosive. Today was the first day of the trial and we've found out that Tori was cheating behind Ethan's back multiple times. Can you believe it? And there's rumours of a new witness coming forward that is going to blow the case wide open. What are your thoughts? I'm still on the fence as I think there's more to this trial than anyone knows. I'll be watching closely tomorrow.'

I'm about to end my recording when I remember I haven't done my usual sign-off.

'Don't forget if you have any ideas for celebrity court cases or even true crime that you think I should report on, give me a message. Also please follow me and check out my pinned videos. And remember, the truth is always grey.'

I publish the video to the app. I scroll through TikTok when one video catches my attention.

'You will not believe what has happened to Tori Simmons. The Daily Gossip has just posted the photographs of her cheating on

Ethan. Obviously they are all super blurry but this is proof that she's been having affairs. We don't just need to take Ethan's word for it.'

Photos appear in the video. The guy was right, they are incredibly blurred but there's enough in the photographs to fill in the blanks with a creative imagination. The photographs have been blurred in a certain way that still maintains certain shapes, if you know what I mean.

'How can she try and defend herself by saying she was telling the truth about Ethan when she's clearly not to be trusted? I've lost all respect for her. Tori, if you happen to be watching this, give up now. Just pay Ethan the money he's owed after you smeared his name in the mud. He deserves better than someone riding his coat tails for fame after your solo career failed to make any waves.'

As soon as the video ends, the next video starts from a different user.

'Oh my gosh have you seen the photos? I was always Team Tori and thought Ethan was a slimy prick but you can't deny these photos are proof Tori was cheating. People always said she was only with him as he was doing so well as an actor and his star was only getting brighter while Tori was losing her fame and nobody cared about her anymore. I thought it was just people tearing a woman down as usual but now I'm questioning everything. Why did she lie?'

And then the video ends, and the next video starts and it's on the same topic.

'Do we think the videos could have been doctored? I don't know, it's hard to tell.'

And the next.

'I've seen the full unredacted photos. I can't show them here as I will be banned but just type the words on the screen into Google and you'll find them. They're disgusting.'

I don't want to look for them. I know I don't want to see them, but my morbid curiosity takes over. That's the thing about all of us true crime podcasters, our quest for the truth is more important to us than the need to respect people. I need to see these photographs. I open up a new private browsing tab and type in *Tori Simmons explicit photographs*. They don't appear straightaway and most of the results are news articles talking about the fact they exist but only showing the altered ones. But in my search for answers about Alice I've learnt how to find things that shouldn't be found and it only takes a few minutes for me to track them down.

They are worse than I thought and I can't help but feel ashamed that I sought them out. They are the sort of calibre you'd find on a porn website. Tori is in extremely degrading positions in some of these photographs. The photographs are all date- and time-stamped and they are all dated since Tori and Ethan began their relationship. I wonder if they are real. Having worked in video editing for so long I have contacts that edit photographs all the time; they'll be able to work out if these have been faked. I send a quick message to my friend Sam, warning him about the graphic nature of the photographs but asking him to check if there's any evidence they are faked. It's not like the validity of them has been checked by anybody.

I can't help but wonder who took them and how. Did Tori know they were being taken? There's a knock on my door. Odd. I'm not expecting anybody. Perhaps it's the cleaners but it looks like they've already been. Perhaps it's the mysterious account.

I check through the keyhole to see who it is; after all, you can never be too careful these days. It's cops. I open the door.

'Hi.'

'Are you Riley Grey?'

'Yes, that's me. What's going on?'

'I'm Detective Sergeant Taylor and this is my colleague Detective Constable Hayes from the Metropolitan Police. There has been a development in the search for your sister. Are you able to accompany us to the station?'

'What's going on?'

'Oh, did you not know we were coming? We contacted your parents who told us you were staying here. We thought we'd have to do the entire thing over Microsoft Teams or something but it's really helpful you're here,' DS Taylor says.

'I don't understand.'

'We'd like you to come with us to help identify a body recently discovered in East London. Based on identity documents and personal effects found on the person, we believe it to be your missing sister, Alice Grey.'

And then my world collapses.

Chapter Eight

VICTORIA 'TORI' SIMMONS

It took everything not to break down in the courtroom and keep my composure but as angry as what Ethan was saying made me, nothing prepared me for what was to come after. Jessika had warned me I'd need to hide my face from the paps and luckily I had my sunglasses in my bag. They're all looking for a photo of me crying to plaster on the front cover so everyone can laugh at my expense. What did I do to make people take pleasure in tearing me down?

The media have been hounding me ever since I left court a couple of hours ago. On the drive home we had to take the back roads to avoid being followed. Jessika lent me her jacket to hide under as people kept trying to take photographs through the taxi windows when we were stopped at the traffic lights. It's not just the professionals anymore; there were amateurs, onlookers with phones trying to get a glimpse. I've never related more to a zoo animal.

When we got back to the house the media had already set up outside. They operate in teams so while some were following me from court, their colleagues were coming from elsewhere to beat the traffic. It's a like a full-scale man hunt, or woman hunt in my case. Dozens of photographers and reporters littered around – I'm sure the neighbours aren't impressed. This is an affluent neighbourhood; there's other celebrities living nearby who don't like their privacy invaded.

Jessika has closed the blinds to prevent anyone looking in; they're so intrusive they don't care that this is my home, my private space. I could call the police as they are technically on my property but in my experience the police don't tend to be very sympathetic to celebrities moaning about attention, not when so many people pay for it.

'Why didn't you tell me about those photos, Tori? How am I supposed to prepare for a shitstorm like this when you don't keep me in the loop?' Jessika paces back and forth across my living room, her stilettos thudding against the wooden floor. Her phone starts to vibrate in her hand. 'The news outlets are calling me non-stop. They all want to interview you to get your side of the story. I've had to ignore them all because I have no idea what to say because this is all news to me. What do I always tell you? I need to know everything to do my job.'

It's the reaction I predicted.

'What will your label think about this? You need to think about these things.'

'That's not me in those photographs.'

'I've seen them, it's clearly you. I don't care if you cheat on your husband. Do whatever the hell you like, but at least tell me so I can be prepared. Seriously, this is a trial all about infidelity!' She throws her hands in the air like she's about to shake me but thinks better of it. She drags her palms down her face. 'Did you tell Faye at the very least?'

I shake my head. She'd accosted me briefly afterwards to ask about them but I fobbed her off and lied about a call from my dad to get away.

'She's going to be pissed. You need to get her over here so we can discuss strategy for tomorrow. If there are any other hidden secrets about to come out we need to know. Also if there's any reason we can give to explain those photos we need to know. Is it what it looks like or is there something else going on?'

Ethan has worse secrets on me than just those photographs. I never thought he'd go so far. I'm scared if I try to defend myself too much that Ethan will do much worse in retaliation. This I can handle. There are worse things than this.

'It's so low of Ethan to do this. Bringing up Tori's past like it's some sort of weapon? Who cares if you used to like a party? You were young and in a girl group. You were probably the tamest one of us all. Ethan is no saint, they didn't used to call him the playboy of Hollywood for no reason. Such a dick move,' Shelley says.

Jessika's phone vibrates again.

'They did the same thing with me when I had my defamation trial even though it had nothing to do with what I was accused of saying. Tried to make out that because I had a social life in my teens and twenties I couldn't be trusted. The media published so many unflattering photographs of me drunk to try and discredit me. And everyone called me sloppy and a disgrace as if they've never been on a night out before. They're pigs.'

Jessika's phone vibrates for a third time and she finally turns it off. 'I can't deal with all these media requests until we've worked out how to deal with this. We need a media blackout right now. Nobody talks to the media, nobody says anything, posts anything, or sends a message to anyone with talking to me first. And I mean nobody. That includes you, Shelley.'

'I wasn't going to say anything! I bet he's feeling so smug

right now. Slimy little prick,' Shelley says and stops typing on her phone, a sheepish grin on her face. I have no doubt she was in the middle of a post ranting about Ethan.

'Can you call Faye, Tori?' Jessika says. I've never seen Jessika look out of control but there's sweat above her brow and her hair is unusually unkempt.

I do as I'm told, almost in a trance-like state. 'Hey, Faye, Jessika told me to—'

'I'm already on my way. I just had to go back to my office to get all my case files. We are going to be up most of the night trying to deal with this. I'm sure Jessika has already told you but do not speak to the media about this. I'll be there in fifteen minutes. Ava is with me.'

She hangs up, short but sweet. She's hiding her anger to be professional but I heard it in the tone of her voice. I can't blame her.

'I'm going to make a cup of tea, anyone want one? I'll make some snacks too,' I say, heading to the kitchen. Shelley and Jessika both ignore me but I have to keep busy.

I grab everything I can from the cupboards. A big bowl of crisps. Chocolate. Some cheese and crackers. Some fruit. It's not exactly the most balanced and nutritious meal but we are going to need food to get us through the next few hours. Once Faye and Ava arrive it's going to be all hands on deck.

I bet my record label has already gotten in contact with Jessika. They'll be worried about what the negative attention will do to my album sales. They say there's no such thing as bad publicity but I've learnt that is a myth. So much is on the line with this trial, it has the potential to destroy my career and my reputation, and if we don't find a way to respond to Ethan's revelations then I'm going to lose.

As I bring the food into the living room I hear the doorbell. It must be Faye. I don't even need to ask, Jessika is already on her feet and checking. Thankfully Faye and Ava rush in as the door is opened and I hear the crowd outside roar. I can imagine the headlines already – *BARRISTER VISITS TORI FOR CRISIS TALKS*.

'Take a seat, Victoria,' Faye orders me, even though it's my own home. I sit and wait for my dressing-down.

'How bad is it?' Jessika asks.

'Bad. I'm not going to mince my words. I'm sure I don't need to tell you how bad social media is right now.'

'We've not been looking – I thought it best to have a media blackout until we decided what to do,' Jessika says.

'Good. That's good. And you've not made any press comments?'

'Of course not.'

The pair of them won't let me speak. Them talking about me as if I'm not in the room makes me feel like a child.

'Good. Okay, Victoria. So this wasn't brought up in court so it shouldn't form part of the case against you, but the judge may be unfairly prejudiced. It's not a criminal trial so the press aren't prevented from reporting about the trial while it's ongoing. I also can't in good faith stand up there and pretend you're completely innocent in all this, having seen those photographs. I'm only going to ask this once as there's no use wasting time on this but why didn't you tell me or any of us about the photographs? If I knew this was coming I could have prepared for it. I'm sure Jessika could've managed to keep things out of the newspapers. If you'd told Ava, it would have been helpful to know during settlement discussions.'

I take a deep breath in.

'It was before I was with Ethan. You know I had a bit of a wild girl past. I wasn't cheating with Ethan as I wasn't with him when these were taken. He must have doctored the timestamps.'

Faye sighs. 'I had one of the juniors print these off for me. I admit I don't usually spend so long staring at photographs of this nature but my job is to make sure that I know everything about this case and anything Ethan's team can use to try and destroy your reputation.' She takes an A4 brown envelope out of her bag and pulls out the papers inside, throwing the contents onto the coffee table next to me. 'If these were taken before you knew Ethan, how are you wearing your wedding ring?'

I can't even bring myself to look at the photographs because I know she's right and I should've thought of a better lie. Unfortunately for me, my wedding ring from Ethan is unique, it's a large emerald with clusters of diamonds either side on a gold wedding band. It looks more like an engagement ring.

'If you lie to me, I can't help you. If you lie to me, we may as well admit defeat now and just pay Ethan all the money he is asking for, which, as we both know, is more than you can afford. If you keep lying to me, you better find yourself new representation.'

'Harsh,' I hear Shelley mutter.

I'm surprised Jessika hasn't added anything but Faye has said enough for both of them.

'Okay. Yes, you're right, I was lying. The truth is Ethan liked…' I don't know how to say this. 'Ethan liked to watch me with other men. It was his thing. And I didn't really want to do it, but I did it for him, to make him happy.'

'So he was involved? He was there?'

'Every time.'

'Then why are there no photographs of Ethan?'

'I guess he was smarter than me. And he was the one that wanted to remember it. It didn't bother me.'

'Why were you so upset then about him cheating on you then? Why did you go to Jasper?'

'It was supposed to be a thing we did together, a bonding thing. I was never into it but I was trying to keep him happy. I eventually told him I couldn't do it anymore because it made me feel used. So he started sleeping with other women. I think to get back at me.'

'Right. I'm not sure I see the difference but it's not for me to judge.'

'So what do we do then?' I can't see what other options I have right now.

'We need to forget about trying to make you look better, that is not what this trial is about. This trial is about Ethan, about us proving that when you said he was a cheater you were telling the truth. All of this is to discredit your character. It's a distraction.'

'But I'm not a liar.'

'So let's shift the focus from you back to Ethan. We need to assassinate Ethan's character. Go after him and show him to be a cheat. Ethan needs to be taken down.'

'I think I have just the thing,' I say.

Chapter Nine

ETHAN SIMMONS

I watched Tori run from the media, from the flashing lights and chorus of questions. I say run; of course she was in heels so it was more like a hobble. I watched as most of the reporters took off in cars behind her to chase her back home. Maybe I shouldn't feel so smug but Tori has just got a taste of what I've had to go through all these months with the media slating me after I lost my role and ad campaign. Before I brought proceedings and the real reason became public, there was a lot of speculation. The media printed horrible stories about me, made up lies just to grab attention. They said I had a drug problem, a drink problem, an anger problem. Every type of problem you can name. The worst story though was when one particularly trashy magazine suggested I was caught messaging the director's underage daughter inappropriately. I have never done anything like that and never would. Once I've finished this trial, I'll be going after that paper for their lies.

'I think I'm going to go talk to the press,' I say to nobody in particular as we prepare to leave the court.

'Wait, is that a good idea? It's in the heat of the moment,

emotions running high. How about you and I go for a drink and work on a statement you can put on your social channels? That way we can have more control over it. You don't want to go out there unprepared, who knows what sort of questions they'll ask?' Owen chimes in.

'So you're suggesting I go out there and say nothing?'

'Exactly. Do what Tori just did. Ignore them.'

'I don't want to do that. Tori was hiding because she was embarrassed. I don't need to do that. This was a good day for us.'

'It's risky. We need to see how people react to what's happened.'

'You've seen the news, right? Everybody is slating Tori.'

'Have I taught you nothing?' Owen puts his hands on my shoulders. 'Things can change quickly. Sure, it seems like everybody is against Tori right now but people are fickle. If I was her and her team, I'd be putting out something that paints her as the victim. People are so sensitive now about not cancelling people for fear of the consequences, soon enough people may stop piling on her and ask everybody to be kind to her.'

I roll my eyes. I know Owen is the expert but I don't agree with him. He's supposed to advise me and look out for my best interests but that doesn't mean he always knows the best thing to do. Besides, it's not like I'm Owen's only client. He's spent most of the time since we left court typing on his phone. I heard one of his clients was arrested for drug possession earlier so he's distracted. He just wants me to go back to the hotel so he can give that his undivided attention. That client just got a number one single so they're making him far more money in commission than I currently do.

'I need to make a quick call, when I'm done we'll get a car back to your hotel.'

Owen walks off and I hear him mention Johnny's name – the client that's just been arrested. I can't get his attention when we are standing in court at my trial, not even after today went so well. Owen has always had favourites – even when I was at the peak of my career I still wasn't in the inner circle. To be honest, I worried he would drop me when I lost the *Aces & Diamonds* series. If this trial doesn't go well, my days as an actor will be over and my career will be limited to being an extra in some trashy comedy show – if that. A true graveyard for actors. Then he'll most likely drop me.

Screw this. I know what is best for me and I want to talk to the media. I shouldn't be listening to someone that clearly isn't focused on my career; he has one foot out of the door already. People are realising that Tori isn't the victim in all of this and now is the time to capitalise on it. If Owen is right and people might change their opinion on Tori, I need to get my story across before that happens.

I push the exit doors and stride outside. There's a natural swagger in my step as a result of feeling like a winner. As far as I'm concerned, this trial is already won. It takes a second but heads turn towards me and eager journalists rush forward.

'Ethan, how was the first day of trial?

'Ethan, how are you feeling?'

'Are you happy with how it went?'

'Do you feel vindicated?'

I smile, taking it all in. It feels like my redemption parade. This is my moment, my time to finally feel like how I used to feel, to have the media treating me like royalty instead of like something they've trodden in on the sidewalk. I stand outside the court with microphones and cameras pointed in my face like I'm the president about to give an important speech. What I'm about to say will hopefully mark the rebirth of my career.

'I'm really happy with how court went today. It's been a

hard few months dealing with the fallout from Tori's allegations. You have no idea how hard it is to have everybody turn on you when there is no proof behind anything she said. I didn't want to resort to such a public forum because I didn't want to hurt my wife. I still love her, after all. But her lies hurt me and I couldn't let the lies stand. I don't know how those photographs got leaked to the press but at least it proves I was telling the truth.'

'How long has Tori been cheating on you?'

'Too long. I was silent for too long. I shouldn't have put up with it but I was ashamed to admit what was going on. No guy likes to admit that they're being cheated on, that they aren't enough for their wife.'

'How many guys did Tori sleep with?'

'How did you find out what was going on?'

'Why are there photos? Who took them?'

'Is this just a distraction technique? What about your cheating?'

The final question makes my jaw clench and my right hand forms a fist at my side. This isn't the point of this victory lap. I ignore it.

'I don't know how many there were, I think I'd rather not know. Sometimes being in the dark is much less painful. It's difficult to talk about how I found out about the cheating. I walked in on her. I was supposed to be at an all-day audition in central London for a new TV pilot. It was for a new fantasy TV series that was going to be a limited series, only a few episodes. My agent thought it was the perfect match for me in between shooting for *Aces & Diamonds*, and having something to shoot in London would mean I could spend more time with Tori.' I clear my throat. 'But unfortunately the audition didn't go well. I guess I should've brushed up on my British accent. I didn't even make it to the afternoon round of auditions so I went home early and that's when I found them.'

'What did you do?'

'Who was he?'

'I don't know who he was. I never saw him again. I walked in on them, in our bedroom, writhing around naked. I couldn't move, I was in shock. I ran out, stormed out of the front door and sat in the nearby park for hours until I could face going back home again. I agreed to forgive her. She promised it was the only time, that it was a one-off. I stupidly believed her. I hired a private investigator just in case and he's the one who took those photographs.'

'Who was the guy?'

'Where did you get the photos?'

'What about the waitress in Jacksonville?'

'Do you think Tori will settle now?'

'My client has answered enough questions for today, thank you.' I feel a firm grip on my shoulder as Owen interjects and leads me away from the circus and towards a waiting cab. He's holding on slightly too tight and I can feel his nails digging into my shoulder.

'I told you not to do that. What were you thinking?'

I shrug. 'I wanted to say my piece. I don't think it went badly.'

'You'd better hope this doesn't come back on us,' Own says, opening the cab door for me. 'You do realise that this will be broadcast all over the news, right?'

'So? Isn't that the point?' I slide along the leather seats as Owen clambers in.

'Can you take us to The Hidden hotel in Baker Street? Thanks.' He turns to me. 'Tori and her team will have been watching that little stunt.'

'I still don't see the issue. I don't care if she sees it.'

'It's not Tori that I'm concerned about, it's her barrister. She is going to be dissecting that footage because tomorrow she is going to be cross-examining you about those photos. And I swear if you get one detail even slightly wrong, she will pounce on you and rip you to shreds. Your little soliloquy could end up costly.'

Shit. I didn't even think. I was so wrapped up in myself, enjoying being in the spotlight once again, that I forgot that the trial isn't over, that there is still a long way to go. Today was easy because I was the one speaking and I knew the questions Thomas was going to ask me because we'd already practised my answers. It was more like reciting lines from a script than anything else; I was doing my job. But tomorrow will be different. I don't know what Tori's barrister will ask me so I need to know my story inside out.

'I'm sorry, Owen. I should've listened to you. I didn't think.'

'I turn my back for one second to make a phone call … it doesn't matter now. The damage is done. Just please, next time I tell you not to talk to the press, listen to me. I don't say these things for my own amusement, you know, I have experience in this industry.'

The cab pulls to a stop outside my hotel. There are a few paparazzi waiting nearby, they've already figured out where I'm staying. I stopped living with Tori a while ago and have been staying at The Hidden ever since. She's been staying in the London house to deal with the trial preparation and going back to her Cotswolds home near her family as and when she can. I could've rented somewhere else but I enjoy not having to worry about cooking and cleaning. Tori used to do all of that for me.

I head straight to the hotel bar, in a quest for something to take the edge off after the ordeal of the first day of the trial. I've spoken to other celebrities that have been through this so I had an idea of what to expect but nothing can prepare you properly. I unlock my phone but the stream of notifications has my head spinning so I immediately turn it off.

Tomorrow will be difficult. But at least I'm not the only one speaking tomorrow. Jasper is supposed to tell everyone what Tori said to him that night.

I don't see how she can come back from this.

Chapter Ten

@THETRUTHISGREY

I can't even think about the trial today. All I can think about is what happened last night. The cops came to my door and told me they might have found my sister. It turns out the person they think might be my sister is the same Jane Doe being discussed on the radio in the taxi that day I arrived. They said that 'due to various reasons' the body was difficult to identify but they didn't go into them and I didn't dare ask. I know what that means; that animals have probably gotten to her. At least, I'd rather it was that than part of how she died. My mind was swimming with questions and what-ifs. Of course I pictured every worst-case scenario.

They told me that the body they found was female. And that they'd found my sister's passport and wallet with the body and that had led them to look up her name and realise there was an open missing persons investigation into her whereabouts. I don't recognise either of the cops from when I was in London a few months ago so I suppose it's a different team. I got a call from my dad shortly after I got into the car.

He was distraught that he hadn't managed to catch me before they arrived.

When we got to the station, I assumed I'd be led into a room with the possible body of my sister and have to identify her as they pulled back the sheet covering her, like it always happens in the TV shows. My hands were sweating just thinking about it but that isn't what happened. Instead I got shown into a room with no dead bodies in it. It wasn't a morgue, just a regular square room with a nondescript table and chairs in it. One solitary window. No paintings or anything on the walls except the paint peeling in the corners. I had to wait in the room for what felt like ages.

By the time the officers came back into the room with photographs I'd bitten down my fingernails to the skin. They spread the images of the body out in front of me and asked me if the person in the photographs was my sister. I automatically placed my hand over my mouth to stop myself puking. The person barely looked human; they had no eyes, just empty bloody sockets and scratches across their face.

I had to tell the cops I didn't know who the person was. It could have been Alice but it could have been anyone. Their face was so disfigured and twisted. The hair was similar but that wasn't enough. The decomposition was so bad that I couldn't see my sister's tell-tale tattoo – the one inspired by Alice in Wonderland on her right wrist. As much as I wanted answers, I prayed that it wasn't my sister because I couldn't have that as my final image of her – I wanted to remember her for the ray of sunshine she was.

It feels like I have failed Alice by not being able to identify the body. I should have known, had some sort of innate feeling. How could I not do this one last thing for her? I asked the detectives if I could see the body but they strongly suggested I didn't due to the nature of the injuries. I thought about demanding to, but having seen the photographs I knew I couldn't handle it. I got the impression that even they were struggling with the images.

They don't know how she died yet because the post-mortem is scheduled for tomorrow. They're going to take DNA and dental records to attempt to identify her because I couldn't help, so I should know over the next couple of days whether it's Alice. I will get answers either way, except if it is Alice, there would still be a lot of unanswered questions about what happened to her. I did ask the officers how long she had likely been dead for. They can't say for sure until after the post-mortem but they think several months at least. The dates line up.

How do I concentrate on this trial when I'm waiting to find out if the body is that of my sister? I didn't want to go to the court today, I wanted to stay in bed, the sheets over my head so I could block out the world and pretend nothing was happening. I'm in limbo and paralysed until I know the truth. The only reason I'm here is because if it is Alice, I want to know how she ended up rotting in a disused carpark in East London.

There's still an hour until the proceedings begin today. I'm watching the stream on my phone so there's no need to actually be there. I could stay in this hotel room and slowly decay. I decide to get out though, knowing it is what I need. Any type of distraction is welcome at this point.

When I get to court, I find a space in the courtyard outside and set up to watch, headphones in, tripod in front of me, which I remembered to bring this time. The feed is patchy today; there is background noise and the picture quality is slightly fuzzy. They get the formalities out of the way and then things really start.

'Ethan, when we spoke yesterday you made some

revelations to this court about your wife, Mrs Simmons. You said she had been unfaithful,' Ethan's barrister asks.

'Yes, that's correct. She cheated on me multiple times.'

'Some might ask why you've never mentioned this cheating before. We all know Mrs Simmons has called into question your fidelity, in fact, that is the very reason we are all here today. So, why have you not rebutted those statements with evidence of Mrs Simmons's indiscretions until now?'

'I was embarrassed. I didn't want to admit that I was being cheated on. Also I knew that if I said that in response to Tori's lies nobody would believe me.'

'And to this date, Mrs Simmons has produced no evidence of you cheating on her?'

'None at all – there isn't any, because I haven't done anything wrong.'

'Moving on, I want to talk about somebody called Blair Priest. She was meant to be taking the stand today but has suddenly withdrawn her cooperation. Do you know this name?'

'Yes. She's a … shall we say a colleague of Tori's?'

'Colleague? I thought Mrs Simmons was a solo artist. Do you mean she worked in the music production team?'

'No. Blair Priest is a singer.'

'So she was a backing vocalist on Mrs Simmons's new album?'

'No. Not quite. Blair Priest is the singer on Mrs Simmons's new album. Tori doesn't sing a word.'

'So you are saying, Mr Simmons, that Mrs Simmons hired Miss Priest to impersonate her?'

'Yes. Tori's solo career hasn't been going very well for some time. Her label were about to drop her. It sounds harsh to say this but Tori doesn't have the vocal ability to be a solo singer, it's very different to being in a group. My friends in the industry tell me you don't have to be a good singer to be in a pop group as it's all about performance and chemistry. On her own she struggled. I had many conversations with her about it. Next thing I know, I walk into the recording studio at the Cotswolds house and find somebody else singing the songs on Tori's new album.'

'And that person was Blair Priest?'

'Yes. I challenged Tori on it as I'd heard Tori recording the songs the week prior so I recognised them. It turns out she was paying Blair to sing the songs for her as she knew she needed help. Or maybe her label were. Maybe Jessika was. I don't know.'

'But wouldn't people realise the singer on the album wasn't Mrs Simmons?'

'No. Blair sounds scarily like Tori … but better. I think Tori probably auditioned thousands of women until she found the closest match. Besides, with some creative musical production you can do anything. I told Tori I didn't think it was right.'

'And why didn't you think it was right?'

'She's deceiving her fans and profiting off somebody else's talent. I know Blair will be getting paid but it won't be anything compared to what Tori will make if the album does well. All the opportunities it will get her.'

'So it's the deceit that gets to you?'

'Yes. I just don't think she should be profiting off lies. Us actors, we obviously can't do that and when I'm on a screen it's me that you can see, it's my hard work paying off. Whereas it felt like Tori was using money and connections to get ahead.'

'And why did you think it important to bring this up today?'

'Because it shows that Tori is a liar. She lied about the affairs she was having. She's been lying to her fans about her new album and she also lied about me cheating on her. It will sound harsh, but part of me wonders if she is a compulsive liar, maybe she can't help it. But I've got to know my wife well throughout the last few years and you can't believe a word she says.'

'As you'll be aware, Blair Priest agreed to verify all of this, but just this morning she revealed she is too unwell to attend. Does that seem like a coincidence to you?'

I missed all of this. I don't know if it was reported in the news this morning because I didn't check it.

'She signed an NDA although I didn't know that before today. It means she can't talk about what she was contracted to do. Someone in Tori's legal team must have made her aware of the consequences of breaking it.' I catch Ethan glancing at someone from the corner of his eye. I can't tell who it is from this angle but my bet is on Tori or that barrister of hers.

'No further questions, my Lady.'

Ethan's lawyer takes a seat. It's a hell of a line to end on. In just over twenty-four hours, Ethan and his lawyer have managed to completely reverse the public opinion on this case. Before things started, I thought that Tori was the victim of Ethan's cheating and that the trial was just a way for Ethan to try and grab some money. Now it seems like Tori has been the villain all along. A cheat. Now a liar.

Tori's lawyer stands for her turn. I have to say, if I had to pick someone to represent me I would've chosen her. Tori's lawyer is the perfect advocate for her, she's glamorous yet fierce, a younger Miranda Priestly in *The Devil Wears Prada* compared to Ethan's lawyer who seems experienced but old-fashioned and weird.

'Mr Simmons, do you have any evidence that my client paid Blair Priest money to sing on Tori's album?'

'Well, I saw her in the studio and when I confronted Tori she told me that she was paying Blair Priest to perform the vocals for the album, or rather the label was. Blair also told me herself, and she would have told the court before you put a stop to her.'

'Mr Simmons,' the judge cautions him.

'I will ignore that allegation. So you are expecting us to believe that Tori told you that this was the arrangement?'

'Yes.'

'And I assume you have evidence of that conversation then? A recording perhaps? Maybe a detailed note?'

'Well, no. I don't. But it happened.'

'So, we just have to take your word for it that this conversation happened?'

The judge cautions her line of questioning.

'So if you don't have evidence of the conversation in which my client allegedly told you about this plan, is your only evidence that you found Blair Priest recording my client's songs in her home recording studio?'

'Yes, but that seems quite damming to me. Why else would she be recording them?'

'Have you listened to my client's new album?'

Ethan appears unsure of what to say, his eyes darting around the room.

'I, well it's not that I haven't listened to it … I mean, I've been busy.'

'Is that a no?'

'I've not listened to it. Not properly. I heard snippets being recorded, that's all.'

'If you had listened to it, you would know that a lot of the songs have backing singers featured, including her song, "Payback is Sweeter than You". And in that song in particular, the backing vocals are present throughout almost the entire song. Is this the song that you heard Blair Priest recording?'

'I couldn't say.'

'Let me give you a refresher of the chorus in case that helps jog your memory.

You treated me so bad and you made me so sad
You were all that I had, all that I had
You brought another girl into our home
So many times I watched those wandering hands roam
You said it was all in my head, all in my head
Then I found you fucking her in our bed, in our bed
So I told everyone what you did, that it was all true,
And now I know payback is sweeter than you.

'Does that ring a bell, Mr Simmons?'

Listening to the lawyer with the posh English accent read out the lines to Tori's latest bubble-gum pop number makes it worth watching this. I wonder how many times this clip is about to be reshared across social media. This will be a viral trend on TikTok, I'm sure.

'I don't know.'

'I put it to you, Mr Simmons, that you couldn't know if my client was paying Blair Priest to record songs for the album, especially given that Blair Priest has now refused to provide any witness testimony in this case. There is no evidence of any such arrangement and what you describe is very likely to have been Blair Priest recording backing vocals for my client's album. And if you look in the credits on the album you will see that she has been credited for that work.'

Ethan doesn't respond.

'No further questions.'

Ethan sits next to his barrister, his part in the trial now done. Tori's lawyer did a good job of refuting the accusations but sometimes accusations are enough to ruin a career even if they can't be backed up by any proof.

Ethan's barrister, whose name I can't remember, stands. Luckily the streaming service shows the name on screen each time somebody starts speaking. Thomas Grantham KC. He clears his throat.

'The claimant calls Jasper C Morris.'

The director's turn. Everyone thinks that he is just going to confirm what we already know. That Tori told him exactly the things that Ethan is alleging. Tori never denied that she did.

'Mr Morris, can you please confirm your relationship to Ethan Simmons?'

'I am the film director of the *Aces & Diamonds* movie series based on the popular YA fantasy book series. Until December last year, Ethan Simmons was contracted to play the lead male character, Leo Trax, in that series,' Jasper says. His Nashville twang has disappeared over the years but I can still hear it as he pronounces certain words.

'And what happened in December last year which meant Ethan Simmons was fired from his role of Leo Trax?'

The courtroom is quiet as everybody waits for his answer.

'Ethan was fired because he breached his contract. I became aware that he had breached his contract from his wife, Tori Simmons.'

'And what did Tori Simmons tell you?'

'She told me that Ethan had been unfaithful in their relationship. She also told me that she had become aware from a friend in the media that a major magazine was planning to publish an exposé on Ethan Simmons.'

'An exposé? But that hasn't appeared, even after this whole trial business.'

'No, it hasn't.'

'And what happened after Tori told you this information?'

'I talked about it with the rest of the crew and the studio. Because of my ethics and the studio we work for, we insist that all actors and actresses have a morality clause in their contract.'

'Why?'

'Over the Rainbow Studios, which produces the *Aces &
Diamonds* series, primarily produces children's films with the
occasional YA film. *Aces & Diamonds* is slightly racier than the
studio's usual content but we kept it incredibly classy and
produced a lower rated version along with the explicit version
for different audiences. The studio has put a lot of money
behind *Aces & Diamonds* but the board do not want bad press
associated with any of its stars that could lead to blowback on
its other projects.'

'And what does this morality clause say?'

'Essentially the actor can't engage in a lifestyle that could
bring them or the studio into disrepute. From what Tori told
me, I believed that Ethan had done that and so I terminated his
contract.'

'What evidence did Tori provide you with backing up her
allegations?'

'She didn't provide any.'

'So you just took what she said at face value and acted
on it?'

'Yes.'

'So to be clear, you were never given any evidence that
Ethan Simmons cheated on his wife, yet terminated his
contract anyway?'

'That's correct.'

'No further questions, my Lady.'

Chapter Eleven

VICTORIA 'TORI' SIMMONS

The judge asks if Faye has any questions for Jasper but she declines to question him. I can tell from the whisperings behind me people in the courtroom are surprised by this answer. Faye had already told me this was her strategy but I can't help feeling anxious. Is she making a mistake? She said that we had nothing to gain from questioning Jasper because I wasn't denying what I said to him. I hope she's right.

'We're going to break for lunch and then you'll be up,' Faye says as she pushes her piles of paper into an overflowing lever arch folder as the people in the courtroom file out of the door. She cradles it in her arms and follows the crowd. 'Don't panic, you'll be fine. We've been through it enough times.'

It is easy for Faye to say as somebody who spends as much time in court as she does at home. I've never been to court, which actually these days is unusual for a celebrity. It feels alien to me and the thought of having everyone's eyes on me makes the contents of my stomach fester in the back of my throat. This is going to be the performance of my life.

Faye must spot my nerves over lunch as she keeps

reassuring me with every other sentence. She tells me that the first part is easy. She's only going to ask me the questions we've already practised together, and all I need to do is recall the answers we've rehearsed. There are no surprises. The difficult part is when Ethan's barrister cross-examines me, but she tells me it won't be as bad as I imagine. He will be trying to catch me out but I just need to keep my composure and stick to what I've already said – don't give him anything new to latch onto. Faye calls him a rottweiler and tells me I can't throw him a bone.

Back in court, once everyone is seated, I'm instructed to take my place at the front. It's uncomfortable looking at all the faces staring back at me, and the cameras are livestreaming everything to thousands more anonymous faces online. A bead of sweat drips down my forehead despite the cool temperature in this room. I don't know what to do with my hands. If only I had pockets, but I don't, so instead let them rest by my side.

Faye rises from her seat and this is the cue that it's beginning. I take a deep breath through my nose like they teach us in my yoga classes. It's not enough though, I can feel my heart pulsing. I've had a lower heart rate during a SoulCycle class.

'Tori, how long have you been married to Mr Simmons?'

'A year. We've been together for two.'

'You had what many called a whirlwind romance, correct?'

'Yes, we got engaged a year after meeting and then our marriage took place a couple months after that. They say when you know, you know. Ethan was everything I wanted in a partner. He was handsome and we had a lot of fun together, at first anyway.'

'And when did things start to change?'

'When I first met Ethan, he was filming the first *Aces & Diamonds* film. It was Ethan's first major role. The fame was so new to him. It was different for me, I was part of Lipstick Lasses as a teen and I'd been in the spotlight for all of my adult life. The thing is, fame can change people. And that's what happened to Ethan.'

'What do you mean?'

'Well, when we first got together he was enamoured by me. He did everything for me and I felt truly loved. But then shortly after we got married and the success of the film became unprecedented, things went downhill. I had to move back to London because my mother is sick so we went long-distance which is hard for any couple. He started spending more time out partying and making excuses why he couldn't travel to see me or why he wasn't free for a call. And then there were all the rumours about his co-star.'

'And that would be Nikki Feldman, correct?'

'Yes.'

Nikki is exactly the type of woman that people worry about their husband spending too much time with. She is beautiful in a Victoria's Secret Angel type of way. Obvious. Seductive. She was not only an actress, but also a model and is regularly featured on luxury perfume adverts. She looked good on screen – she's the Megan Fox of this generation. I've been jealous of her even before I met Ethan.

Nikki turned heads even amongst the Hollywood stars used to being surrounded by the genetically blessed. The films already had the young girls hooked with Ethan and those who were fans of the books, and then they got the male audience in with Nikki dressed in tiny shorts and crop tops. And of course, all the girls wanted to look like Nikki. Every magazine article for months was about her workout routine or her skincare regime.

The media saw it as a chance to make a story out of nothing. I would be pictured without Ethan and the papers started saying it was because we'd had an argument when the truth is that he was out with friends or working. Ethan would be pictured with Nikki on set and the papers would crop it so it looked like they were together outside of work. Every time I left the house they'd hide in the bushes and take photographs of me, find the one where I looked the most miserable and publish things like 'Tori looks glum after rumoured trouble in paradise' and 'Tori's heartache over Ethan's rumoured affair'. And none of it was true. Until it was.

'My Lady, I'd like to draw your attention to exhibit SIM004. Mrs Simmons, do you think Ethan cheated on you with Nikki Feldman?'

'Yes.'

I don't like to be that person but it was the media's fault that it happened. The constant headlines and photographs eventually did the trick and got to me. And so we fought and fought. I became paranoid, jealous. He became secretive. I started snooping on his phone. He started changing his passwords. It was a game of cat and mouse and eventually I caught them.

'Do you have any proof?'

I sigh. 'No. I caught them, saw it with my own eyes. But no, I don't have any photographic evidence. I'm sure if I looked through Ethan's phone, looked at his card statements, there would be a trail of breadcrumbs.'

'But unfortunately Ethan's phone with potentially incriminating information is not available, is it?' Faye asks.

'No. Apparently he accidentally left it in his jeans pocket and it didn't survive the washing machine. The data on it was irrecoverable.'

'How convenient,' Faye says and I notice the judge purse her lips together. 'What happened after you walked in on Ethan cheating?'

'I confronted him about Nikki and he admitted it and we agreed to start afresh. Put all the trouble behind us.'

'This was in September, so a couple of months before the party at Jasper Morris's house?'

'Yes.'

'And he moved to London in October?'

'Yes. Although he wasn't permanently here, he was still flying back and forth as he'd started filming for the second film. I made him agree to be based here though to get away from the toxic lifestyle he had.'

'That's not the reason you told people publicly, is it?'

'No. We told people that I wanted to be closer to my family. We knew if the media found out about the affair that we would never hear the end of it. Unfortunately the move to London was only just the beginning. Things got worse quickly.'

'Did Ethan cheat on you again once you moved to London?'

'Yes. He became a serial cheater. He also became more brazen about it. Each time he'd apologise and tell me he'd never do it again but he got around more than most single men I know.'

'What possessed you to finally talk about Ethan's infidelity? And to Jasper, of all people?'

'It was when he met Alice. Alice in Wonderland came into our lives and our marriage fell down a rabbit hole.'

TROUBLE IN PARADISE? TORI LOOKS GLUM AS LOVERBOY ETHAN CUDDLES UP TO SMOKING HOT CO-STAR NIKKI

Tori was spotted looking upset as she ventured out to the gym in Soho yesterday. She was seen sporting a two-piece from Lululemon and her hair was piled on top of her head in a messy bun. The bare-faced singer was alone as her beau, Ethan, was seen spending the day out with his co-star Nikki Feldman. No doubt the star was in the gym working hard to maintain that svelte physique of hers to edge out the competition. Last year Nikki was voted America's sexiest woman and her Instagram is full of bikini-clad photos of the model turned Hollywood starlet. Tori is older than Nikki and must be feeling the pressure.

<tori-alone.jpeg>
Tori was spotted looking fed up as rumours swirl about Ethan and his co-star.

Ethan and Nikki have been spending a lot of time together lately. An anonymous source told us that Ethan and Nikki's on-screen chemistry has been spilling into their off-screen time together. The duo, who fans have already coined 'Ekki', have been seen enjoying time together in their rare breaks from filming in Vancouver, far away from Ethan's wife Tori who is currently in London.

<nikki-and-ethan-together.jpeg>
Ethan and Nikki spend time together

Sources close to Tori have said she is 'reeling' and 'upset' after seeing the photos of the pair together. Apparently the previously loved-up couple have been arguing more lately and sources say Tori worries Ethan might be involved with Nikki. Tori notably hasn't been to visit Ethan in over a month. It looks like it might no longer be smooth sailing for Hollywood's most loved up couple.

It wouldn't be the first time co-stars have got together and broken up relationships. Last year, Eleana Barker was devastated when her boyfriend of two years broke off their relationship to pursue things with his co-star Rebecca Watson.

<Rebecca-watson-affair-with-troy>

Enjoyed this story? Why not leave a comment below?

Comments:

Nikkiisfit2883
He definitely traded up if he went with Nikki … can't think of any woman hotter than her right now!!

Alex_A_TUF
Does anyone think Tori has put on a bit of weight lately? Only hitting the gym and taking care of herself because she's worried she'll lose her man! Maybe if she'd put some effort in before she wouldn't need to worry.

Leah_Farmer2710

Think the comments about Tori's weight are unfair. She's tiny. Last month you were all saying she was too skinny and should eat more. Women can never win can we.

Tash_Tasha

Maybe she's pregnant??

Chapter Twelve

ETHAN SIMMONS

Bitch.

I knew that Tori would fight back against everything I said. I should have known that she'd play dirty. After all, she already showed her true self when she blabbed about our private life. She is just doing this for sympathy, but I know Thomas will tear her to pieces; she has no evidence.

'What possessed you to finally talk about Ethan's infidelity? If, as you say, he started cheating on you in the summer of 2024, why did it take you months to speak up?'

'It was because Alice was different than the others.'

Tori glances at me as she says it, smirking. A wicked glint in her eye. Nobody in this room, in this world, knows the significance of what Tori has just said. The Alice in Wonderland reference will be nonsense to everyone else. They'll think she's playing games and right now she's just landed the checkmate. I'm sure the media and TikTok wannabes will dissect that sentence and wonder what she means. Maybe somebody will find some deep meaning behind it and say Tori was using symbolism or something like that. But the truth is that Tori knows exactly what she is doing.

'Who was Alice, Tori?'

'Alice was Ethan's girlfriend. The others, it was about sex. It was difficult to deal with and made me insecure but I could handle it. It was a physical thing. I convinced myself he just needed an outlet but he still loved me and that if I removed the temptation he'd stop eventually. A lot of men in Hollywood cheat all the time. The public don't hear about it because the agents are good at keeping it out of the press. But Alice was different.'

'And what made her different?'

'He loved her. And I think he was going to leave me for her.'

'What made you think that he loved her?'

'I went through his phone. I saw the texts he sent to her. The others, it would be sharing photos or videos. Telling them they were hot and arranging times for them to meet. He didn't do that with Alice. Their messages were about the future. They arranged dates, not hook-ups. I think they met in London but she was actually American so maybe she reminded him of home.'

'These texts which don't exist anymore?'

'Because Ethan's phone was destroyed, yes. If it was still around, it would validate everything I was saying. It's convenient for Ethan that it's not.' Her eyes meet mine and the stare she gives me could turn me into stone. My beautiful Medusa.

I know Thomas doesn't want to go anywhere near this line of questioning. Yes, all the messages no longer exist. Yes, my phone was destroyed because I accidentally left it in my pants pocket when I washed them. The technical teams tried their best but they couldn't recover anything. It was such a shame it could never be used as evidence in this trial.

'Moving on, you thought the evidence you found was enough for you to think he was going to leave you?'

Tori nods. She's looking straight at me now as she speaks. I've never seen my wife look so in control. I'm mad at her right now for the poison that she is spewing but she's never looked more alluring, more enchanting.

'I followed them once. To one of their secret meeting places. You know the one I mean, don't you, Ethan? It's well hidden, isn't it?''

'Ms Simmons, please do not address Mr Simmons directly,' the judge warns.

Tori is talking in code, more mind games. But of course she's talking directly to me. She doesn't want anybody else to understand but she needs me to know how far she is willing to go. Hell hath no fury like a woman scorned and I've well and truly pushed Tori past her limits.

'Anyway, they were together. I mean, not *together* together, they were still fully clothed.' Tori grabs a tissue from her blazer pocket and starts wiping at imaginary tears. 'It was hurtful.'

'What happened then?'

'I was so upset but also furious at how I was being treated. She was just a young girl, she knew all about mine and Ethan's marriage and was continuing to plot and scheme with him without ever thinking of what it was doing to me. I had to confront them both. I wanted Alice to see that I'm a real person behind all the tabloids and I wanted her to know the destruction she was causing.'

'What did Ethan and Alice say when you confronted them?'

'Well, that depends.'

'Depends on what? I don't understand.'

Tori's solicitor's brow is furrowed. I watch as she checks her notes, quickly turning the pages. I'm guessing Tori didn't fill her in on this part of her plan.

'Shall I tell the world what happened next, Ethan? What I saw when I walked in? What happened to the girl who held the seven of diamonds playing card in her right hand?'

Tori's barrister wasn't expecting her to say this.

I grab Thomas's sleeve and tug, leaping up and whispering in his ear. 'You need to stop this. You need to stop this now.'

There's a break in questioning while Tori's barrister frantically flicks through her notes. Thomas ignores me so I press my mouth against his ear and through gritted teeth tell him to stop.

'If you don't ask for a break now I will make a scene.'

I can't have Tori continuing with her testimony – not until I know how far she is willing to go with it. She's been cryptic enough with her riddles that hopefully nobody watching will be able to put the pieces together, but if she keeps talking along these lines, if she identifies who Alice is and what actually happened, then all hell will break loose. Tori cannot spill that secret. I will take that secret to my grave one way or another.

'My Lady.' Thomas finally stands and not a second too soon. 'My client has a family emergency. Can we adjourn to tomorrow morning?'

She seems to consider it. She too must be confused at the state of events but hides it well. She could say no, she could demand that Tori continues. If I was her, I'd want to let this play out. I'd have to find a way to stop it. 'Very well.'

We rise as Justice Shellings leaves the courtroom. My heart rate finally returns to normal but the fabric of my shirt still sticks to my lower back and I smell my natural odour overpowering my overpriced cologne.

'You'd better tell me what that was about after I just

embarrassed myself in front of this entire court.' I've never seen Thomas this angry, not at me. I can see now why he has a reputation for provoking tears in even the most hardened of witnesses.

'Not here.'

We leave the courtroom and Thomas drags me to the corner. He folds his arms across his chest. 'Spit it out.'

'I think I want to settle out of court,' I say, bracing myself for Thomas's reaction. Thomas mentioned settling to me numerous times after I came to him wanting to pursue the claim against Tori. He tried to explain to me that celebrity defamation trials were receiving so much attention recently that the additional attention could mean unscrupulous actions from my past are brought up, not just by Tori's team but by the media and the social media sleuths. But I said no each time. We've come so far, to only get this far.

'You are joking? Ethan, we have had countless pre-trial discussions about settling and every time you were adamant that you wanted this to play out in a trial. I believe your words were that you wanted "to show the public the real Tori Simmons"?'

His memory is impeccable. 'Yes, I may have said that.'

'So why are you now changing your mind? I told you I thought settling was smart but now that the trial has already begun the advantages of settling have gone out of the window. If you settle now, people may infer that it's because you think your case against Tori is too weak.'

'Do you think it is too weak?'

'Not at all. I didn't follow the latest part of her testimony and I'm not sure her own barrister did either. Either way, I would say that the case is still heavily weighted in your favour. Tori's testimony may have sounded persuasive but she hasn't managed to produce any concrete evidence of your infidelity, it has all been conjecture and coincidence.' Thomas pauses as a group of people walk past. 'If you want to settle because you're worried about the outcome of the case, I must implore you not to. You are in as strong a position as ever.'

I sigh. I don't know what the right thing to do is. Thomas is right, I can see the headlines now. They'll parrot that I settled because Tori was telling the truth all along about me cheating. I can visualise Tori capitalising on my weakness, becoming the public's darling. She will come out shining while I'm dragged through mud.

'Why did you make me stop proceedings? You can't just stop proceedings.'

I don't have an answer for him. How can I tell him the truth? The truth that I was worried Tori was going to tell everyone what we did to Alice Grey. And if she does that ... I might never see the light of day again. Then again, neither would she.

Chapter Thirteen

@THETRUTHISGREY

I've been staring at my phone, as if the longer I stare at it, the more likely it will ring. That a message will pop up. That anything will happen. It has only been a day, not even twenty-four hours, but I haven't heard from the cops yet. And all I care about is finding out if my sister is dead. I have played out every scenario in my head, lived every eventuality and played out my part. But nothing, nothing will satisfy me until I have my answer.

The trial is proving an interesting distraction. Alice in Wonderland. Tori said Ethan was dating Alice in Wonderland. She also said she held the seven of diamonds playing card in her right hand. Tori was talking about my sister, *my Alice*. It couldn't be anyone else. That was originally my nickname for her but Alice used to refer to herself as Alice in Wonderland too. She was obsessed with the book and the film, would quote it constantly. It reminded her of our childhood. And maybe, maybe, I could convince myself that was a coincidence, there are a lot of small, blonde girls in London.

But that's not all Tori said. Alice loved the book so much that she got an Alice in Wonderland related tattoo. It was a pair of playing cards, like the playing cards that are servants for the Queen of Hearts. She got them on her right arm near her wrist. And the card that was closest to her wrist, on her right hand? That was the seven of diamonds because seven was Alice's lucky number.

If Alice's body is lying in the police station, Tori and Ethan know something about what happened to her. It is selfish of them not going to the police with what they know. How dare they use my trauma for gossip fodder and as part of their games? I thought she was about to reveal everything but court proceedings got interrupted. It wasn't clear on the livestream what happened but it was Ethan's barrister that engineered it so that the proceedings would be over for the day. Ethan must be scared about what Tori was going to say.

I don't know what to do first. Do I seek out Ethan and Tori and confront them? If I tell them she's my sister, maybe they'll tell me the truth. That's doubtful considering it looks like they are about to settle out of court just to avoid the truth coming out. How would I even get anywhere near them without security intervening? I could broadcast what I know on my TikTok channel. Maybe there are others out there that could help put the missing pieces together.

'Shocking news from the courtroom just now as court is suspended for the day. The rumours are that Tori and Ethan are thinking of settling out of court.' Oskar 's voice rings in my ears outside the court as he speaks directly to his phone. 'What do we reckon? Is this because Ethan doesn't think he can win the case anymore or is something else at play here? I don't know about you but Tori's last testimony confused me. Who is this Alice girl Ethan was seeing? Anybody know who she is?'

I want to interrupt him and tell him I know exactly who the Alice girl that they are talking about is. I restrain myself though, because I know acting impulsively is not the smart thing to do. I've been waiting so long to find a new lead in my sister's disappearance and now that I've been handed one, I don't want to mess it up by charging ahead like a bull. I need to be strategic about this. If my sister is dead, the missing person investigation suddenly becomes a murder enquiry. And I've found my prime suspects.

> **@thetruthisgrey**
> How did you know that Tori was going to talk about my sister today? What do you know?

> **@thetruthisblackandwhite2011**
> I can't tell you how I know.

This user is frustrating. I don't understand why this person can't reveal their identity.

> **@thetruthisgrey**
> Are you Tori? Is that how you knew what she was going to say today? Is that why there is all this secrecy?

> **@thetruthisblackandwhite2011**
> I'm not Tori. I'm just somebody that has a vested interest in the case and seeing justice done.

> **@thetruthisgrey**
> What do I do now?

> **@thetruthisblackandwhite2011**
> Nothing. Just wait.

Wait? That can't be the answer. I can't find out what Ethan and Tori know about my sister's disappearance by doing nothing.

> **@thetruthisgrey**
> Waiting can't be the answer. I need to do something.

> **@thetruthisgrey**
> Hello?

> **@thetruthisgrey**
> Please give me a sign.

> **@thetruthisblackandwhite2011**
> You need to trust me. I can't help you if you don't trust me.

They told me I'd find out more about my sister by covering the trial. They told me that Tori's testimony today would shed further on the link to my sister's case today and they were right. I thought she'd say more though; all she has done so far is allude to a connection I already knew existed from the anonymous user. I know Ethan was dating my sister. I want to know what his involvement was in her going missing.

I look at my phone. I should be doing what Oskar is and reporting on the trial. It's a major piece of news and I can hear the other media outlets surrounding the court spilling their thoughts about what Tori's testimony might mean. It's ironic, the one time I have precious information that others don't and I don't want to broadcast it.

'Tori made some odd references to Alice in Wonderland in her testimony today. What do you think that means?' I hear one news reporter ask another.

'I think perhaps Ethan was dating a young girl. Perhaps she was underage. It wouldn't be the first time that a celebrity has been in trouble for dating someone younger than they should have. If that was the case, it would be a devastating blow to Ethan's career if it were to come out. Hollywood has stopped turning a blind eye to such activity.'

I hear another speculate.

'I think Alice in Wonderland was a code word. I still maintain that this entire trial was a PR stunt set up by the couple's agents to boost their popularity. I've always thought it was more than just a coincidence that Tori's album launched the week before the trial. I don't know what the code word is meant to mean but I think Tori was trying to give Ethan a message. Maybe about settling.'

I can't handle this. I need answers now. I stride towards Oskar, interrupting his livestream by grabbing his phone from his tripod and turning it off. I'm not his biggest fan but I have to admit that he's good at what he does. He manages to get information quicker than anyone else on the platform. He always knows things others don't, the prime person for breaking a scoop. I don't know who his sources are but they must be genuine. If anyone can help me, it's him.

'What the hell do you think you're doing? Give me my phone back now.'

'I need to talk to you.'

'Yeah well I'm busy. Go find someone else to disturb.'

'I know who the Alice is that they're talking about. And I'll tell you. But only if you help me.'

'How do I know you're not lying?'

'You know me, Oskar. I've never bent the truth when reporting on cases. I have integrity and I always have done.' I don't add *unlike you* to the end of the sentence as that won't make him more likely to help me.

'Fine. What do you need me to do?'

'I need you to help me track someone down.'

My phone rings, interrupting our conversation. It's an unknown number.

'Sorry, I need to get this,' I say. 'Hello?'

'Riley Grey? It's DS Taylor. We have the results of the DNA testing.'

Chapter Fourteen

VICTORIA 'TORI' SIMMONS

I knew I was going to get an earful from Faye as soon as we left the courtroom. She ushers me to one side, pinching my arm as she drags me away as if I'm her child rather than her client.

'What were you doing in there? We had a script. We practised the questions and answers. Why did you deviate? You can't deviate,' Faye says. 'We were up all night going through this.'

'I know I was supposed to stick with what we've discussed but I thought of a new plan on the spot and decided to go with it.'

'You can't do that. You completely blindsided me. How am I supposed to act on your behalf if you go off piste? You're in luck that Ethan's barrister asked for the proceedings to be adjourned or I'm not sure what we would've done. You can't do this again. I will not represent somebody who jeopardizes their own case.'

Ava hurries over with Jessika, as if things can get any worse.

'What's going on?' Jessika says.

'You need to tell your client to buck her ideas up. She can't just make up her testimony on the spot and expect to win this case.'

'I don't understand, Tori, I thought we spoke about how you were going to talk about Ethan's history of lying. You were going to talk about how he lied about having gone to certain acting schools to land his agent. You said you also had evidence he lied about his upbringing in interviews to gain sympathy. I thought that was the game plan?' Ava says.

'I know. I know. But I realised that strategy wasn't going to work. Nobody thinks Ethan can act anyway. He got cast in *Aces & Diamonds* because he's hot so nobody is going to care. I thought this would be a better idea.'

'And what even is your idea? What were you talking about on the stand and why were you being so cryptic?' Ava asks, hands on her hips. I've never seen my solicitor so animated, she's usually so mild.

'It's something that's just between me and Ethan for now. I can't explain what I'm talking about.'

'You've got be kidding me,' Ava says.

Faye laughs.

'Why won't you tell us? If you have something on Ethan that would help your case, why wouldn't you use it?' Faye asks.

'You don't understand. It would ruin Ethan's life.'

'So?' Jessika says. She has no empathy for anyone. I've always thought she's particularly bullish but I suppose you have to be in her business.

'I can't say more, not without talking to Ethan first. But what I know about Alice is so much more than some silly little affair like I know you're thinking it is. It's more than you could even imagine.'

'If you don't use it, you are going to lose this trial. I know you're protecting Ethan for reasons I don't understand but it's a choice between you or him right now,' Faye says. I can see the hope in her eyes knowing that she might have an easier route to win this trial.

'The thing is, what I know won't just destroy Ethan's life, it'll destroy mine too.'

'Hasn't Ethan already done that? He leaked your nudes. You're going to lose this case,' Faye tells me.

'Your record label told me this morning they are going to drop you as a client. They said your name is tarnished,' Jessika adds to the list of my worries. 'I know Blair didn't end up coming to court but what Ethan said was enough to spook them. Your music career is over.'

'So, please tell me why you are protecting this man?'

'I ... I don't know.'

'Tori, I spoke to my friend at *HotCelebGossip!*, the first newspaper to post about the photographs. He told me his source after I gave him some very juicy information on one of my other clients in return. He said those photographs came from an email address belonging to Ethan Simmons. He didn't even get Thomas to do it, he leaked those photographs himself,' Jessika says.

'He's going to keep going until you can't come back from this. If you have anything to use against him, we need it now,' Faye says. 'Wait, one second. I'll be right back.' She rushes off.

'I don't think what he's done is the end of his campaign against you,' says Jessika. 'My contact told me that he had something else up his sleeve. That he should expect to run more stories on you over the next few days.'

'Like what?' I ask.'

'I don't know, but he's not to be trusted. You need to destroy him before he destroys you.'

Chapter Fifteen

ETHAN SIMMONS

I need to talk to Tori. I need to find out if she's really willing to sacrifice herself in order to bring me down. Is she really going to tell the truth about Alice? We've kept the secret for the last few months, buried it deep. We made a pact. *We'll take it to the grave*, we said. I can't answer Thomas's questions so I make an excuse, escaping to the men's bathroom. Thankfully it's empty. I lean over the sink, running the tap and splashing cold water over my face to try and cool down. I can't stop sweating.

The door opens with such force it slams against the wall. 'Why did you run off? We were in the middle of a conversation,' Thomas says.

'I need to talk to Tori. Can you arrange that?' I ask Thomas.

'Is this about your idea of settling? As I said, we are going to win this case, I don't see why you would want to do that.'

'Thomas. Can you arrange a meeting with Tori or not?'

He nods. 'I can. I'll approach her legal team and see if Tori would be opening to discussing a potential settlement. Do you have a figure in mind?'

'No, not at the moment. I just need to talk to her. Alone.'

'I really wouldn't advise any conversations take place without your legal team.'

'Thomas. I am instructing you to do this. Do I need to find another barrister?'

'I'll go and find Faye.'

He disappears, leaving me to my thoughts. I leave the bathroom and find somewhere to sit while I wait for Thomas. What is the worst-case scenario here? The worst case would be if Tori gets back up on the stand tomorrow and tells everyone what happened with Alice. But maybe it wouldn't be too bad if she doesn't have any evidence. And there isn't any evidence. We both made sure of that. Right?

'Ethan,' Thomas calls as he makes his way towards me, beckoning me with his fingers.

I approach.

'Tori has agreed to talk to you but not without legal representation. We are going to speak back in my chambers as it's slightly closer than Faye's. Let's get a taxi with Roger and meet Tori and her team there. Did you want to call Owen?'

I think of my constantly distracted agent and the answer is easy. I don't need his opinion to make things more difficult for me. Owen is the one that pushed for this trial after he saw the rising fame of the celebrities that were tangled up in it, how they were all that was talked about. There is no chance he wants me dropping this. He cares more about this trial than I do.

'No, I'll text him to let him know,' I lie. Owen wasn't even in court today. Apparently he had a 'conflict' that he couldn't get out of. I'm glad really, because I didn't need him to see me stopping court proceedings.

We are the first to arrive at Thomas's chambers. He takes a seat behind his desk but I can't sit still. I pace around the office, glancing at the window to see if I can see Tori and her team approaching the entrance outside. Roger and Thomas engage in boring conversations about settlement strategy that I don't have the concentration to engage with. Luckily they realise there's no use trying to speak to me and discuss it amongst themselves.

'Why are they taking so long?' I say.

'Perhaps they got caught in traffic.' Thomas sounds unamused, disinterested.

'Or lost,' Roger says.

'They should've been right behind us. How would they be caught in traffic when we weren't?'

Thomas doesn't answer.

'Maybe I should ring her. See where she is. Just in case she's changed her mind.'

I take out my phone and scroll through my contacts to find Tori's number. I'm about to hit the 'call' button when Thomas's hand appears over the top of my phone as he takes it from my hands.

'I don't think that's a good idea. If she has changed her mind, it would only be courtesy for Faye to inform me that they weren't coming.'

Thomas's phone rings as soon as he finishes his sentence. He flashes me a look of surprise as he picks up the receiver.

'Thomas Grantham KC.'

I can't hear who is calling.

'Yes. Is that so?' Thomas says. I wish I could hear the other side of the conversation. 'Okay, thanks for informing me. I'll let him know.'

He hangs up.

'They're not coming, are they?' I slump into the chair behind me.

'Oh, I don't know. That wasn't Faye. It was about another case. I do have other clients, you know.'

I exhale deeply with relief, running my hands across my face. Tori should still be coming. There is still a chance we can talk this through. I can make her see sense. We can put all this trial business behind us. I thought the trial would help reignite my career after I lost the *Aces & Diamonds* contract but I care more about not letting what happened to Alice come out than my career.

Thomas's phone rings again.

'Thomas Grantham, KC.' A brief pause. 'Thank you, Antonia, please send them up.' He hangs up. 'Tori and her team are here, you'll be pleased to know.'

Tori and her entourage arrive. Faye greets me but Tori notably doesn't, avoiding eye contact. Jessika gives me a smirk and an insincere wave. We've never gotten on. When I first started dating Tori, I overheard her telling Tori that I wasn't good for her image and that dating a playboy like me would never end well. She wanted Tori to date another client of hers that was also in the music business. It was going to be a PR relationship to help both of their careers. Maybe things would have been better for both of us if Tori had listened to her then. Ava trails behind them all. She's noticeably out of place; much quieter, fades into the background.

'Right, have a seat all of you. My client has requested we meet today to discuss a potential settlement out of court. Now we've invited you here to—'

'Actually, can I talk to Tori alone first?' I interrupt. I need to see where her head is at before we go any further. I look at her to gauge her reaction but she still won't make eye contact with me.

'Ethan, that would be quite unusual for your legal counsel not to be present. I must advise you against that course of action,' Thomas says.

'I agree. I wouldn't advise any conversation occurring

without Thomas and I being present while we are in midst of court proceedings,' Faye adds. 'Ava and Roger too.'

'Tori, please. You know why we need to talk alone. We can't talk freely about … things … in front of our teams. You said you wouldn't speak any further about … things … if I agreed to settle. And I'm saying I'm open to settling but I want to talk to you alone before we start discussing any agreement.'

Tori makes eye contact with me for the first time since she arrived. Our eyes lock and I widen mine to signal my distress. I need her to talk to me, to reassure me that this whole thing was a scare tactic. Would she really destroy us both in the name of revenge for what I did to her? I need her to know that I'm sorry, that perhaps I went too far circulating her nudes.

'Actually, I came here because I wanted to tell you that I don't want to settle. I've thought about it and I think the whole world needs to know the truth. The whole truth. I have evidence to present too,' Tori says, picking up her bag and standing to leave. 'We were late because someone threw this through the window of our taxi.'

She hands me a plastic bag. I take out the contents and find a brick with the word *WHORE* written across it in what looks and smells like shit. I instantly drop it on the floor which causes Thomas to sigh.

'I hope tomorrow you realise that all actions have consequences,' Tori says. 'And maybe you'll realise why you should always clean up the mess you make.'

Tori spins and strides out of the room.

'Oh, Thomas, I'll be in touch this evening. We are going to submit some additional evidence in light of Tori's testimony tomorrow,' Faye adds. 'You'll want plenty of time to go over it given the impact this will have on your client's case.'

Faye and Jessika follow Tori without looking back at the destruction they have left. What evidence could she mean? We agreed that we'd get rid of all evidence of what happened to Alice … but … Tori was the one that dealt with everything. Did she keep something just for this moment? Was this her plan all along?

I can't let her tell everyone the truth.

Chapter Sixteen

@THETRUTHISGREY

The words of the phone call have been replaying on a loop since I heard them, like a sadistic pop song that never ends.

'It's not your sister.'

That's what he said. Despite the body carrying my sister's identity documents, the DNA result proved that whoever they found was someone else. The cop said that they were going to run the DNA though their database to see if it matched any other DNA on file.

I didn't know, and I still don't know, whether to feel happy or upset. There was a part of me that was relieved to finally have a conclusion to what happened to my sister. I can't begin to grieve properly until I know what happened to her, and this could have been the start of processing what happened. But knowing it's not my sister, it means there's a small hope that she's still okay. But hope, especially against all odds, often lends itself to bitter disappointment.

I ended up ditching Oskar after the call ended as I needed time to process. But I still think the right move is to involve him to get answers. I send him a message in the app asking if he's free to talk.

I spent the entire night lying awake thinking about Tori's testimony and the words she said. I spent hours replaying the online recording, analysing each word to see if I've missed something. I watched every video about the trial, read every article and listened to every opinion. I hoped that somehow I'd hear or see something that would make things clearer for me. Nothing.

I've been restless waiting for proceedings to start today. They don't start the live broadcast until they are ready to begin so I've been refreshing the page even though I know they start at 9.30am and never earlier.

Oskar writes back that he's free, sending me his number. I call straightaway.

'You rushed away pretty quickly yesterday.'

'I know, sorry. I had something to take care of. Once you help me, I'll explain everything.'

'If you say so. So what is it you need my help with?'

'There's someone that's been sending me messages on TikTok. I need your help tracking them down.'

'Is it a troll? Because honestly you just need to ignore them. Block, delete and move on.'

'No, not exactly. Look, can you help me find out the identity of a user on TikTok? But discreetly. I can't have them finding out I'm looking for them. If I send you their username, can you ask around your contacts to see if anyone knows who they are?'

'I can try. But you'll still tell me about this Alice person even if I don't find them?'

'Yes, don't worry. I'll keep my end of the bargain.'

'Okay. DM me the name. I'd better go as the trial is about to start. Media seem amped up this morning so something is going on.'

He ends the call before I can respond.

Oskar's right. The livestream has started. The judge has taken her seat. Tori should be the first one to speak today and I'm hoping her testimony continues with what she was talking about before. Maybe this is the day the truth comes out. I might not even need Oskar's help.

There have been a lot of rumours that Ethan and Tori are going to settle the case and that this morning the proceedings will just be a formality to state that they have settled and then it will all be over. Hopefully those rumours are wrong.

Tori's barrister stands.

'My Lady, I'm afraid I need to ask for a stay in the proceedings,' Faye says. 'I have been unable to locate my client this morning.'

The livestream microphone picks up murmurs in the courtroom, the sound of people shifting in their seats, no doubt all eyes fixed on where Tori should be. I didn't even notice that Tori isn't sat next to Faye and Ava like she always is.

'Very well, but Ms Robertson, I won't be staying proceedings again so I suggest you find your client quickly.'

The livestream cuts out. What is happening? I need to know what is going on. I order a taxi on my phone and start searching social media for any more information. There's nothing yet. I need to get to court to see if anybody knows anything. What is going on? This meant to be her big day. Everyone has been waiting for this.

During the taxi journey, the updates filter in. It's all piecemeal at the moment. Tori didn't show up for court this morning. She didn't answer the door to her friend Shelley when she visited this morning. Some people are speculating that she's had a breakdown and that the stress of the trial was too much and she's done a runner or is perhaps in some fancy celeb facility for treatment. Some think this is all for attention. I should message the anonymous account to see if they have more information. I send a message. I message Oskar too as he's always in the know. He knows more than I ever do.

The cab can't get close to the court. Not surprising. Apparently the roads are gridlocked with news vans and traffic. I jump out of the cab and run the last few blocks to the court. When I arrive there is a sea of cameras. The court has been busy the whole time but this is different, there are unfamiliar faces and logos for news channels I've never heard of. I find Oskar in his usual spot.

'Oskar, Oskar!' I yell as I run towards him.

'Guys, I need to pause the livestream quickly but I'll be right back,' Oskar says towards the camera.

'Seriously, Riley? I was in the middle of a livestream. You'd better have a good reason for interrupting me. Just because my coverage is getting way more hits than your lacklustre attempt is not reason to try and sabotage me.' Everything sounds blunter in his German accent.

'Get over yourself. Do you know what's going on with the trial? The livestream ended abruptly.'

'No. All I know at the moment is that Tori is missing. Apparently her bed wasn't slept in. Her phone is off and she didn't tell anyone where she was going. I know people are saying it is for attention but something doesn't feel right.'

'Have you heard any inside information? What are the news reporters saying?'

The news reporters always hear more information than we do. Sometimes they're kind enough to feed us tips in exchange for us crediting them.

'What, so you can use it on your own channel?'

'Fuck, no. I won't use it on my channel. I just need to know, Oskar, please.'

'Look, I don't know much, okay? But I did hear that apparently despite what everybody was hinting at, Tori and Ethan weren't going to settle.'

'Really?'

'Really. Apparently Ethan wanted to settle but Tori refused. She was going to continue whatever she started yesterday.'

'Thanks, Oskar.'

'Now, can I get back to my livestream?' He points at his camera. It's phrased as a question but I know it's rhetorical as he inserts his AirPods in his ears. 'Welcome back to my livestream everyone. Sorry for that brief pause, I was just talking to one of my contacts close to the case about what is going on. So a quick recap for anyone that has been living under a rock – day three of the Simmons trial and Tori has failed to show up to court…'

I walk away from Oskar and his livestream, letting his voice slowly fade out. I can't be bothered to listen to him any longer. It is interesting what he said about Tori not settling with Ethan. That means she was about to tell the truth, the truth about my sister. And then she didn't turn up to court. Almost like somebody knew the secrets she was about to spill and put a stop to it.

There's a change in the tone of the noise surrounding me. What was a general wave of confusion turns into something much bigger. Panic. People start talking in hushed voices. Running. Something has happened. I can sense the change in the air.

If anyone knows what's going on, it will be Oskar. I rush towards him.

'What's going on?' I ask.

'I don't know, but we've been told we all need to leave right away.'

'What? Why?'

'I don't know but it sounded pretty serious. I'm going to get going. Continue the livestream from somewhere else. Apparently some of the news reporters are going to move to Trafalgar Square to get some shots.' He slings his bag over his shoulder. 'See you there?'

'No, I'm not going.'

'Guess I'll see you around,' he says with a shrug.

I spot a policeman in the crowd talking to the departing reporters. I approach him for clarity.

'Hey, is it true we have to leave?'

'Yes. We need to clear this area, please.'

'Can I ask why?'

'You can ask, but I'm not going to answer. The police want this area cleared in the next five minutes so I suggest you head on out.'

Is it because they're worried about Ethan's safety? There's going to be even more attention on him without Tori to share the limelight.

'Miss, can you please leave the area? I don't want to have to keep asking,' the same cop says.

'Yes, sorry, I was just going. Do you know when we will be allowed back?'

'Not at the moment.'

There's a café across the street. I go in for a coffee and grab a seat next to the window. A window that clearly faces the Royal Courts of Justice and has a front-seat view of whatever is happening there. The area is almost empty now with just the final crews packing up their equipment.

There are now news reports that there was no settlement agreement on the table, so Oskar's information was correct.

Everything is still speculation but from the sounds of things nobody has heard from Tori. All the big news outlets report having reached out to Tori's and Ethan's teams but they have not had any comments from either of them. What is going on inside that courthouse?

Some of the updates have noted that they are going to pause broadcasting while they move locations. It doesn't look as if the police gave any of them any reasoning for having to leave the area – I thought perhaps they would tell someone more official than a TikTok sleuth the real reason.

I keep my eyes firmly glued on the entrance to the Royal Courts of Justice. What if there is another way out? If they are worried about Ethan's safety then they might have him use a less public exit, but then what would have been the purpose of evacuating everyone? I've given up hoping to spot something, maybe it was a bad idea to stay here. I should go back to the hotel and wait for any news. If Tori is missing then the potential lead on Alice might have disappeared.

Only the dregs of my overpriced coffee remain. The door to the courthouse opens and people trickle out. I can't tell if Ethan is in the crowd as a swarm of people leave. It doesn't help that it's raining and the umbrellas obscure my vision. A car pulls up and several people file in. It's followed by a second car.

That was probably Ethan leaving along with his team.

I take the underground back to the hotel. I have no signal so it's only when I surface that I see my phone pinging with messages. There's a ton of comments on my last TikTok video asking me to comment on the news about Tori. I stand in the concourse of the station checking my phone to work out what news they are talking about. It comes up as soon as I type Tori's name into the search bar.

SINGER TORI SIMMONS REPORTED MISSING

5 June 2025 12:31pm

Singer Tori Simmons, who is currently embroiled in a tense defamation trial with actor husband Ethan Simmons, has been reported as missing. She has not been seen since 11pm last night at her home in Hampstead. Police are currently investigating but are treating the disappearance as suspicious.

This is a breaking news story. Follow *TheLondonNews* on Facebook, Instagram and X for live updates. Got a story? Email us at hello@thelondonnews.com.

Related Topics

Missing People

News articles from other websites lack any further details. The critics accusing Tori of disappearing from the trial because she was seeking attention have been silenced. She would only have been reported as a missing person if there was cause to believe something had happened. It hasn't even been twenty-four hours since she was last seen and Tori isn't a vulnerable adult.

What has happened to Tori Simmons? And does it have anything to do with her testimony about Alice? Maybe somebody didn't want the truth coming out.

After The Trial

Chapter Seventeen

VICTORIA 'TORI' SIMMONS

Chapter Eighteen

ETHAN SIMMONS

'I need to know what's going on. What's the latest?' I ask Owen. We came to my hotel room immediately from the courtroom to avoid the commotion. I didn't want to go to Thomas's stuffy chambers again and Owen's office is on the other side of London through gridlocked traffic. He's finally made an appearance given what is going on. From a celebrity slander trial to a missing persons case. I think that's a first.

'Tori has been reported as missing. Apparently her agent and barrister couldn't find her this morning and she wasn't responding to calls or texts. They got in touch with her parents and they can't contact her either. Her phone has been turned off since 1am this morning,' Owen responds. He has connections to help get this information for me. I tried asking at the courts but they wouldn't tell me much. 'The police went to her address due to the high profile of the case and declared that her disappearance is a result of foul play.'

He says it so calmly. *Foul play*. What does that even mean?

'I keep trying to call her. It's going straight to voicemail,' I say, taking a sip of whiskey as I dial her number again. It may only be early afternoon but it's already been a difficult day. They had to sneak me out of the court as they were concerned I would be mobbed by paparazzi. We found a taxi with tinted windows so nobody could follow us. The hotel let us in through a side exit. Owen says the hotel has already had a few complaints about the media camped out front who are refusing to move despite the hotel's requests.

'Well, I think everybody already tried calling her before they reported her as missing.'

I side-eye Owen. 'I'm not just everybody though. I'm her husband.'

'Not sure you're her favourite person anymore.'

'Fuck you, Owen.'

'Just being honest.'

'Do they think somebody took her? Is she okay?'

'I don't know anything more than I've told you. You'd need to talk to the police, not me.'

'Whatever. This isn't helping. What happens to the trial?'

'I would've thought that was the last of your concerns, mate,' Owen says, his tone bitter.

'Easy now, tensions are high but we need to remain calm,' Thomas says. I'd forgotten he was still here, perching in the corner.

'No, it's not that I'm concerned about it. I just mean, I assume we aren't going to court tomorrow?'

'The trial will be suspended for now. I've already talked to the judge. Obviously with Tori missing we can't finish her testimony and so it would be prejudicial and unjust for us to continue without her,' Thomas answers.

'So is the case over?'

'For now. I did have an interesting conversation with Faye though. She said that after she left Tori's house last night, Tori had promised to send across some important evidence. She wouldn't tell me what it was, but she did tell me that Tori never sent it.'

'I wonder what she was going to send,' Owen says.

'Given the suspension of the trial, I think it best I take my leave for now. This must be a difficult time for you, Ethan, so I don't want to impose. If either of you have any questions do give me a ring. If I hear anything more from my end I'll be in touch but I would think the legalities will be firmly on pause until Mrs Simmons is found.'

Thomas shakes our hands as he leaves, grabbing his umbrella and coat. The hail outside crashes against the hotel windows. You wouldn't believe it is summer. If Tori is out there, she'll be cold, alone, terrified.

'Maybe I should call her parents,' I say, although I know they won't want to hear from me. They hate my guts. I was not the person they had in mind for their daughter. When I met her parents for the first time, her dad looked me up and down and rolled his eyes. Later, when talking about my movies he made a comment about how what I did couldn't be classed as acting and suggested I consider auditioning for 'proper' roles.

I wish I could call my own parents or my brother to help but it's early in the States right now. Besides, there's not much they can do. Even if they jump on the next flight to support me they wouldn't be here until late tonight or even tomorrow and it's not like they can find her. Should I be out there, looking for her? But where do I even start?

'Sounds like a good idea,' Owen says, texting as he answers so I'm not convinced he actually heard what I said. 'By the way, I've had a lot of journalists contacting me about Tori's disappearance. I suggest we go "no comment" for now. If any of them try to ambush you in the hotel, don't answer their questions.'

'Why? I've got nothing to hide.'

'I know how much you *love* talking to the media but you need to actually stay quiet this time. I've been checking the social media coverage. Asked my assistant to scan the reports for anything mentioning your name that came up. And I'm afraid there's a troubling narrative developing,' he says.

'Troubling? What do you mean?'

'People are accusing you of having something to do with her disappearance.'

I slam my whiskey glass onto the table. 'Are you joking? What do you mean, they think I had something to do with it?'

'People are saying you were worried you were going to lose the trial and were scared about what Tori was going to say so you made her disappear.'

'Seriously? I'm an actor, not some criminal mastermind. Should we speak to the media and set them straight?'

'You're not listening to me. Relax. It's not the mainstream media that are circulating this nonsense. It's all the armchair detectives theorising. Nobody takes those sorts of people seriously but given what they are saying I still think it's wise to exercise caution when it comes to talking to the press. Look, hopefully Tori appears tomorrow and everything goes back to business as usual. I'm sure she's just gone to clear her head somewhere and is having a digital detox.'

'I hope you're right. I can't imagine what will happen if she doesn't.'

'I've gotta go. Look, just lay low for the rest of the day. Order some room service, watch some Netflix and try not to pay attention to the news or any gossip. Don't check social media whatever you do. ' He stands up to leave. 'And don't drink too many of these,' he says, tapping his nail against my tumbler on the coffee table. 'Not wise to have an unclear head at times like these.'

I don't like being alone. Once he's gone I'm left to my

racing thoughts. It's probably the first time I've felt properly alone in the last few months. I've constantly been surrounded by Owen and the legal team, the paparazzi, my fans, my haters – only left alone to sleep. But now I'm a prisoner in this hotel room – there may as well be bars on these windows. I could call some friends to keep me company. But really, I don't have many friends here. I have drinking buddies, people I hang out in expensive bars with, but I wouldn't call them to discuss any actual issues going on in my life.

I ignore Owen's warning and head to TikTok, typing my name into the search bar as I have done so many times before. If that is where these crazy theories about me being involved in Tori's disappearance are circulating then I need to know what's being said about me. I can't defend myself if I don't know what I'm being accused of.

The highest rated video is from a user with the handle @celebgossdesk.

'Has anybody heard the MAD theory that Ethan Simmons is behind his wife's disappearance? Hear me out, yesterday I told you how bizarre Tori's testimony was, how she acted like she had some big secret of Ethan's that she was about to reveal unless they settled. Well I reported earlier that I'd heard from my inside sources that Ethan had tried to settle but Tori had declined. So if Tori was about to reveal something about Ethan to the world and he didn't want it getting out, it's a bit of a coincidence that Tori has disappeared, don't you think?'

Where do they get this nonsense from? It's unfair that anybody can say whatever they like on the internet these days and it can gain traction and ruin people's lives. He has no proof or evidence to back up these claims. The irony is that he has done exactly what Tori did – committed slander. You would think they'd learn. When this is over maybe I'll make an example out of him. I'd like to see his smug face in court.

Another video appears. This one from an account called @celebnewsanchor:

'I hold my hands up that I was one of those people who thought this whole defamation trial was some sort of PR stunt set up by both teams in order to boost their popularity. So when Tori went missing I thought it was some sort of ruse to elevate their stardom even higher. But now I'm starting to think I was deeply wrong. Is anyone else worried about Tori's welfare? It's not like she can just wander around London with nobody seeing her. Somebody should have found her by now...'

I never thought Tori was doing this for attention. If Tori wanted attention she would've come to court and spilt all our secrets. Or she could've gone straight to the papers. Or the cops. Disappearing isn't her style, and she wouldn't make her parents worry by not being in contact, not with her mom being so sick.

I dial the contact number I have for Tori's dad, Daniel Scott, and hope it is the right one. I've never needed, or wanted, to message him but Tori gave me his number once when her phone was out of battery and she wanted to check in. He might not even pick up given his feelings towards me, which I'm sure have only intensified during the trial. Her mom is nicer but she doesn't really know who I am. Tori told me she has early-onset dementia and her memory is slowly fading. It's why she spent so much time in England rather than with me.

Daniel answers on the second ring. He must have his phone close by in case it's news about his daughter.

'Ethan. Are you calling with news about Tori?' he asks. Always straight to the point.

'I wish. Sorry to disappoint. I just wanted to see what you know... Have the cops said anything to you? They haven't really spoken to me about it,'

'I should think that's because of the trial. You know, it was causing her a lot of stress. I just hope it wasn't too overwhelming for her especially after what was said in the papers. You should never have … it doesn't matter now though, I guess.'

'I'm sorry. I really am. You think Tori left because of the trial? Is that what you think?'

'I don't know. That's what I thought originally but the police said there are signs that she didn't leave by choice. If there's anything you know that you could help us, you need to tell me. Or the police. Please. She's my only child.' His voice breaks as he says the last sentence.

'Have they said what sort of signs? I haven't heard from her but if I hear anything I'll let you know.'

'I've told you all I know. So,' he says, clearing his throat, 'I'd better keep this line free in case the police call. Goodbye, Ethan.'

He hangs up.

Chapter Nineteen

@THETRUTHISGREY

Tori has now been missing for over twenty-four hours. The news sites continue to be updated frequently but there's no real news, they keep rehashing the same information over and over hoping people don't notice. TikTok is awash with various theories about what has happened. Some seem possible, some are wacky. I saw one saying that Tori had been abducted by aliens and that's why there's no sign of her. I quickly scrolled past that one.

There is a prominent theory emerging and it's one I think might have traction. People suspect that Ethan had something to do with Tori's disappearance and it all relates to Tori's testimony at the trial. People think Tori was about to reveal a secret of Ethan's that he didn't want coming out so he made her disappear. Some have gone so far to allege he might have shut Tori up permanently. Is Ethan a killer? If he killed his wife, I have no doubt he could have killed my sister. Tori is his wife, the love of his life. And now, now I might never find out what she was about to say.

At one point I thought I was so close to finding out what

happened to Alice. The trial, the body with Alice's ID documents. Everything was lining up for a conclusion and now, somehow, the truth feels even further away. For every step forward I take three back.

My phone buzzes. It's a text from Mom.

Mom [15:01]
How is it going in England x

I shoot back a response telling her that England is fine. I really should have messaged her more but I know she doesn't like me being here. My calendar today reminded me that there's a documentary featuring Alice's case airing tonight. It feels like forever since they asked my permission but apparently they moved the episode forward after the discovery of the body in East London. If it had turned out to be Alice, I think they were planning to capitalise on it.

Luckily, as it's airing in the UK I won't have to stay awake until a silly time to watch it. I check the TV guide. It's on at 10pm on one of the crime channels – clearly it wasn't a documentary with a lot of money behind it. I know the bleak truth about missing persons cases – if they haven't been found within the first forty-eight hours, it's unlikely that they will be. Not alive, anyway. I hope for Tori's sake that isn't true and she's found before then. I hope the next time I watch one of these documentaries it's not her face filling the screen.

I message Oskar to see if he's found anything about @thetruthisblackandwhite2011. The account has been quiet ever since Tori went missing. It could be a coincidence, sure, but I'm not that naïve.

A FaceTime request pops up straight away. One thing I can rely on Oskar for is always being on his phone.

'Hey, did you find anything?'

'Well the account was created on 6 April 2025.' That's the

date that the trial was announced. So whoever made this account started planning whatever this is months ago. 'The only account that they follow is yours.'

I already knew that.

'There are no videos on the account.' They deleted the video of Ethan and Alice, which is not surprising – I noticed they did it not long after I watched it.

'I mean, that was all public. Did you find out anything else?'

'Hold on. I asked around about the account to see if anybody else had received messages from them. I particularly asked people I knew were focusing on the trial but nobody has had anything from them.'

'So it's just me,' I say. At least this confirms that the account is targeting me specifically.

'I messaged the account to see if they'd reply to me but they didn't. Sorry I couldn't get anything else.'

'Well thanks anyway.'

'You should put out a callout. Set your followers on it. Let them do the digging for you.'

'Perhaps. I'm worried what will happen if I provoke them.'

'Well I can do it if you want, they blocked me so won't see the video.'

'Wait,' I say, 'when did they block you?'

'Yesterday.'

I end the call, promising Oskar that I'll send him the information about who the Alice in Wonderland reference was about. After all, I need him on my side and Oskar has double the amount of followers I do, so him looking into this can only be a good thing.

If Oskar was blocked by @thetruthisblackandwhite2011 yesterday, that means either somebody other than Tori is in charge of that account or, if it is Tori, she's alive somewhere.

It's almost time for the documentary. The hotel TV doesn't have many channels so I find a stream on my iPad. Alice's face is featured in the opening sequence. *Missing: Where are they?* That's the name of this new TV series. The intro promises to 'use all the techniques available to police to find new leads in unsolved missing persons cases' – whatever that means. Alice hasn't been missing that long so I'm not sure that there've been any breakthroughs that would make the difference on Alice's case.

We get to the second advert break and they still haven't mentioned Alice. My impatience is getting worse these days. It feels like I'm constantly waiting for answers that are never going to come.

'*And now,*' says the narrator, '*we turn to the missing person case of Alice Grey.*'

An image of my sister fills the screen. Her waist-length straight blonde hair framing her face. Her bright blue doll-eyes piercing through the screen. She always turned heads.

'*Alice Grey was last seen on 20 November 2024. Originally from America, she came to the UK to study and then decided to stay after she graduated. She was reported missing by her flatmate when she failed to return home from work. Alice was last seen on CCTV entering Mill Hill East tube station in North London. Alice seems to disappear once she enters this tube station, never being seen again, not even seen exiting. Alice's movements from the tube station weren't able to be traced and the leads eventually went cold. To this day, Alice's family have not heard from her since she disappeared last year.*'

A second photo flashes on screen. The three of us. Alice, Mom, me. We all look so happy, so unaware of the pain that is about to be inflicted on our lives. We don't even look like twins here, Alice's long blonde hair versus my pixie cut which was blue at that point. It's only when you look at our eyes, our smile, the dimple in the right side of our cheeks.

I remember that photograph. It was taken at a 4 July party at a family friend's house. It was always Alice's favourite holiday. When she moved to England she told me she used to make all of her English friends celebrate it by throwing a party at her flat. She sent me photographs – she used to go over the top because that was Alice's personality. Bunting with American flags on; an inflatable Statue of Liberty; a ridiculous spread of food. She couldn't even cook so I don't know how she managed it. I hope that Alice is found before Thanksgiving this year.

'Police investigating Alice's disappearance believe she got into a vehicle almost immediately on exit from a tube station in a blind spot not covered by the CCTV cameras. Once she was in that vehicle it would have been impossible to trace. Our investigators understand that police were viewing surveillance footage outside of popular tube stations to try and work out where she exited,' the narrator continues.

I remember this was a particular bone of contention of mine. I couldn't understand how Alice could have just disappeared in one of the most surveillance-heavy cities in the world. I thought the police were incompetent. I'm pretty sure I told them that during one particular despair-filled rant.

'Police initially suspected that a serial killer could be at work, as Matilda Green, another young woman, disappeared without a trace after entering the tube network, only six weeks earlier, but no link between the two victims was ever made.'

There is a video on screen of the trains running underground while the voiceover continues to speak.

'Where did Alice go? It's not like she disappeared underground; she must have exited somewhere.'

The next frame is a woman on screen. You can tell she's a

scientist because they've made sure to dress her in a white lab coat and glasses. Her name appears on screen: Samantha Viper – Forensic Investigator.

'*I'm sure some of our viewers at home have noted that Alice only disappeared recently so wondered what scientific techniques could have developed since then that would break this case. However, Alice's case is a little different. We received new evidence in this case from an anonymous source.*'

I sit up at this. It is the first thing I've heard that I didn't already know.

'*What evidence did you receive?*' a female voice behind the camera asks.

'*A jacket. It was sent to the producers of this programme wrapped in clingfilm with a note that said, "The jacket Alice was wearing when she disappeared". Alice Grey wasn't originally going to be featured in this programme but somebody must have wanted the producers to pay attention. We listened.*'

'*And is this indeed the jacket she was wearing in the CCTV clips we've just seen?*'

'*There is a strong possibility that is the case. It matches what she is wearing in the CCTV footage of her last movements and hair fibres found on the jacket match the hair samples we recovered from Alice's flat.*'

'*And were there any other significant findings?*'

'*Yes. We found blood. There were two distinct profiles found. The first matches Alice Grey which makes it even more probable that this was her jacket. The second sample is unidentified.*'

'*What does that mean?*'

'*It means that whoever the DNA belongs to isn't in the criminal database. That means they've never had their DNA taken by the police before. They are unknown to the police.*'

A second set of DNA on Alice's clothing. I wonder if this could be Ethan's. I don't think he's ever been arrested before so it would make sense his DNA isn't in the system. Why don't I know about this? Surely they must have told the police.

'*Is that unhelpful?*'

'*Yes and no,*' Samantha continues. '*At the moment we can't do anything with it but that doesn't mean that will always be the case. People get arrested all the time and have their DNA taken. And if that was to happen to whoever's blood is on this jacket it would flag up in the database as a match. But it doesn't necessarily have to be that person. Any blood relation would help us narrow down the search parameters.*'

'*And what about this anonymous source? Can you shed any light on their identity?*'

'*Unfortunately not. The note was typed. We did test for fingerprints and try to trace its source location but it didn't reveal anything.*'

'*A new potential lead in the disappearance of Alice Grey. Next, an unsolved disappearance dating back to 1981 with no suspects may have new leads thanks to new DNA evidence.*'

Before the picture flips to the next victim, a blank slide with text appears.

Update: Since the production of this documentary, a body was discovered in East London believed to be that of Alice Grey. Identification is ongoing.

Ongoing because I couldn't recognise my sister in the photos I saw. There's no further update. On one hand, it appears that there's no new leads for now as the DNA isn't in the system. But somebody had that clothing and sent it in to the producers. It must be the same person behind the anonymous account.

But there's a more chilling revelation from that programme. They said there was blood on the clothes that Alice was last seen wearing. They didn't say how much blood but the fact they didn't show any images of the jacket makes me concerned. Maybe there was a lot of blood and they realised it might be upsetting or triggering. Either way, blood means Alice was likely hurt on the day she went missing. Or worse – but I can't let my mind go there.

I should contact the producers of the show. Maybe they have more information than they are revealing – after all, they can't just throw out accusations. We know what happens when you accuse someone of something without backing it up.

I draft an email to the contact details I have from when they originally contacted me about the show.

From: Riley Grey <thetruthisgrey@gmail.com>
To: Enquiries <info@missingtvshow.com>
5 June 2025 11:15pm
Re: Tonight's Episode

Hello Tanya,

My name is Riley Grey. We've been in contact previously when you alerted me that you were planning to use my sister's case for your TV series. I've recently finished watching the first episode which aired tonight at 10pm.

My sister's case was discussed in the episode tonight. The episode claimed that an anonymous source had sent the clothing she was last seen wearing to the producers of the show and that it had blood on it. As her sister, this new finding is significant given there have been no new leads on Alice's disappearance for some time. I wish I'd been given a heads up.

I wondered if you would be able to tell me more about

what was sent to you? Was there anything that was left out of the show that you can tell me? I trust the evidence has been handed over to the police?

Looking forward to hearing from you,
Riley

I hope for a speedy response. It might be there isn't anything else to tell me but I need to at least try. I need to mention this new evidence on my TikTok. I set up this whole account to try and find more evidence about Alice and now that more has been uncovered I need to make the most of this new momentum to bring attention to the case.

Riley [23:32]
Mom - did you watch the show?

If Mom has worked out what the blood means like I have, I hate to think how she's feeling right now.

While I wait for Mom to reply I set up my camera to record a TikTok about the jacket. I need to compile images from the TV programme as a backdrop and report on the news. I've noticed some videos already springing up which is good because all attention is good attention.

I clear my throat.

'Hi everyone, did anyone else just finish watching the first episode of Missing: Where are they now? For those of you who know me and my channel, you'll know that one of the people featured in this documentary is my sister, Alice Grey. Alice went missing in November last year and hasn't been seen or heard from since. All my pinned videos on my channel go into further background on the case.'

I pause the video to have a breather. This isn't live and I'll edit it before it's posted. It's important to get it right.

'I started this account to make people aware of my sister's case. I hoped that somebody would realise they've seen something and that could lead to new information. Sadly there have been no new leads. But today, this episode showed that there is somebody out there that knows what happened to my sister. They had the clothes Alice was wearing and sent them to the producers. They found blood on the clothes. My sister's and somebody else's.'

I pause the video and take a sip of water. Talking at the camera without interruption makes my mouth dry.

'They don't yet know who the blood belongs to. Their identity is a mystery for now. Whoever it is – they might be responsible for my sister's disappearance. They might have hurt her. This is a direct plea to whoever sent this evidence to the production team. Please get in contact with me. I need to know what happened to my sister. Please.'

I pray it reaches enough people to make a difference. Before posting, I add another clip.

'There is somebody on the platform that I think knows something about what happened. Their name is @thetruthblackandwhite2011. They know what happened to my sister but won't tell me. If you can help me find this person, please help.'

I quickly edit it and post it to the platform before I can change my mind. It might be a mistake but I'm not going to wait for that account to do the right thing. I've seen social media sleuths make real progress in cases. We all know about the cat lovers that brought a murderer to justice through a Facebook group. That could happen here.

I message @thetruthisblackandwhite2011.

@thetruthisgrey
Did you send the jacket? Are you behind
all of this?

No response.

Chapter Twenty

VICTORIA 'TORI' SIMMONS

Chapter Twenty-One

ETHAN SIMMONS

Tori is still missing.

I've been lying low just like Owen told me to. The hotel have hired extra security personnel because of reporters trying to sneak inside to get a snap of me. Apparently people have tried bribing reception to find out my room number, giving them money for a candid photo taken on their phones. I don't think any have been successful – yet. I haven't dared go outside the hotel; I don't think I'd make it very far. Luckily I have everything I need here even though I feel like I'm going crazy from not leaving these four walls. Why am I made to feel like a prisoner when I'm the victim in all of this?

There's a knock at my hotel room door. I freeze. Could it be that one of the journalists has managed to get past hotel security and find my room? I haven't ordered any room service and the maid has already been. I don't answer, hoping whoever it is gets the message I don't want to talk.

They knock again. 'Ethan Simmons, open up. It's the police.'

The cops? What are they doing here? Maybe there has been

news about Tori. It makes sense they'd tell me before it appeared in the news. I'm still her husband despite the trial and everything that has happened lately but if they are here, that can only mean the worst has happened, right?

I open the door.

'Is there news about Tori?' I ask, hopeful.

Two officers enter the room. 'DS Jay Taylor. This is DC Derek Hayes. Can we come in for a moment?'

DS Taylor is taller and looks older than DC Hayes. He has a smartly shaved, dark brown beard. Skinny – needs to hit the gym. DC Hayes is larger and shorter. Ginger curly hair and clean shaven. Also should probably hit the gym but for different reasons.

I allow them to enter and they take a seat on the sofas in the room.

'Is this about Tori? Have you found her? Please tell me you found her,' I plead.

'We aren't here to update you on Tori's whereabouts. We wanted to ask you to attend a voluntary interview at the station to assist with some enquiries. I know that there's a lot of media attention surrounding you right now and so if you are willing to go now, we would like to accompany you to ensure the press don't give you any grief,' DS Taylor says.

'You want me to come to the station?' I ask.

It isn't what I was expecting. I felt for sure this would be news – good or bad – about finding Tori.

'Yes. To assist with enquiries,' DC Hayes replies.

'And you want me to go now?'

'Is there something else you need to be doing right now?' DS Taylor asks. It's accusatory and I notice his eyes lingering on the half-empty whiskey bottle on the coffee table.

'Do you mind if I call my solicitor?' I ask.

'Of course not. Go ahead. We'll wait here,' DS Taylor says.

I pull out my phone and find Roger's number. It feels weird dialling his number and not Thomas's.

He answers quickly. 'Ethan, is that you?'

'Yes, it is.'

'Are you okay? I'm surprised to hear from you with the trial being suspended pending your wife's disappearance. Anything I can do? Are you holding up alright?' he says.

'Not really. But I'm not calling about the trial. I'm calling because the cops have just arrived at my hotel room.'

'Are they there about Tori?'

'Yes,' I say, darting a look at the officers. 'They want me to attend the station for a voluntary interview. Do you think I should go?'

'Ah, Ethan. I'm not a criminal solicitor so I'm not sure I'm the right person for you to be asking. I deal with civil matters like your defamation trial, not criminal investigations. But my understanding is that if it's voluntary you can say no. Or you could go and simply refuse to answer their questions by answering "no comment". But given it's your wife's disappearance, if you were to refuse they might think it's because you've got something to hide.'

'So you think I should go?'

'Well, it's your choice. Either way, you have a right to legal advice but I'm not the right person for it. I'll give my friend Ellen a call. She works as a criminal solicitor and is better suited to something like this. I'll tell her to meet you at the station or send a colleague. Did they tell you which station they are taking you to?'

'No, but I can find out and text you the address.'

'Okay, great. And when you get there, if Ellen hasn't arrived, you have the right to wait for her before they ask you any questions, okay? It doesn't make you look like you have something to hide by requesting legal support. It's there to protect you. The police should know this but if they try to be a bit underhanded, stand your ground.'

'Thanks, Roger.'

I hang up and return to where the officers are sitting.

'Okay, you can take me to the station now. Can you let me know where we are going so I can text my lawyer?'

The officers escort me through the hotel, past prying eyes and the other hotel guests desperate to get a look. We take the elevator to the basement-level carpark. I'm glad for the discretion because I wouldn't want to be seen leaving the hotel flanked by cops – can you imagine what the headlines would say? They lead me to their car which is thankfully unmarked so I don't need to worry about being spotted through the windows but I brought a cap and a pair of sunglasses with me just to make sure – I've become used to being incognito.

The journey to the station isn't short. My hotel is in central London and the traffic is always heavy here. I think it's because the road system here is so illogical. Why can't this country have straight roads? The officers attempt to engage me in light chit-chat about soccer and my films but it's stilted and unnatural. I let Roger know the address of the station and update him on our ETA.

Once we arrive the officers ask to me wait in reception. I take a seat and flick through some magazines as if I'm at a spa waiting to be called in for my treatment.

'Ethan Simmons?'

I raise my head at the sound of the woman's voice. I stand up thinking it's the receptionist and notice it's someone else, a stranger. She has a thick ring binder clasped to her chest. Grey suit. Brown hair slicked back into a bun. She's older than me.

'That's me. Who are you?'

'I'm Ellen. Roger asked me to come down here as a favour.

He said you would be expecting me. Can I sit?' She gestures to the seat next to me.

'Sure.' I shrug and sit back down.

'So, Roger told me about your current defamation trial although I already knew most of it from the news. But he said the police have asked you to come to the station voluntarily to answer some questions?'

'That's right.'

I'm sure this woman is a good lawyer – Roger wouldn't have recommended her otherwise. And I'm sure she's competent. But she doesn't know me and I don't feel comfortable being in these strange surroundings where my only support is somebody I've just met. I don't know how the legal system works in this country. I don't know why I've been brought here.

'And did they tell you what they wanted to ask you questions about?'

'Tori's disappearance. She's been missing for a couple of days and nobody has seen her. I haven't seen her since she came to Thomas's chambers so I don't know how they expect me to help.'

'They will be trying to cover all the bases. I'm sure you know that when married women go missing it's always the husband they look at first.' I shoot her a look. Is she flat-out calling me guilty? 'Not wrongly either as more often than not they are the person responsible. So I wouldn't worry too much as this seems very standard procedure and doesn't mean they suspect you of anything. I need to tell you that how far you want to cooperate with their enquiries is up to you. You can state "no comment" to any of their questions or stop assisting at any time. At the same time, if you want to answer then that is your choice.'

'Yeah. That's what Roger said.'

'Good. But if there is something incriminating you think they might bring up, then it's best to let me know before we get in there so I'm not on the back foot. Do you understand? Is there anything I need to know?'

I shake my head. 'There's nothing you need to know.'

'Ethan Simmons. Do you want to follow us?' DC Hayes calls.

I take a deep breath. I think I'd rather take my chances with the overzealous journalists than be in here. We follow him down the corridor and into a small room. It isn't inviting. A small plastic table with cheap-looking chairs. No windows either. There's a jug of water on the table and some plastic cups so I pour myself a drink, managing to spill half of it over the table. The effect of last night's whiskey is settling in. There's no air in the room and my throat feels like there's a cord around it gradually twisting, constricting my airflow.

'Thanks for agreeing to come down and answer a couple of questions. I don't think this will take very long,' DS Taylor says.

They have a brown A4 folder in front of them. DS Taylor opens it and start to flick through the pages.

'It is police procedure for this interview to be taped. I'm going to start the recording now,' DC Hayes says. An unpleasant high-pitched noise sounds. 'This interview is being conducted by DS Jay Taylor and DC Derek Hayes at Colindale police station on 6 June 2025. Can you please state your name for the tape?'

'Ethan Simmons.'

'Also present in the room is Ellen Pilkington from Dawson and Edwards Solicitors. I must remind you that you are not under arrest and are free to leave at any time. You have the right to legal representation which you have exercised. Before we continue I must let you know this interview is under caution. You do not have to say anything but it may harm your defence if you do not mention when questioned something which you later rely on in court. Anything you do say may be given in evidence. Do you understand?'

I nod.

'Can you please vocalise your response for the tape?'

'Yes, I understand.'

'Do you know an individual by the name of Alice Grey?' DS Taylor asks.

The world stops. My stomach turns. I see spots of black and my vision blurs. Why are they asking me about Alice? This is supposed to be about Tori. I glance at Ellen for a way to answer, hoping she can see the panic on my face. We didn't discuss this. I don't have time to think of what to say. Didn't they say that they were going to ask me questions about my wife? Or did I just presume they would because I didn't think they had anything else to question me about? Until now…

'My client was led to believe this interview was about the disappearance of Tori Simmons? Is that not the case?' Ellen's interjection is a welcome relief while my thoughts continue to swim.

'I think your client assumed there. We never informed him of the purpose of the interview. There is a team working on his wife's disappearance but my team is focused on the disappearance of another woman – Alice Grey,' DS Taylor says.

I stay silent.

'Correct procedure is for you to inform my client the reason he is being questioned,' Ellen remarks. 'That should have been done before you brought him in here to be questioned.'

'We're awfully sorry about that. Must have slipped our minds,' DS Taylor says.

DS Taylor and DC Hayes exchange looks.

'Allow me to refresh your memory. Alice Grey was a

twenty-three-year-old female, originally from America, who lived in North London with her flatmate Catrin. She went missing in November last year and was last seen entering Mill Hill East underground station. This—' DC Hayes takes a photograph from the brown folder and slides it across the table in my direction '—is a photograph of Alice captured from the CCTV camera near to the station. This is the last known photograph of Alice. Do you recognise her?' DC Hayes asks.

I swallow, hard. *Of course I recognise her.*

'Do you have an answer for us?' DS Taylor says.

'No. No comment.'

'To confirm, your answer to whether or not you recognise the woman in this photo – Alice Grey – is no comment or no?' DC Hayes asks.

'No comment.'

DC Hayes flicks through the folder and pulls out three further photographs, placing each of them in front of me.

'For the tape, I am showing Mr Simmons images AG288, AG289 and AG290. Is or was your phone number the one displayed in the first of these images, ending in 701?' DC Hayes says.

It was. Right before my phone was put through the washing machine and I had to get a new phone. The first image is a photocopy of an invoice from a mobile network provider displaying my old phone number. It clearly has my address on it and my full name. They already know that it's my previous number but they'll make me go through this circus of questions. What do they have on me?

'No comment.'

'Moving on. In the next two images you will see exchanges between this number and a second number. Do you recognise these messages?'

'No comment.'

'Did you send the messages in these images to the phone number ending in 389?'

'No comment.'

I recognise the texts.

Ethan

I miss you so much. I wish we were together right now.

Ethan

One day I promise we will run away together. We could go back to America and live near the beach.

Ethan

You're the one for me, Alice.

I sent them. I remember my feelings as I typed them and it all comes flooding back as if it was yesterday. My phone was destroyed though, the computing experts couldn't recover anything off it for use in the trial, so I don't understand how they could have these texts when I was told the phone was unreadable.

'You didn't message: "You're the one for me, Alice"?' DC Hayes asks.

'No comment.'

'I believe my client has already answered that question in his previous response,' Ellen interrupts.

'When you agreed to volunteer to answer some questions I did hope you'd be more forthcoming than you have been,' DS Taylor says.

I don't respond. I just need to get out of here, everything is closing in on me, I can't breathe. I grip the edges of the table, burrowing my fingernails into the plastic. Ellen said I could stop cooperating at any time. I could leave right now, get out of here. But I can't. I need to know what they know. *How* much they know.

'Okay, let's move onto the next item. This evidence was recovered off a mobile phone that was sent to us anonymously yesterday. For the tape I am showing Mr Simmons item AG279,' DC Hayes says, producing a plastic bag with a mobile phone inside it. An iPhone, one of the newer models, it looks like. It has a pink case on it with love hearts plastered over it. That's not my phone but I know exactly who it belongs to. That's Alice's phone. They found her phone and that's how they have the texts. But how did they find it? Tori told me she disposed of it.

'Did you know a body was recently found suspected to belong to Alice Grey?'

'A body?' I say, almost forgetting my 'no comment' stance. Did they find Alice?

Ellen lightly presses her heel into my foot which I take as a reminder to keep quiet.

'Yes. A body was recovered a couple of days ago and this mobile phone was delivered this morning. Our technology experts have managed to recover these messages.'

I need to know if it's Alice's body but I can't ask. If I ask then I may as well admit I knew Alice.

Ellen breaks the silence. 'Was the body you found this Alice Grey?'

'No. We thought the body belonged to Alice, but further identification testing has confirmed that it does not. Oddly though, it had Alice's passport and purse on it. And then a few days later somebody sends us her phone. It all seems very concerning. Alice's parents confirmed this morning that the phone belonged to Alice and that was her number.'

'Who did the body belong to?' Ellen asks. I'm glad I have her there to ask the important questions.

'The body has been identified as belonging to Matilda Green, although that information has not been made public yet.'

'So is this line of questioning about Alice Grey or about Matilda Green?' Ellen says.

'Well, did you know Matilda Green, Mr Simmons?'

'No. I did not.'

Ellen sighs.

'Do you recognise the phone, Mr Simmons?'

'No comment.'

'Maybe you recognise these.' DC Hayes reopens the brown envelope and pulls out even more photographs. I brace myself for more messages, of which I know there are thousands. Most of them were explicit, but instead it's photographs.

'For the tape, I am showing Mr Simmons a copy of an item marked AG298. Do you recognise the female in these photographs?'

'No comment.'

'Do you recognise the male in these photographs?'

'No comment.'

'No comment? Are you sure you don't recognise him? I'd say that looks an awful lot like you, don't you think? Is this a photograph of you engaging in sexual activity with Alice Grey on 2 November 2024?'

'No comment.'

'These were taken from the photo library on the iPhone that has been confirmed as belonging to Alice Grey. Why does Alice Grey have intimate photos of the two of you on her iPhone?'

'No comment.'

'My client has answered the question. I'd appreciate it if you stop badgering him and move onto the next question.'

'Indeed, indeed. Badgering wasn't our intention,' DS Taylor

says. I've noticed he takes over whenever Ellen questions their behaviour.

'Do you know why Alice's passport and purse were found on Matilda Green's body?'

'No, I don't.'

'I think, for now, that is the end of our line of questioning. You are free to go although I would stick around the area if I were you as we may have further questions. This is an *active* investigation.'

The emphasis he puts on 'active' makes my pulse quicken. I thought the world had forgotten all about Alice Grey. I thought we'd gotten away with it.

'Recording ending,' DC Hayes says as he pushes the button on the tape recorder. 'Thanks for coming in.'

It feels surreal leaving the room. Everything has changed since I first set foot in here. I thought this was going to be an informal chat about Tori to see if I knew anything that could help the investigation. I never thought this was going to be about Alice. After Tori bringing Alice's name up a few days ago I should have been more prepared for this. I should have known somebody would eventually work out what happened to Alice Grey.

Chapter Twenty-Two

@THETRUTHISGREY

'Breaking news. Our sources have learnt that Ethan Simmons, the husband of Tori Simmons, has been taken into the police station for questioning. We understand that he has not been arrested at this time and has been let go pending further enquiries.'

The images on the screen are of Ethan leaving the police station, his hands stuffed in his pockets, head down. He looks like a guilty man. There's no footage of him leaving his hotel room so maybe someone tipped them off that he was in there. He's trying to hide his face from the camera with a hat and sunglasses but it's still clearly him. Ethan is six foot three inches which makes him perfect for a swoon-worthy male lead but makes it harder for him to hide.

'Tori Simmons disappeared two days ago having last been seen at her address in Hampstead in North London at 11pm on 4 June. No contact has been made with her since and her whereabouts remain unknown. Before her disappearance, Tori was the defendant in a multi-million-pound defamation trial. It was touted as the biggest trial of the decade and was the first in the UK to be livestreamed following the success of livestreaming in the US.'

Do the police suspect Ethan of having something to do with Tori's disappearance? Everything I learn about Ethan makes me more suspicious of him. His wife seems to have disappeared on the cusp of revealing some great secret, likely about my sister. He was involved with my sister who also went missing. It's not like it's a normal thing for everyone you have a relationship with to end up missing. Maybe my sister and Tori weren't even the first women to fall victim to Ethan's charms.

But there's hope that Tori is okay because somebody using that account I think belongs to her blocked Oskar. My followers haven't managed to uncover anything about the account yet but lots have commented to say they are digging. One of them will turn up something. They're an army. A weapon in the right hands.

'We have reached out to Ethan's legal team but have received no comment.'

I rang my mom last night to talk about the new evidence they found on the TV show. I was furious we hadn't been told about the new development but it turns out the cops had told my parents about the jacket some weeks ago. They chose not to tell me about it because they thought it was a fruitless lead. I slammed the phone down in anger – them choosing not to tell me has made my investigation harder than it needed to be. Who knows how things would be if I'd had that information from the start?

I don't know how it works but maybe they can take Ethan's DNA or maybe they already took it when they questioned him. They can check to see if it matches the blood on the jacket.

A notification pops up on my phone.

@thetruthisblackandwhite2011
Did you enjoy the show??

They are back, whoever they are.
I rapidly type a response.

@thetruthisgrey
Did you send Alice's jacket to them? Do
you know what happened to my sister?

@thetruthisblackandwhite2011
Yes

@thetruthisgrey
Can you tell me then???

This person knows the truth about what happened to my sister. They won't tell me but why haven't they gone to the police?

@thetruthisblackandwhite2011
All in good time. There is a plan. Did you
see Ethan was questioned by the police?

@thetruthisgrey
Yes in connection with Tori's
disappearance. Do you know what
happened to her?

@thetruthisblackandwhite2011
That isn't why he was questioned.

@thetruthisblackandwhite2011
They questioned him about Alice's
disappearance.

@thetruthisgrey
How do you know that?

@thetruthisblackandwhite2011
If you want me to keep helping you, I'd
call off your followers.

@thetruthisgrey
I will. I'm sorry, I just need answers. How
do you know why Ethan was
questioned?

There is no response. The account seems to message me when they want and then go dark as soon as they've told me what they want me to know. It's infuriating that they know so much but are unwilling to share it except on their terms. I delete my video asking for my followers' help. I can't risk it.

I need Tanya to reply to me. I send a chaser email.

From: Riley Grey <thetruthisgrey@gmail.com>
To: Enquiries <info@missingtvshow.com>
6 June 2025 4:30pm
Re: Re: Tonight's Episode

Hello Tanya,

Did you get the email I sent yesterday about the evidence from my sister's disappearance? Sorry to chase so soon.

Thank you,
Riley

There's another email in my inbox, one that piques my interest. It's from my friend Sam. I forgot that I sent him the explicit photographs of Tori, asking him to work out if they are authentic. He's one of the most skilled photo editors I know, if anybody will know if they've been faked, it's him.

From: Sam Young <sam.young@samyoung.com>
To: Riley Grey <thetruthisgrey@gmail.com>
6 June 2025 3:50pm
Re: Can you check these?

Hey Riley,

Long time no speak. How are you doing?

I've checked the photos for you – thanks for the warning about the content. I wasn't expecting something of that nature from you! Anyway, I'm not sure what you've gotten yourself into and I won't ask. I ran a lot of checks and in my opinion, every single one of those photographs is faked due to inconsistencies in shadows, texture and tone. The date stamp was definitely inserted post-production too. It's pretty good work so looks like a professional has done it and it would fool most people. Not me though!

Hope that helps.
Sam

That's interesting. So the photographs leaked to the press of Tori's sexual activity were faked. I wonder who by. Did Ethan know they were fake? It looks more and more like Ethan is guilty of something.

I can't rely on @thetruthisblackandwhite2011 to get the truth. I can't rely on Tanya, considering she hasn't responded. If I'm going to find out what happened to Alice, I need to do it myself, outside of the online world. I can't rely on my TikTok followers finding some important lead that will reveal everything. I need to put myself at the forefront of this investigation.

I need to track down Ethan and confront him myself.

Chapter Twenty-Three

VICTORIA 'TORI' SIMMONS

Chapter Twenty-Four

ETHAN SIMMONS

It's been leaked to the press already. My face is splashed all over the magazines, social media and the internet. Memes have already been generated using my 'mugshot', AI used to create something that doesn't even exist. The headlines vary from slightly incendiary to outright accusing me of murdering Tori. The silver lining is that they've all assumed that the cops were asking me questions about my missing wife, and I'd much rather people believe that narrative than know who they were really asking me about. I need to keep that secret under the radar as long as I can. As Tori and I said, what happened to Alice Grey is something we will take to the grave. To the grave.

'This is bad. This is very, very bad,' Owen says. He paces back and forth across my hotel room, wearing the carpet thin with his steps. 'You should've called me. I could've handled this. I shouldn't be finding out my client was questioned by the police after the fact. For god's sake. I found out because one of my colleagues saw your face on *HotCelebGossip!*'

Owen kicks the wall in rage and winces, holding his toe and hopping about the room. He's such a weakling.

'I know. I'm sorry I just didn't realise the seriousness of the situation when they asked me to go in. It sounded like it was just a casual interview and I made sure nobody saw me leaving the hotel. I don't know how anybody would've known I was there so I didn't think it was a big deal.'

I fill the glass tumbler with whiskey from the decanter on the coffee table. 'Want one?' I offer Owen.

'I shouldn't,' he says before changing his mind. 'Actually yeah, I need it. Having you as a client is going to put me in the ground before my time.'

I pour Owen a generous measure and hand him the glass. It gets him to sit down on the sofa next to me which is a welcome development as his frantic movements were making me feel worse, nauseous almost.

'There must have been a leak somewhere. They probably tipped off the media so they could be there for the money shot when you left the station. You can't trust anyone.'

'I didn't tell anyone. Do you think my solicitor did?'

'Doubtful. Wouldn't look good if it got out. My money is on the staff at the station. It probably got out that you were there or someone saw you. Passed it around to their colleagues and any one of them could have phoned in. Some papers pay money for a photo opportunity like this so it's worth their time.' He finishes the whiskey quickly, discarding the tumbler on the coffee table and hanging his head. 'My phone won't stop ringing with people asking me for a comment on the situation. Honestly, I'm not sure we can keep working together if you don't keep me in the loop about things.'

It's not a great surprise. I've had a feeling Owen didn't want to continue representing me. Ever since I lost the film contract and the ad campaign, I've not been successful enough for him. In fact he will have earnt zero commission from me in the last few months. I know he wanted to use the trial to re-invent my career but with this whole mess that has ensued, any potential upside for him has disintegrated. For a while there was hope that I could be a star once again, but now that star has burnt out and all that is left is a black hole where my career used to be.

'It's not like they arrested me. Surely it's a good sign that I left the station? If they had evidence I'd done anything wrong then I'd be locked up. Things could be worse.'

'The media don't care if you're actually guilty. It's the speculation that will drive their sales. The reporting on Tori was starting to wane. Nobody has heard from her and there's no new information so there's nothing to report. Now you're the big juicy carrot for them to latch onto.'

'But I didn't do anything.'

'What did they ask you about?'

'Who?'

'The police. What did they want to know?'

I haven't directly lied yet. I could tell Owen the truth, that they were asking about Alice, but I can't. As much as Owen is meant to have my back, I've always had a niggling feeling that he'd throw me under the bus to get ahead. And now that I'm a dead weight, I'm sure he wouldn't mind if I gave him the tools to sever our connection for good.

'Just about our marriage. If there was anywhere I thought she might go. How her general mindset was. Things like that.'

'So they didn't seem to be suspicious of you?'

'No, like I said, it was a casual chat. The media is turning it into something else.'

'And you didn't have anything to do with her disappearance, right? Because if you did I need you to tell me.'

'Of course not.'

'Good. Good. Okay, I'm going to go back to the office and try to—' He stops, a notification on his phone distracting him. 'Oh my fucking god. What is this?' His eyes are wide. It's not anger, its fear.

'What?'

'The media has a new headline, Ethan.' He thrusts the phone in my lap. 'Things have turned from pretty bad to astronomically screwed.'

ETHAN THREATENED WIFE TORI JUST BEFORE SHE DISAPPEARED.

6 June 2025 17:02

The London News has uncovered evidence showing Ethan Simmons threatening his wife after she was reported having last been seen. The video, received exclusively by *The London News*, shows Ethan arriving at Tori's home address in Hampstead on 4 June at 11.38pm. Previously, Tori's agent was the last person known to have seen Tori at 11pm when she left her home after an intense de-briefing following court that day.

The video shows Ethan telling Tori not to appear in court the next day and warning her there would be 'grave consequences' if she went ahead and talked about someone named Alice. The video does not contain any details about who this 'Alice' is that Ethan refers to but Tori mentioned an Alice at court the day before she disappeared. Ethan then appears to grab Tori's collar and whisper something inaudible in her ear which causes her alarm.

The London News has authenticated the video and it is being shared with the police. This is a breaking news story. Follow *TheLondonNews* on Facebook, Instagram and X for

live updates. Got a story? Email us at
hello@londonnews.com.

'Have you seen the video?' I ask Owen.

'No. But I can probably get it from my contact at *The London News*. Is it true then? Did you threaten your wife before she disappeared?'

'They make it sound much worse than it was. I wasn't really threatening her. It was more a stern conversation between husband and wife. And obviously I didn't know anybody was filming me.'

'It's never how it looks with you. You had the conversation on her bloody doorstep! It's well known where your wife lives and the media have been at her house during the trial trying to get the inside scoop. You bloody idiot.'

'Okay – I get it might not have been my smartest move but you don't understand.'

'No, I don't. What is it with this Alice chick that you're so desperate not to come out? Did you knock her up or something? Because I can easily handle the media side of that. Trust me, many a client of mine has had an affair and got somebody other than their wife pregnant. Or is she underage? That's more difficult…'

'Can we drop it, please?'

Every time I think I see a way out of this mess, things get more chaotic. I thought the cops questioning me about Alice was bad enough but now this video? It's almost as if somebody is trying to destroy my life.

'Seriously? You're not going to tell me?'

'I think you should leave.' I can't deal with Owen trying to find out about Alice. Things are only bound to get worse if the cops pull me back in for questioning or if anybody finds out what they were really asking me about. Everything is unravelling, everything spilling out, the mess for all to see.

'You know what, Ethan, I was told representing you would be a disaster. That you were just another Hollywood heartthrob who had an ego and would ultimately screw his career. And you did exactly that. And I did have sympathy for you when I thought you were telling the truth about Tori spreading lies about you cheating but from the sounds of things that's exactly what you were doing with this Alice person. Consider yourself dropped, Ethan. Find yourself new representation.'

Owen grabs his coat and slams the door on his exit. It shouldn't surprise me that he doesn't want to be my agent anymore. If anything, I'm surprised it took him this long. Losing an agent can be a crucial mistake in show business but right now Owen is the least of my problems. I need to focus on trying to clear my name. I'm happy to let Owen think that the worst thing I did was cheat on Tori with Alice.

I pour myself another glass of whiskey. I'm going to need to order another bottle from room service. I dial 0 on the phone to be put through to reception.

'Mr Simmons, how may I help you?'

'Can I have another bottle of whiskey please?

'Of course, I will organise that right away. The same brand as before?'

'Yes please. And can you send up some food? Literally anything will do. I'm starving.'

'No problem. Anything else?'

'That's all.'

I hang up. I could get used to living in a hotel room although the cost of this place per night is extortionate. I convinced myself it was fine because I'd be getting a payday from Tori once I won the trial. Perhaps I should slow down on the spending but that sounds like a future Ethan problem. Although ... a dark thought enters my mind. If Tori is missing then what happens to her estate? I'm her next of kin and we have no children so surely everything would go to me. The house in the Cotswolds is owned outright by her and I know it's valuable.

I open up my browser and type *when is a missing person declared dead* into the search bar. The answer presents itself in a big bold writing at the top of the page. *Seven years*. Seven years? That's a hell of long time. Perhaps I shouldn't be counting on Tori's savings to tide me over.

There's a knock at the door. 'Room service.'

The maid wheels in a gold tray with two levels. On the bottom is another bottle of whiskey and a fresh glass with ice perfectly moulded into identical sized squares. On the top is an array of dishes covered with a silver cloche. I always know I'm in a good hotel when the food is almost like a surprise waiting to be revealed. The maid places the fresh bottle of whiskey next to the almost empty one and replaces my now empty glass with a fresh one. She places the food down beside me and then leaves, wheeling the cart with her.

I haven't had to cook a meal or wash up since I've been here but as much I enjoy that, I do want to get out of here. Owen advised me not to go outside because he didn't want me talking to media – he obviously never had any trust in me. But I'm sick of hiding out in here like I'm some sort of criminal and now that Owen has dumped me he can't tell me what to do anymore. It's only making me look more guilty. I need to show everyone that I am the victim here. I'm the one that the media is tarnishing – just because Tori has gone missing doesn't mean she's a saint. Do these people crying over her being missing forget how they called her a whore a couple of days ago?

I shovel some food in my mouth and take another swig of

whiskey, then grab my shoes and head to the hotel lobby. I'm going to use the front exit this time, something I haven't done since the day I checked in. I can see the media outside already. News of the video must have travelled fast. I spot hushed whispers as reporters spot me and question whether it's really me. I'm about to make their day. As I get closer to the doors, cameras start flashing and I hear people scream my name. There is nothing quite like the feeling I get from people calling my name over and over.

'Mr Simmons.'

'Ethan. Ethan.'

'Ethan Simmons. Ethan. Ethan Simmons.'

A chorus of voices chant my name like I'm some sort of deity and I revel in it. This is why I wanted to become a celebrity in the first place. I wanted people to want me like this. I soak in the attention that I've missed so badly holed up in my room, preparing myself to make a statement that will clear my name.

'I want to talk about my wife,' I start. 'I have a few things I need to say. I need to set the record straight.'

I stand at the top of the hotel steps. The sun is bright and I stumble slightly as the glare blinds me.

'Have you been drinking, Ethan?'

'Is it true you threatened your wife?'

'What did the police say?'

'What happened to Tori, Ethan?'

'Did you kill her?'

'No, I did not kill my wife. Please let me speak. I have some things I need to say.'

As I stare into the crowd of flashing lights and murmurs, my head feels fuzzy and confused. I thought I had the perfect speech planned out but now I'm here to deliver it, it all seems rushed and disjointed. It had seemed like such a good idea moments ago to talk to the media but now I wonder if Owen was right. I can feel the food I devoured so quickly in the back of my throat.

'I have nothing to do with Tori's disappearance. I just want her to come back home and safely. I wish we'd been on better terms when she vanished. I know there's a video circulating about me that looks bad but you need to know that I would never hurt my wife,' I say with conviction. I hope it's enough to appease the circus.

'Did you threaten Tori?'

'Do you have any idea where she is?'

'Why did the police question you?'

'What happens to the trial?'

The voices overlap and the questioning is constant. My palms sweat and my heart beats faster. My stomach starts to turn and I feel the whiskey I drank earlier in the back of my throat.

'I have no further comments to make. I need to go.'

'Is it true the police questioned you about the disappearance of Alice Grey? Were you her secret boyfriend?'

The noise stops. Time stops. Everything is still. *Alice.* I search for the identity of the person asking the question. Did I just imagine it? It's not a face I recognise. I don't know all the journalists in London but the same ones crop up in these situations. Something about her is familiar though. She doesn't seem like she belongs here – her accent is American for a start. She has pink in her hair. A piercing above her right eyebrow. She's dressed like she should be at a Green Day concert rather than accosting me at the front of my hotel.

'Didn't you cheat on Tori with Alice Grey?'

I don't answer. I can't answer. The only logical solution I can think of is to ignore it and hope it stops. Hope nobody else picks up on what she's asking. Hopefully they see how inappropriately she is dressed and assume what she is talking about is nonsense and that my lack of response implies that is the case.

'You know I'm telling the truth, Ethan. Don't make me prove it. I have evidence of what you did.'

I turn my back on the reporters and walk into the hotel. The sweat seeps through my pores, dampens the armpits of my shirt. I can hear the whispers behind me. What does she know and how does she know about Alice? There's only a handful of people who knew about my connection to Alice and I made sure all of them were dealt with. But with Alice's phone, passport and purse showing up, and now this, somebody is trying to expose everything.

I hear the doorman telling the reporters that they can't come inside the hotel and ordering them to clear the entrance. I wait for the elevator to take me away from all of this so I can drink myself into such a state that I'll forget it all.

'Mr Simmons?' I hold my breath, worried a reporter has somehow gotten inside or, worse, that girl with the pink streak in her hair. I can't face the barrage of interrogation much longer. It's exhausting me. The mental stress is radiating throughout my entire body.

But it's not a reporter. It's one of the hotel staff. I check the name tag and notice it's the manager. Celia.

'Yes?'

'Do you have a minute?' Celia asks. 'I need to speak to you about your stay.'

I want to get back to my room but I get the impression that's not an option.

'Sure. What about it?'

'How much longer were you planning on staying with us at The Hidden? As you know, our guest list here features prominent individuals and we've had a number of complaints about the constant media presence at the front of the hotel,' Celia says, her voice soft.

'When I booked here the hotel said they were used to having celebrity clients. My agent assured me that all the staff had been warned about the attention the trial was drawing and that it wouldn't be an issue.'

'Well, yes. But things haven't turned out exactly as planned. Things were manageable during the trial, and the trial was only supposed to last for a week, but with the sensationalising of your wife's disappearance it's become overwhelming. People are trying to bribe guests to give them any information about your whereabouts. Staff are being grabbed on their way to work. Our booking numbers are down. I'm afraid it's making it very difficult to run our business here and guest satisfaction is our number one priority.'

'What about my satisfaction?' I don't know where I'll go if the hotel kick me out. I could try other hotels but now that Owen isn't working for me I'll actually have to do it myself. And even then, they might feel the same way The Hidden does and not want my business. I'm more trouble than I'm worth. It's not like I can go and stay with family when they are in back in Dallas. I could call a friend but I doubt they want me in their house, knowing their privacy will be invaded.

I could go and stay at our second home in the Cotswolds. I haven't been there for a while. I never liked living there anyway; it was always Tori's house. She lived there before we met and so moving in felt like I was invading her space. We tried to make it feel like my home too, but with me always being in America or Canada it felt like staying at an Airbnb. It was my idea to buy a place in London. I couldn't stand being out in the countryside anyway. There's nothing to do there.

I can't stay at the London house where Tori was staying for the trial – I assume the cops are all over it. I'll have to go back to the home in the Cotswolds. It's much bigger than the house in London and it'll be far quieter than it is in this busy city, fewer journalists and less noise in general. Hopefully the chaos won't follow me. Surely everything will quieten down soon and I can go back to my old life. Write a tell-all book and sell it.

I can even dedicate it to Tori.

Chapter Twenty-Five

@THETRUTHISGREY

It felt so good asking Ethan about my sister. The look on his pretty-boy face when he realised somebody was asking him about what he'd done, that maybe somebody could see past the lies he was trying to spin. For a moment I thought I saw recognition in his face and wondered if he knew I was Alice's sister. Did he see her face in mine? But then it disappeared and the look was replaced with contempt, the corners of his mouth pinched, his jawline tight. It's not as if we ever met but could he have seen a photo of me before? Would Alice have told him about me? I don't think he connected the dots though; I was just another nameless reporter to him.

I wanted to go further. I wanted to ask him outright if he killed my sister. I wanted to run up to him, scream in his face and demand the truth. And I probably would have if the coward hadn't scurried away into his palace. The best part was that all the reporters wanted to know what I was talking about; they saw the look on Ethan's face and knew that I was telling the truth. They knew I wasn't just spouting some conspiracy theory.

So I told them everything I know. I told them I was Alice's sister and that I'd received a tip-off about why the police were really questioning Ethan. I told them about the episode and the mysterious DNA on the jacket Alice was last seen wearing. I told them about the video of Ethan and Alice together proving they were in a relationship. I wish I'd downloaded that TikTok video when I had the chance as I can't back it up.

They all nodded their heads and asked questions. I hope they all go back to their desks and write about it and bring attention to my sister and Ethan's involvement. If enough people start pointing the finger at Ethan he won't be able to hide anymore. And the fact his wife is missing only adds fuel to the fire.

I haven't left the area outside of the hotel. I'm still high off adrenaline and I don't want to go back to my room. I bought myself a coffee and some snacks and have been camped on a wall opposite. I keep getting suspicious looks from the doorman but he hasn't told me to move on yet. It's getting dark and most of the other reporters I was with have left, sure that Ethan won't be venturing out again today. I think he's learnt his lesson. There were murmurs that he was drunk when he was giving his impromptu speech. Some closer to him said they could smell the alcohol on his breath. He did seem to be stumbling around and slightly slurring his words. It's interesting hanging out with journalists; they told me things I didn't know. Apparently Ethan has a bit of a drinking problem but his agent has always managed to keep it out of the news. I wonder if he's a violent drinker.

The email I've been waiting for has arrived.

From: Enquiries <info@missingtvshow.com
To: Riley Grey <thetruthisgrey@gmail.com>
6 June 2025 7:21pm
Re: Tonight's Episode

Hi Riley,

Thank you for reaching out. The team is always interested to hear from viewers who have enjoyed the show. I hope you feel that we did your sister's case justice and I hope there is renewed interest in the case following our broadcast. There isn't much else to tell you about the evidence item that was sent to us. It was sent to us by an anonymous source and we were not able to determine the sender of the item. The outside packaging was tested but there was nothing indicating their identity. It contained a note which told us we needed to air the case. It piqued our interests so we fast-tracked getting the jacket authenticated. We weren't originally planning to include your sister's case at all given how recent it was.

The parcel was sent tracked so the only thing we were able to decipher was that the parcel was sent from a village post office in the Cotswolds. Chipping Campden is the name.

I wouldn't usually divulge this but considering you are her sister I wanted to help out. We have passed the evidence onto the police. We did so as soon as we'd finished with it. We have very strict evidence-handling protocols and we always follow procedure. I don't know what has happened to it since, you'd have to follow up with the police yourself. Let me know if I can be of any further assistance.

Tanya

I need to find the contact details of the cops I spoke to about my sister's disappearance. If I tell them what I know, maybe I can persuade them to test the mystery DNA against Ethan if they haven't already. Do I have enough though? It seems to clear to me but when I try to set it all out there's not enough to prove Ethan's guilt.

I'm so lost in my thoughts I almost don't notice Ethan slipping out of the doorway of The Hidden. He has a baseball cap on to obscure his face but I know it's him. For one thing, he's dressed in the same clothes he was wearing earlier. He's clearly waited until dark to make his escape. But he doesn't look like he's just getting some fresh air because he has a large duffel bag slung over his shoulder. I wonder where he is going.

I have to know. I have to get closer to this man. What if he's running away? I haven't yet seen any media coverage about him being questioned about Alice Grey but I'm sure everyone is just corroborating what I told them and it won't be long until the floodgates open. Soon I hope Ethan being Alice's boyfriend will be a well-known fact and one he can't escape from.

I follow him. I've never followed someone before so it's not surprising that I don't know how to act. Should I be keeping a safe distance? Hiding in case he turns to look behind? Everything I know about following people I've learnt from movies. But I shouldn't worry because Ethan is oblivious, never once turning to look behind, barely taking any notice of his surroundings. He's typing away on his phone, nearly bumping into onlookers who curse his rudeness, attracting car horns as he brazenly crosses the road, flipping the cars off as he saunters past.

Where is he going and why is he not taking a taxi? I haven't thought this plan through but for the moment I'm going to keep walking. It's all I've got. I don't know what I'm expecting but this is where things have led.

As Ethan turns the corner into a street complete with fancy looking houses, the road becomes busier. More noise, more people strolling on the street. More cars. Everyone seems to be heading to the same place as Ethan and then I see why. Paddington station is up ahead. I don't recognise the name but this must be Ethan's destination. He's going to get out of London. The question is, to where?

I move closer, now cloaked by the crowd of tourists. Nobody pays attention to Ethan, which shows how oblivious people can be. I watch as he purchases his ticket and heads to his platform, still anonymous. Surely someone must recognise him considering his face has been plastered over the news recently? I spot the destination of the train he steps onto. Cheltenham Spa. The destination names scroll past on the screen overhead. None of them ring a bell but why would they? I've only really heard of London and Exeter.

I could buy a ticket and follow him on to the train. It would be hard to stay close enough to know when to alight without giving myself away but it's a risk I need to take. I could easily end up stranded miles from London without finding Ethan. If I give up now, if I turn back and go back to my hotel room and wait for justice to be served, then Ethan might walk off into the sunset after potentially being involved in my sister's disappearance and his wife's disappearance. Something tells me he's used to his problems going away. Well, not this time.

The train leaves in five minutes. I grab a ticket from the machine, choosing Cheltenham Spa as my destination. It's not cheap, just under £50, so it better be worth it. There might not be any return trains and I'll have to get a hotel. My funds aren't unlimited and I've just spent more than I could afford on that ticket. As much as I need to be in London to feel close to my sister and investigate, I'm going to have to go back to the US soon. I can't afford to stay here much longer.

A noise behind me interrupts my thoughts.

'Police. Out of the way, please. Police coming through.'

Behind, the crowd is parting like the Red Sea. A string of cops decked in all black jog through the station heading towards the 20:08 train to Cheltenham Spa. The train staff open the ticket barriers for them to flow through. There's a commotion and the station is stunned into silence, eyes firmly towards the train that Ethan just boarded.

There's yelling in the distance but I can't decipher the words. Something is happening on the train. There's a collective gasp and whispers as figures emerge from the train. Cops first, but then follows a man in handcuffs escorted by more cops. He's struggling. They're getting closer to me.

'You do not have to say anything but anything you do say...'

It's Ethan. And he's in handcuffs.

Chapter Twenty-Six

VICTORIA ' TORI' SIMMONS

Chapter Twenty-Seven

ETHAN SIMMONS

'You're under arrest for the murder of Victoria Simmons.'

I repeat that line over and over in my head. It still hasn't sunk in that I've been arrested. I can't keep track of what the cops are after me for. First Alice, now Tori. I was almost free, already on the train to our home in the Cotswolds, waiting mere minutes for it to depart. I knew I should have gotten a cab but I thought getting the train would draw less attention, would be less expected.

Murder. They didn't say disappearance, they said murder. Is Tori dead? Have they found her body? When they arrested me, I didn't know at first if it would be for Tori or for Alice. Maybe it's only a matter of time before they arrest me for that too. If Tori really is gone, I'm left to deal with any fallout on my own.

I'm back at the same police station as before, but everything looks bleaker now, which I didn't think was possible. Muted, grey. My lawyer has been called and is on the way, apparently. I've known so many of my celebrity friends get arrested but it's always for things like DUIs. It's never taken very seriously in the business, it's almost like a rite of passage. We all laugh at the celebrity mugshots and rate whose is worst. Magazines run entire articles on it but this doesn't seem so frivolous. I've been arrested for murder. This is more than just questioning. This might have been my last night as a free man.

I'm sure news of my arrest has already spread across the internet faster than a deadly virus. When I got off the train I saw the scores of witnesses filming on their phones, gossiping with their friends, my hands restrained so I couldn't even hide my face. My baseball cap had been knocked off in the struggle. It was worse when we stepped outside and suddenly the media were back, the flashing lights in my face, the screeching of my name. It wasn't like it usually is. This wasn't an adoring public worshipping me, this was a bunch of hyenas ready to tear roadkill to shreds.

Just over a week ago I felt like the apex predator. On top of the world – about to go into a winnable trial, my career looking up after my inevitable vindication. And now it couldn't be worse. Arrested for the murder of my wife. Questioned about my relationship with Alice. I was even tossed out of my hotel.

Being at the police station is different from the last time. I'm not waiting in the front reception for them to call my name. Instead I'm shown to the back, shoved into a square, grey room with a metal bed and no windows. There's an acrid smell of piss in the air and I try not to gag. They spoke a lot to me as they led me in but the words didn't sink in. Something about me being held in custody, another interview. Being held here for twenty-four hours.

They took my possessions. Searched me. Took my fingerprints. Stuck a nasty-tasting cotton swab in my mouth and made me gag. Took my photograph. I've been photographed so often lately but I've never felt humiliated by it. I felt like livestock the way they prodded and poked me. I hope Ellen turns up soon. Without my phone I have no way of contacting anybody. I'm alone with my thoughts in this empty room. Just four blank walls.

I lie on the bed and close my eyes. The only thing to do is to sleep, but my mind is racing and I can hear unfamiliar sounds. Aggression, shouting. Swearing, banging, screaming. I'm scared. I have no concept of time so I don't know if it's been ten hours or ten minutes when there's a pounding on the door that lights my senses on fire.

'Simmons. Your lawyer is here. Step away from the door.'

The metal door opens and I'm led to another room. Slightly nicer but not by much. At least it doesn't smell as bad. Ellen is ushered in. 'Let us know when you're done,' the guard says to her, his voice gruff, low.

'Ellen. I'm so glad to see you. I've been going out of my mind in here. You've got to get me out of here.'

'Okay, here is what I know. They've arrested you on suspicion of murdering your wife. They've found something. I'm not quite sure what yet but whatever it is they think it's incriminating enough to arrest you. Now they have twenty-four hours to hold you in custody while they gather more evidence and question you. Once those twenty-four hours have elapsed they'll either charge you with the murder or release you.'

'And what if they charge me?' I ask.

'If they charge you it means they think they have enough evidence that there's a reasonable prospect of them winning at trial.'

Trial. There's a bittersweet irony that this all seems to have started with a trial. Maybe it will end with one too.

'And,' she continues, 'given the serious nature of the charge you wouldn't be released on bail so…' She pauses. 'If you're charged then I'm afraid you'll be remanded in custody. You won't be getting out.'

'But even if it went to trial, I could be found not guilty, right?'

'Yes. But you'd be in custody until the trial, which could be months. You wouldn't be held here, you'd be in prison. There's a big backlog at the moment. Technically it's not supposed to be longer than six months but I know of people who have been waiting almost two years for their trial date.'

I don't know what to say. How has this all happened?

'You should rest up. It's late. I'll be back in the morning as I understand they want to interview you then. Do you need anything?'

'Some water would be nice.'

'Sure thing.' Ellen stands up. She's in stark contrast to me with her smart suit. I've never felt so inferior to someone. I judged her before, thought myself better than her, but how the tables have turned. She will be going home to her family – assuming she has one. She will spend her night in a comfy bed. I will be on a lumpy single mattress. I'm not going to sleep a wink.

'Guard, I'm ready to leave now.' The door opens. 'Can you bring my client some water please?'

'Of course.'

'Goodnight, Ethan. Try to get some rest.'

She leaves and the door is slammed shut. Once she's gone, I'm escorted back to my room. I hear the bolts being slid across and darkness consumes the room once more. I wait for someone to return with my water, my throat scratchy and my lips parted. I wait and I wait but the water never comes. Nobody checks up on me. I've never felt truly alone until this moment.

I hug my knees to my chest as I blink through the tears

sliding down my cheeks and spooling across the thin blanket. I wish Tori was here right now. She's all I can think about. After all, she is the reason I'm here. There was a time where Tori and I were on top of the world and now I've been arrested for her murder.

When did everything become so toxic?

Chapter Twenty-Eight

@THETRUTHISGREY

Ethan has been arrested.

I can't believe I saw it with my own eyes.

It's been leaked already. I guess that's what happens when you get arrested in the middle of a busy train station. Ethan has been arrested for the murder of Tori Simmons. Not suspected in her disappearance but suspected of killing her. All this time I still thought Tori might be the one messaging me on TikTok, behind the campaign to make sure Ethan sees justice. But if the police have arrested Ethan for her murder there must be good evidence that she's dead. I'm guessing they've found her body and there's incriminating evidence that Ethan was involved. Everyone has seen the video of him threatening her but I reckon they must have DNA or something pretty damning to arrest him like they did.

Will they take a DNA sample as part of the arrest? An internet search suggests it's standard procedure. If they take his DNA tonight, once they analyse it they might get a match on the blood from the jacket Alice was last seen wearing and they can arrest him for Alice's murder too. I might finally learn what happened to my sister. If Ethan can murder his wife – a famous popstar everybody will be looking for – he can murder my sister, an unknown victim who can vanish without a trace. I've been the only one looking for her all this time. The media haven't posted anything about what I told them yesterday about Ethan's connection to my sister, but I suppose that news is small fry now they've got the biggest hook of the moment.

There's an article in *The London News* about Ethan's arrest. It has a contact email at the bottom. I draft an email to send. In it I tell them everything about Ethan's connection to Alice. I tell them everything I've found out from the documentary and the helpful stranger on TikTok. I don't want to leave any stone unturned. I link all my relevant TikTok videos on the case. I make it emphatically clear that I think Ethan killed my sister. This is the hook for the media. They sadly don't care that much about a cold missing persons case but they will care if it appears a Hollywood star not only killed his wife but somebody else. And maybe it's not just them, maybe Ethan is actually a serial killer. A serial killer in Hollywood, how more twisted can this man's life be?

I leave my phone number at the bottom of the email, letting them know that they can call me if they need any further information. I copy the email and find every single news article about Ethan's arrest. They don't all have contact information but for the ones that do, I send an identical email to them. The scatter-gun approach will yield the most success. By tomorrow morning, I hope that the name Ethan Simmons becomes synonymous with the name Alice Grey.

I'm not going to risk it all on the editors though. They can be fickle and I can't depend on them picking up the story and posting it. I pleaded with reporters to keep posting about Alice when she disappeared but none of them would listen to me. One of them was callous enough to tell me that Alice wasn't even the only person to go missing in the week that she did and that they couldn't report on everyone.

Speaking of missing persons, I got a call from the cops about the unidentified body they found that didn't belong to Alice. They found out it was Matilda Green's. She went missing a few weeks before Alice and everyone thought there could be a connection between them, both young, attractive women in London to vanish without a trace. There was speculation about a new serial killer. Matilda being found dead might be further confirmation that Alice met the same fate.

I need to use my own platform to tell everybody the truth. My account stands at 732k followers. That's a lot of people I can tell about Ethan Simmons and my sister. I was too scared before, scared of him taking to me court for slander like he did with Tori – after all, I can't afford to keep staying in London let alone legal costs. Tori had the money in the bank to fight back but I don't.

Now that Ethan has been arrested, I'm not worried anymore. He's definitely got bigger problems on his plate than what I'm saying or doing – besides it's not like he can take the moral high ground anymore. He's already public enemy number one – he can't be seen to be going after somebody who is grieving their sister.

I set up my camera to record the video. I piece all the evidence together in a sort of slideshow, making it nice and easy for the viewer to understand what's going on. I link all the other videos. I include excerpts from the documentary. I tell them that Ethan will have his DNA taken from him when he's in custody. I tell them that in a few days we should know if his DNA matches the mystery DNA on the jacket my sister was seen in when she disappeared. The one covered in her blood. When I'm happy with it I write the caption. There's only one choice.

ETHAN SIMMONS – THE HOLLYWOOD SERIAL KILLER.

If that doesn't grab the attention of people mindlessly scrolling TikTok then I don't know what will. I make the cover image a photo of my sister with Ethan superimposed on it along with a big banner with the same text. I need this to go viral. I don't care if I can't prove what Ethan did.

I hesitate to publish the TikTok. Once I post it, it can't be undone. Things are reposted, copied, reacted to so quickly that it becomes impossible to contain; like trying to hold water in your hands, it spills out and you can never get it back.

I take a deep breath in. I have to do this for Alice. I may not be able to get my sister back but I can make sure that the person who hurt her is punished. Not just for me, but for our parents. Nothing has been the same since the day Alice left our lives. She was always the better daughter. The sunshine while I was the grey cloud.

I press publish and sit back in my chair. It starts getting likes instantly. The numbers getting higher and higher. And then the comments come flooding in.

harri_fan08
Is this real?!?

simmons_lufc
Wtf always knew he was dodgy

sammy_labs
@Robinss99: have you seen this? What do you reckon? Still fancy him?

Robinss99
@sammy_labs still wouldn't say no x

Austin__
No way

HollyGardener
I believe it

There are more as the video takes off, the numbers higher than I've ever seen on my account. I suppose this is what they mean when they say a video has 'gone viral'. My videos usually do well but this is something else. I can't keep up with the comments. And then people start filming videos of them reacting to it. The reactions are mixed. Some defend Ethan as if he's a blood relative and some claim they always knew something was wrong with him. I want people to know Ethan is a bad person but more than anything I need someone to come forward with more evidence. I need the police to care as much about linking Ethan to Alice's disappearance as they do about Tori's murder. My sister was never a celebrity but she was my whole world. She was always a star in my eyes.

I get a message on my account. I've had a few come in, mostly from users hoping I'll share more about the Ethan situation. Some are trolls. Some are just nosy. Nothing from @thetruthisblackandwhite2011 but I've learnt that they work on their own schedule. But there is something from a name I recognise. Catrin Thomas. I click on her profile. There are very few videos but I know who this is.

@Catrin_Thomas
Can we meet to talk?

@Catrin_Thomas
There's something I should've told you a long time ago.

@Catrin_Thomas
Meet me in the Wakey Wakey café near Regent's Park tomorrow at 11am?

@thetruthisgrey
I'll be there.

Catrin was my sister's flatmate. I met her only once before Alice went missing. I had come to England to visit Alice. I couldn't come as much as I wanted because flights are expensive from Chicago and I didn't earn that much money as a video editor. But I was really missing my twin and she definitely didn't have enough money to come home. So I took on a lot of freelance work on top of my day job and saved every penny I could. I barely left the house for six months until I'd saved up enough money for flights. Alice was letting me share her bed to save me forking out for a hotel. If only I'd had a TikTok account back then and was able to make the kind of money I do now from posting two-minute videos from my bedroom.

Catrin always seemed nice enough. I think they met through some sort of app for Londoners looking for a flat share as nobody can afford to live in London by themselves. Alice always said she was lucky to only have to live with one other person as some of her friends were living with four or five strangers. Their flat was nice too. Ultra-modern, had clearly recently been redecorated. It was nicer than my parents' home. Sometimes I wondered just how she afforded it. They didn't have much in common on paper but they both had a carefree attitude to life and Alice seemed happy with their living situation.

The next time I saw Catrin was after Alice had disappeared. My family had come to London to be here in case there was news and so we could help with the search. After several weeks went by and the trail went cold, my parents told me it was time to head back to America. I didn't want to leave because it felt like we were giving up but I relented. Before we left we visited the flat to recover some of Alice's possessions. I'll never forget seeing the photograph on her bedside table – a silly photograph some tourist had taken of us outside Buckingham Palace. She'd put it in one of those funny frames that say *I heart LDN*. I took it with me.

I bumped into Catrin as I was leaving Alice's bedroom. I forgot she still lived there. The conversation was awkward. She told me she was sorry for my loss but she couldn't maintain eye contact with me. She then asked me if we had plans to empty Alice's room – apparently the landlord was already putting pressure on her to find a new tenant to pay rent. I knew from the tears in her eyes and the way she kept her head firmly fixed on the floor that she didn't want to ask but had no choice. I didn't know how to react so I told her I'd sort it.

Catrin was involved in the investigation at first, but only to verify the time my sister had left home. She was also the first person to report Alice missing when she noticed she hadn't been home and none of her messages were being read. I never spoke to her again. Maybe I should have. She was possibly one of the last people to see my sister.

What is it that she should have told me? And why is she only telling me now?

Chapter Twenty-Nine

VICTORIA 'TORI' SIMMONS

Chapter Thirty

ETHAN SIMMONS

I wish I could say that the moment I woke up it was all a dream and I was lying in my king-size bed at The Hidden with some half-eaten chicken wings next to me. Unfortunately my eyes open to the sight of the peeling grey walls of the holding cell. There's a sharp pain in my back from the worn-out mattress and my feet are cold from where the too-small blanket has ridden up in the night.

There's a pit in my stomach that I can't ignore. I don't know how it works here. Do I ask for food? It's not a hotel but they can't starve me. Isn't that against my human rights or something?

I bang on the door for attention. The custody officer appears outside. 'What do you want?'

'I'm hungry. Thirsty too. Any chance of getting anything to eat?' I ask. I never thought I'd have to beg for food like this. Usually I dial 0 and the friendly receptionist brings up whatever I want. The Hidden even let me order off-menu. Nothing was too much trouble for them.

'Breakfast will be delivered at 8am.'

He starts to walk away. 'Wait, wait. What time is it?'

He doesn't reply straight away and I worry he hasn't heard me. 'Seven forty-eight am,' he eventually calls back. Not long to wait then.

I spend the next twelve minutes or however long it actually is staring at the ceiling, contemplating how I have ended up in this situation. It's odd having no concept of time. I'm used to permanently having my expensive watch on my left wrist. It feels naked without it. The pain in my stomach gnaws at my insides as I try to block it out. I chew on my fingernails for distraction. I attempt to think of anything else other than food but I can't, each time my thoughts drift elsewhere the rumbling in my core reminds me of how long it's been since I last ate.

I jump up as soon as the tray of food is pushed through the opening in the door. The food isn't the most appealing and usually I'd turn my nose up at it but right now I shovel it into my mouth. The stale bread roll is gone in two bites. I chew so quickly I'm lucky the pieces don't get stuck in my throat. The mushy stew with the unidentifiable meat is devoured despite the texture and the smell. I'm not satiated after the meal but I can at least relax, my body no longer in flight or fight mode.

Eventually the tray is taken away and I'm left to my own devices again. Alone. For someone used to being in the public eye I don't think I've ever spent so long alone with my own thoughts. I wish I had something to do, anything. I'm so used to mindlessly scrolling on my phone to pass the time but they took it away from me so I can't even do that. I see why people work out so much in jail, there's really nothing else to do.

The next time there's a knock at the door for what I think is lunch, the door opens fully.

'Your solicitor is here. The police want to interview you. Come with me.' I can't help but feel disappointed it's not a hot meal.

He looks me up and down. 'Don't try anything or I'll cuff you next time.'

He's a big man. He's unshaven and has a slightly grubby appearance and a hairline that is receding badly. I can't tell if he's overweight or if it's pure muscle but coupled with his height I wouldn't have a chance against him anyway. I may be in pretty good shape but it's all for aesthetics so I have to stay lean and this guy dwarfs me. He walks me from my room and opens the door to an interview room. It could be the same one as before, they all look the same. Ellen is sat at the table alone, leafing through papers and drinking water out of a paper cup.

'I'll give you ten minutes together. Officers will be by shortly to start the interview.' The custody officer shuts the door.

'Ethan, how are you doing?' Ellen asks. She doesn't stand to greet me. She looks like she's wearing the same suit as when I saw her last night and it looks as if she hasn't brushed her hair for a while. Has she even been home?

'I've been better.'

'Are they treating you okay?' she asks, her brow furrowed.

'Yes. Just would rather be out of here, you know?' I take a seat next to her.

'Of course. Of course. Right, let's get to it before the interview starts. So, as I said last night, the police can usually hold you for twenty-four hours. But when the charge is more serious such as murder, they can apply for more time. I'm aware the police have been granted an extension to thirty-six hours.' She looks at her phone. 'It's been about sixteen hours since you were arrested so they still have twenty hours until they have to either charge you or release you.'

'Why have they got an extension?'

'I think the DNA is taking a while to process. But I have

now found out what the additional evidence they have on you is that led to the arrest.'

'Okay, and what is it?'

'Apparently you were kicked out of your hotel yesterday, is that right?'

I groan. 'Yes. The manager didn't want me staying at The Hidden anymore. She said other guests were complaining about the paps outside the hotel – like that was my fault.'

'Well, it seems when you left your room the maids went straight in to clean it. Not normal procedure but my understanding is they wanted to get it tidy as quickly as possible so they could demonstrate to other guests that you had definitely left.'

'Right, what does this have to do with me being arrested in the middle of Paddington station?'

'Well the maid found something and called the police. And—'

The door bursts open, hitting the wall as it ricochets off it.

'Mr Simmons. Nice to see you again.' DS Jay Taylor smirks as he strides in. DC Hayes follows, hugging a pile of documents to his chest. They take a seat opposite.

'I hadn't finished speaking with my client,' Ellen says. She looks annoyed.

'I'm afraid, as you'll know, we are on a bit of a deadline so we need to get things moving. Of course if your client needs to take a break at any time for legal advice then that is his right.'

'My client will be answering "no comment" for the interview, so you are aware.'

It's the same strategy as last time. I want to know what the maid found in the hotel room. I cast my mind back to how I left it. I think I took everything with me. If I left anything it would just be trash, not something that would lead to this arrest. And I didn't have anything of Tori's in that room – she never came to visit me. The only possession I have that has anything to do with her is my wedding ring, and that's still on my finger.

'As you'll remember from last time, it's police procedure to record this. I'm going to start the recording now.' He presses the button on the recorder and the noise is as repulsive as before. 'This interview is being conducted by DS Jay Taylor and DC Derek Hayes at Colindale police station on 7 June 2025. Can you please state your name for the tape?' DS Taylor asks.

'Ethan Simmons.'

'Also present in the room is Ellen Pilkington from Dawson and Edwards Solicitors. Ethan, you have been arrested on suspicion of the murder of Victoria Simmons. I must remind you that you are still under caution. You do not have to say anything but it may harm your defence if you do not mention when questioned something which you later rely on in court. Anything you do say may be given in evidence.'

I get an overwhelming sense of déjà vu. But the stakes are higher this time. This time I'm under arrest. This isn't a voluntary interview; I can't leave at any time. Once the interview is done they'll return to me to my own personal hell. More hours in solitary, alone with my own thoughts.

'How was your relationship with your wife, Ethan?'

'I mean, isn't it pretty obvious? We were literally going through a massive defamation trial before she disappeared.'

There's a loud cough to the left of me.

'So you'd agree your that your marriage was in a bad place?'

'Just meant that things were strained lately because of the trial.'

I feel Ellen's elbow pressing into my side. I turn and our eyes lock and I know she wants me to stop speaking, but the police are twisting my words and I can't let them do that. I don't see how staying silent is going to be help me in any way. I need to stick up for myself.

'Is that why you threatened her the night she was last seen?' DC Hayes pounces on my words.

'Look, if you're talking about that video that was circulating … it isn't what it looks like. It was just a discussion between two married adults. Marriage isn't all sunshine and rainbows as I'm sure you know.'

DC Hayes slides photographs across the table. They are still shots from the video of me threatening Tori. They must be building up to the big reveal.

'Is this you in these photographs?'

'You know it is.'

Ellen sighs besides me. She's given up with her non-verbal hints to stop me talking.

'And who is in the photographs with you?'

'You know the answer to that.'

'Mr Simmons, please answer the question.' DS Taylor interjects.

'It's Tori.'

'And what are you discussing here?' DC Hayes asks. 'It looks like a heated conversation to me.'

What do I say? The media already reported what the conversation was about, so they'll know the answer. If I lie they'll be able to catch me out, but telling the truth is almost just as bad.

'I didn't want her to speak in court about Alice.'

I brace myself for the inevitable.

'And who is Alice?'

In life there's always those pivotal moments that change the course of everything. I know that right here, this is about to be one of those moments. Alice has been my secret for so long.

I can't tell the police everything, but I need to give them something.

'Alice was my girlfriend. I had an affair with her last year.'

'And what happened with you and Alice?'

'I ended things with her when Tori found out. I regretted what I did massively.'

A look passes between the officers and I think they're going to make me talk about Alice more but they switch back to Tori.

'So why were you surprised Tori mentioned Alice? It seems like a pretty good defence considering what you were suing her for.'

'I never thought that Tori would mention Alice in public because it was a very difficult time for us and our marriage. I don't want to go into everything because it's very personal to us but Tori was in a very bad way when she found out about us. I never thought she'd bring it up in court so when she mentioned it, I knew I had to try and persuade her not to speak about it.'

'Why?'

'Because I knew if she did, we'd never come back from it. Call me sentimental but I still had hopes Tori and I would find our way back to each other. We were madly in love once and I knew we could be again. I didn't want her to destroy our relationship once and for all. We'd never survive the press attention.'

'So you brought a multi-million-pound claim against your wife for slander, claiming she ruined your career by lying about you cheating on her, for it to all be true? Forgive me for speaking out of turn but that doesn't make any sense to me.'

I try to stifle my laughter. 'That's because you're not from this world. The trial wasn't real. Well, it was real, but the story behind it wasn't. It was all for show. Our agents concocted it because both our careers were declining. Tori had never been as successful since her pop group ended and her solo career was stalled. When I was single I had a different aura around me that painted me as a lothario but once I got into a relationship with Tori, people stopped looking at me the same way. We all thought the idea of the trial would catapult us back into the limelight.'

'So Tori got you fired from your job so that you could have this trial? Surely the smart thing for you to do would have been to continue starring in the *Aces & Diamonds* series?'

'That bit wasn't planned. Tori was drunk and jealous about Alice and she blurted it out. She's a massive lightweight. Can't be trusted when she drinks. Going along with this trial and letting me appear innocent was her way of making it up to me.'

'So none of it was real?'

'That's showbiz for you. We had it all worked out. We were going to settle after the third day, come to an amicable agreement. We were going to do a commitment ceremony afterwards to reaffirm our love for each other. Our agents were going to secure us a ton of brand deals and exposure. We thought it would be good for us.'

'Okay, but this is slightly sidetracking us here. Are you saying you threatening Tori was all part of this ruse?'

'No. Tori went off script.'

Chapter Thirty-One

@THETRUTHISGREY

I get to the café near Regent's Park ahead of time, too restless to sit and wait. I take a seat at the table in the corner and order a latte and an iced cinnamon bun for the nerves; sweet treats always help me calm down. My mind has been in overdrive, contemplating what Catrin could be about to tell me and what the impact of it will be. If she knows something about Alice that could have helped the police I don't understand why she wouldn't have come forward before. I invent scenarios in my head, play out the possible conversation we are about to have with a different ending each time. I find myself already mad at her for keeping secrets, secrets that could've been the key to the investigation the whole time.

There's been more articles about Ethan's arrest. None of them have mentioned his connection to Alice … yet. I hope they take my emails seriously – perhaps they are still fact-checking. Apparently they have to charge him after a certain amount of time or let him go. I hope they not only charge him for Tori's murder but match his DNA to my sister's clothes and he goes down for that too. It isn't enough if he goes to prison for what he did to his wife, my sister forgotten about and justice not served. Tori may be the prize for everyone else but he might have killed my sister too. I'm hoping that whatever Catrin tells me today will be enough to seal his fate.

Once she tells me what she has to say, I'll be on the phone to the detectives, making sure they are testing Ethan's DNA. I already called them multiple times asking for them to test the DNA and they just told me they'd 'handle it'.

Catrin arrives ten minutes late. My drink and pastry are demolished but my appetite isn't satisfied. I would order another coffee but the prices here are ridiculous, twice what I'd pay back home. She doesn't recognise me at first so I wave at her to grab her attention. She's changed a lot since I last saw her. She looks a lot healthier than she used to. She's always been an attractive girl but she used to have a fragile look about her; her cheekbones and collar bones were slightly too prominent and she always had bags under her eyes. Whatever changes she's made, it's worked well for her.

'You've changed your hair,' she says.

That's right. When I met her my hair was blue, or maybe it was green by the time it started fading out. Not like the pink I'm currently sporting.

'Thanks for meeting me.' She takes a seat opposite and checks behind her, scanning the other visitors in the coffee shop.

I want to ask her outright what she needs to tell me and skip the awkward pleasantries but I resist the temptation even though it's difficult. I can tell from the quiver of her lips that she needs to work up to what she needs to tell me, that it isn't the sort of thing you just blurt out.

'How have you been?'

'Yeah, great. Got a new job. Moved house. Things are a lot better now. What about you?'

A lot better? A lot better than when? She seemed to have things pretty well figured out when she was living with my sister.

'I mean, things haven't been easy since Alice. But I'm managing.'

The small talk is unnatural, forced, but we engage in it anyway.

'Your TikTok channel is impressive. I've been following you for a while. You've got a lot of followers now.'

I didn't know Catrin followed me. I'm sure I would have noticed her name popping up but I get so many notifications some days.

'Thanks. Let's hope it helps me find out what happened to Alice.'

She nods and asks if I want another coffee, stalling. I decline but she insists and I ask for a decaf so I'm not jittery after already having my latte. When she returns we sit in silence. Neither of us wants to be the first to start talking about why we are really here but somebody has to break the tension.

'So, you said you had something you wanted to tell me?'

'Yeah, I did say that, didn't I…' She takes a sip of her coffee. She doesn't respond and I worry she's having second thoughts.

I don't fill the silence. I need her to start talking.

'I don't even know where to begin,' she says eventually with a sigh. 'I want to tell you everything but I'm worried about how you'll react.'

'What do you mean?'

'I'm worried you'll be mad at me for what I did or, more accurately, what I didn't do. I'm not happy about my actions but now I think things are different and maybe I can make up for it by coming clean.'

'Why are things different now?'

'Because Ethan has been arrested. I don't feel as scared about telling you what I should have told you last year.'

I grip the handle of the mug hard, the points of my fingernails digging into my skin.

'So I gathered from your video you know that Ethan Simmons was having an affair with your sister.'

'I know. I didn't know at the time though. It's only something that I've learnt recently. I don't understand why you never mentioned it to us or told the cops.'

'It wasn't just a fling for them both. Alice told me that Ethan was going to leave Tori for her. I don't know how true it all was because I only heard this through Alice so he could've just been playing her but she was serious about him.' She dodges my question.

'Interesting.' But it's not anything big yet. It's useful to hear it directly from someone involved but this isn't going to change anything. There has to be more.

'The thing is, Alice was getting upset that Ethan wasn't committing to her enough. He kept saying he'd leave his wife but then nothing was happening.'

There is more to this.

'She was going to give him an ultimatum. She was going to threaten to tell Tori about their affair unless he left her. Alice had enough of being second best.'

'And what happened when she threatened him?'

'Well, that's the thing, I don't know what happened because the day she went to meet him to tell him this was that day.'

'Wait ... the day she went missing?''

'Exactly.'

'So you're telling me that on the day my sister went missing she was on the way to threaten Ethan Simmons so that he'd leave his wife?'

'That's exactly what I'm saying.'

'And you didn't think it was clear he was a prime suspect in her disappearance? Catrin, if only we'd known this, they could have questioned him.'

'I don't know what I thought. If I'm honest I tried not to think about what happened to her. I felt guilty. I didn't report her missing until two days had passed because I was so wrapped up in my own life I didn't notice she'd not been back to the house, and we'd fallen out over the Ethan situation anyway as I wanted her to stay away from him. I kept thinking if I'd told the police sooner maybe they'd have found something…'

'Why didn't you tell anyone though? It could've changed things. The police never knew about Ethan so he was never considered a suspect. If only you'd told them…' I don't want to let myself think about what could have happened if Catrin hadn't held onto this information. Everything could have turned out so differently. The police never had a chance to find my sister with all the secrets being kept.

'I know. I'm so sorry. You have to believe me.' Tears fall down her face. 'You have no idea the number of messages I've started writing to you that I've deleted.'

'Please just tell me why. Why did you keep this secret?'

'Because I was told to.'

Chapter Thirty-Two

VICTORIA 'TORI' SIMMONS

Chapter Thirty-Three

ETHAN SIMMONS

'What do you mean that Tori went off script?' DS Taylor asks. They are both intrigued, pens paused, waiting for me to speak.

'Like I said, the trial was all preplanned. We rehearsed what we wanted to say. We knew what we wanted to come out.'

DC Hayes interrupts me. 'You're telling me that Tori was fine with those photographs coming out? The ones of her naked … doing those *things*.' He looks visibly disgusted. I wouldn't have taken him for a prude.

'Yes. Somebody had already gotten hold of them, no idea from where. They were trying to blackmail her for a lot of money. Said if she didn't pay up they'd release them. She paid them but then they wanted more money. And then more again. Tori played for time but we knew that whoever had them had no intention of deleting them so we decided to leak them during the trial so Tori could at least control the narrative.'

'So you're saying you knew your wife was cheating on you and you were fine with that?'

'We had an open marriage. That's what made the trial the perfect strategy for us. We were going to settle after the third day, like I said. Tori had affairs and so did I. It wasn't an issue for us, just other people with closed minds. But we used it to our advantage, we tried to play the public.'

The detectives exchange glances. 'I don't buy a word of this. None of this adds up.'

'I'm an actor, DS, I suppose you could say the trial was my most convincing role yet.'

'So if you and Tori had an open marriage, why would she get jealous about your affair with Alice?'

'Our open marriage was just meant to be about physical experimentation but she was jealous because she thought I was going further than that.'

'And how about when you accused your wife of having someone else sing her songs? If the trial was a plan by both of you to improve your careers, why was your wife the only one being dragged through the mud? Anyway, we'll get back to the inconsistencies in this story later. Let's go back to what you were saying before. What do you mean that Tori went off script?'

'Well it was on that last day, the day before she disappeared. Tori's testimony didn't go like it was supposed to.'

'What was she supposed to say?'

'She was just supposed to talk about Nikki.'

'Nikki Feldman?'

'Yeah, she was just supposed to talk about her suspicions that we were having an affair. And then Thomas would cross-examine her and it would turn out she had no proof, although truthfully Nikki and I actually were sleeping together. And then on the third day we were going to settle. We were going to make a big announcement about how the trial made us realise we still loved each other. Tori would say she didn't have any proof for my cheating and say she only said what she said because she was jealous of my female friendships. I'd admit to my part in staying away from home too much and fuelling rumours to help my career. We'd commit to working on our relationship in therapy and then renew our vows in a lavish ceremony.'

'Okay, and then?'

'Well, Tori started talking about some girl I dated that she wasn't supposed to bring up. And then she refused to settle. She stopped cooperating.'

'This "girl" is who Tori referred to as Alice, correct?'

'Yes.'

'And who was she?'

'Nobody well known. Just some girl I'd been dating.'

'So, her name wasn't Alice Grey?'

My heart stops. 'I don't know that name. Should I?'

I hear Ellen groan next to me. 'Not a smart move, Ethan. You were questioned about her disappearance two days ago. And now you're claiming not to know her name.'

I need to think on my feet. I've slipped up. I completely forgot that I was interviewed about Alice. It is all getting mixed up in my head. The drama of the last two days has overridden everything.

'Yes, of course. I'm so sorry, I completely forgot that was her surname. Everything has been a blur lately and I've not really had much sleep.'

'In your interview on 5 June you were asked multiple questions about your relationship with Alice Grey. You were presented with evidence that you were indeed having an intimate relationship with her. You answered almost every question with "No comment" following advice from your solicitor.' DC Hayes shoots Ellen a dirty look. Solicitors advising their clients must make their job a lot harder. 'Is it true that the Alice that Tori was referring to in her testimony was indeed Alice Grey?'

I should have known that they'd piece it together. I think I knew as soon as they brought me in for questioning about Alice's disappearance that eventually somebody would remember Tori's testimony and they'd work out that it's unlikely there are two Alices I'm connected to. It doesn't help that every word Tori said is online for ever, the police can play it back at their leisure and their teams can analyse everything. I wonder if that annoying journalist with the pink hair has been running her mouth too. She somehow knew my connection with Alice before anybody else pieced it together.

I would have been safe if only somebody hadn't somehow gotten hold of Alice's phone and sent it to the police, the phone Tori was supposed to dispose of. It feels like everything is catching up to me.

'That would make two women you've been involved with that have ended up disappearing. Quite a coincidence, wouldn't you say?'

'I know it seems like a coincidence. But that isn't the Alice that Tori is referring to. I told you that my wife and I had an open relationship and Alice was one of the people I happened to be dating.'

'If you were dating her as part of an open relationship then why would you care so much if Tori brought her up?'

'I already answered this.'

'Were you worried about what your wife was going to say on the third day of the trial, Mr Simmons?'

'Well, like I said, she wasn't sticking to the plan.'

'Were you so worried that you would go to her house and threaten her to keep quiet? And if that didn't work, would you be worried enough to make you wife disappear for ever?'

'No.'

'Did you kill your wife?'

'No.'

'Did she know secrets about you that you were scared were going to come out?'

'No.'

'Did you kill your wife?'

'No.'

'Strong-willed, your wife was. I bet she wasn't one to take no for an answer. So when your threats didn't work on her you had no other choice, right?'

'No.'

'So you murdered your wife?'

'No!'

'Enough, officers,' Ellen says. I'd almost forgotten her presence and feel grateful for the interruption. A bead of sweat slides down my forehead and the palms of my hands are sticky.

'I didn't kill my wife. I promise. I don't know what happened to her and I wish I did.'

It's the truth but I can tell they don't believe me. I really don't know what happened to Tori but the police have already made up their minds. So far all they have is the video of me threatening her which I agree looks bad but that surely isn't enough for them to arrest me. I'm waiting for them to reveal what's up their sleeves. They must have something they are waiting to reveal. A slam-dunk they haven't yet played.

'Maybe you didn't mean to. Maybe it was self-defence. An act of passion. There's no doubting that you two were always a passionate couple. Lots of PDA. But we've seen reports in the media that, according to your neighbours, you had blazing rows.'

I scoff. 'I've seen those reports. They're from when we were staying at our Cotswolds home and our nearest neighbours weren't close enough to hear anything. They were just doing it for a few quick dollars and to get back at us.'

'Back at you for what?'

'The neighbours weren't happy after we got planning permission to build an outhouse on our land. They said it would spoil their view or something like that.'

DC Hayes makes a note of my answer.

'Are you going to present my client with any actual evidence implicating him in the murder of Tori Simmons,' says Ellen, 'or are hearsay and hunches all you have to go on?'

'We're getting there,' DS Taylor responds. 'DC Hayes, why don't you ask Mr Simmons about the evidence we found in his hotel room?'

DC Hayes nods. 'Mr Simmons, you were staying at The Hidden hotel until yesterday when we arrested you, correct?'

'Yes.' Technically it's correct, even if I had been kicked out by the time they got to me.

'And you were staying in room 503, correct?'

'Yes.'

'You were kicked out of The Hidden, weren't you?'

'Yes.' It's embarrassing to admit.

'So is it fair to say you left in quite a hurry? I understand from the manager of the hotel that you were told to leave with immediate effect.'

'I suppose so.'

'At 7:23pm on 6 June after Mr Simmons vacated room 503 at The Hidden, the hotel's cleaning staff entered the room to perform the usual room clean following check out. At 7:41pm, the cleaning staff alerted the manager of the hotel to something they had found in your room. The manager promptly called the police and we attended the scene. Shortly after that, the decision was made to arrest you for murder.'

'Is there a question for my client in there?' Ellen says.

'Do you know what we found, Mr Simmons?'

'No?' I honestly don't. Maybe I accidentally left something behind. But by that I mean a stray sock or my toothbrush, not something that would land me here.

'For the tape, I am showing Mr Simmons and his solicitor item TSKRZ1.' DC Hayes slides an item of clothing towards me in a plastic bag. It looks like a red blouse and I don't recognise it.

'Do you know what this is?' DS Taylor asks.

I shrug. 'Should I? I mean it's a woman's blouse but I don't know who it belongs to.'

I hadn't had any female visitors in the hotel room. I knew that would be a terrible idea with all eyes on me during the trial. Of course during the night I often wondered if I could risk it but I never did. The only way something like that could've ended up in my hotel room is if a previous guest left it there.

'You really don't know who this belongs to? Look again.'

I look closer but it's still just a blouse. I don't know what they are expecting me to realise by staring at it longer.

'I don't know what you are expecting from me. It's not mine. It could have been left there by another guest. I don't know.' And I definitely don't know what this blouse has to do with Tori.

'This is the blouse that Tori is wearing in image TSHRU1. For the tape TSHRU1 is a still from the video footage of Mr Simmons threatening his wife, the last time she was seen.'

I look at the blouse and at the photo in front of me. I am at a loss to explain and feel like I must be colourblind because that's the only thing that makes sense. I look at Ellen but her face doesn't show the same confusion as mine.

'The blouse Tori was wearing was white.' I remember it even without the photographs. She'd turned up to court dressed in all white and the magazines went crazy saying that Tori had worn it to remind me of our wedding so I'd end the trial.

'Correct.'

They're really going to make me spell it out.

'And the blouse in this plastic is red.'

'It's white.'

'I don't—'

'Here, maybe this will help.' DC Hayes takes his phone out of his pocket and shines the torch on the blouse. 'For the tape, I'm using the torch on the blouse to aid Mr Simmons.'

And then I realise how foolish I've been and my cheeks redden. It's not a red blouse. It's a white blouse that now looks red because it's covered in blood. *Drenched* in human blood. I push the evidence bag away from in disgust.

'Recognise it now?'

'No! Even if that was the blouse that Tori was wearing I have no idea what it would be doing in my hotel room and I don't know why it would be covered … in blood.' If I'd hurt my wife, why would I bring evidence back to my hotel room, and leave it there? It doesn't make sense.

'Does the blood on the blouse match Tori Simmons'?' Ellen asks. I'm glad to have her in my corner even if I keep going against her advice. But not anymore – I need to keep my mouth shut. I'm not answering any more questions. I don't know where this blouse has come from but all I can think of is that somebody is trying to set me up for Tori's murder. I didn't kill my wife so there is no reason that blouse would be in my hotel room unless somebody planted it there.

'It's being tested,' DC Taylor replies, begrudgingly.

'So, you don't know if the blood on this blouse belongs to Tori Simmons?'

'Not yet, but I'm sure in time the DNA will match what we have on file for Tori.'

'And how do you know this is the blouse that she was last wearing and not just a similar style or the same style but not one belonging to Tori? Have you tested for that too?'

'Of course we have, but we are still waiting for the results on that also. But we are confident that the results will come back exactly as we are expecting them to.'

'Well, let's hope they come back soon because with the evidence you've got I can't see how you can charge my client with anything.'

'Let's end it there for now. The DNA results should be back within the next few hours. We can reconvene then. Interview terminated at 1:32pm.'

DC Hayes presses a button on the tape and a familiar ping sounds. 'Oh and Ethan, I should tell you we are testing your DNA against an item of clothing we have from the Alice Grey case, the jacket she was last seen wearing.

He smirks as both officers stand up and leave. I'm left alone with Ellen again.

'They need those DNA results to come back positive or they won't be able to charge you. If the DNA results don't come back in time they will have to let you go. Of course they can rearrest you if the DNA results then come back in their favour. They could also make another application to extend.'

'I didn't kill her. I don't know how that blouse ended up in my hotel room. I think somebody is trying to frame me. I need you to look into that angle. Somebody must have planted it.'

'Okay, I will look at the hotel CCTV to see if anyone went in your room.'

'Please. I didn't do this. You have to believe me.'

'It doesn't matter what I believe. It's about what the evidence says. I'll see you later.'

But what if the evidence is wrong?

Chapter Thirty-Four

'Who told you to keep it a secret?'

'It was Ethan. He came to the flat after I reported Alice missing. I think he must have found out it was me from the papers. You know Alice, she was always so beautiful and the media just love a beautiful victim. Bad things are only supposed to happen to ugly people.'

I roll my eyes. Although I was obviously glad about the media paying so much attention to my sister, I know it's pretty privilege. There have been so many other girls who went missing since Alice and most of them didn't even get a quarter of the coverage. They didn't quite fit the ideal victim from the newspapers' perspectives. But even for beautiful Alice, too many girls going missing meant her time in the limelight was short-lived. Within a couple of days, everybody had forgotten her name.

'What did he say?'

'He said he knew that I was aware of their relationship. He asked me if I knew he had a wife, which of course I did because it was what Alice and I kept arguing about. He told me that he didn't want his wife finding out so asked if I could keep quiet about their relationship.'

'As in, not tell the mags?'

'No. He didn't want me to tell anyone. He specified that he didn't want me to tell the police either.'

'Why?'

'Well, he said it's because once the police knew, somebody would leak it to the journos and then it would be everywhere and Tori would find out. He said he loved his wife and wanted to make it work. He knew if it got out he'd been seeing Alice that she'd leave him and he'd be heartbroken.' She scoffs. 'I thought it was rich. He had an affair with Alice, told her he'd leave his wife and run away with her, and then tells me that he loves his wife? Bastard.'

'So, what did you say to him? Did you not find it strange he didn't want you to go to the police?'

'I told him to fuck off and I guess I should've thought it was weird but I didn't ever think he had something to do with her going missing.'

'Good for you.'

She grimaces. 'That's not the end of the story. I went to slam the door in his face but he wedged his foot in and came into the flat. His whole demeanour changed.'

'Oh god, did he hurt you?'

'No, no. Nothing like that. But he told me he'd tried to ask me nicely to keep his secret but he could see that approach wasn't going to work so he said he had a different suggestion.'

'Did he pay you off?' I ask. Money talks and Ethan sure had lots of it. I brace myself for her answer, knowing that an important lead in my sister's disappearance might have been hidden because of money. This is why the rich always win. They don't play by the same rules as the rest of us.

'No. It wasn't money. I may be ashamed of what I did but

at least I can say I didn't let my friend down for the sake of some money. He blackmailed me.'

I don't know whether to feel relieved or not.

'What did he have on you?'

She sighs. 'It's not just what he had on me. It's what he had on me and Alice. That's how he got me, you see. The information he had on me would destroy my reputation but that I could live with. What I couldn't live with is that it would also destroy Alice's reputation too. I didn't want to do that to her, to you.'

I don't follow. 'Wait, what did he have on you both?' The deeper I fall down this rabbit hole, the more I realise I didn't know my sister well at all.

She sighs. 'Are you sure you want to know? Even though it might change the way you think about your sister? I've been so hesitant to tell you because I didn't want it to alter the way you remember her. Well, that and the blackmail. But if I tell you I think it'll make you understand why I did what I did.'

My mind is racing with thoughts. What secret could she be about to spill? Is it really so bad that I'm better off not knowing, staying in the dark? No. Whatever it is, it is always better to know the truth. If Catrin had told the truth before we might not be in the situation we are in now. *Alice might be home*.

'Go ahead. Tell me everything.'

'What did Alice tell you she did for a job?'

'We never really spoke about it. She told me was temping while she found her feet after being a student.'

'That was a lie. A cover story.'

'Right … well, what did she do then?'

'She was a dancer.' She pauses, as if waiting to see my reaction. I clearly don't react the way she was expecting because she continues. 'An exotic dancer.'

'As in…?'

'We took our clothes off for money. Like a stripper but they didn't call us that. They gave us some fancy lingerie and some masks with feathers and we performed for rich people and celebrities.'

I don't know what to say. Does it change how I feel about my sister? Of course not and it hurts that Catrin thought it could.

'What kind of club was it?'

'A fancy one. Known as Backdoor, like the poker term. The sort frequented by people that want their privacy. It's in Soho but there's no signage anywhere other than a pair of poker chips. It's the sort of place you only know about from other people. You need to be in with the right type of crowd to get in. They keep it exclusive.'

'But how did you both get in then?' I ask. 'Wait, I didn't mean it like that, I just wouldn't have imagined Alice working in such a place.'

She shrugs. 'I used to dance all my life. Your sister told me she was an ex-dancer too.'

She was, Alice took dance classes since she was five. Although the type of dancing was very different to what I imagine she was doing in that club.

'We were out at a club in Chelsea one time, we started dancing, really going for it, you know? We were drunk and being silly. Anyway some guy came up to us after and gave us his card. Said if we ever wanted some extra money he had a job for us. We were both skint. This was before we lived in the flat you visited us at. We were staying in some really dingy accommodation and struggling to afford food. It was dangerous. Somebody had tried to break into the flat before. We'd heard people yelling. Seen drug deals going on. Alice thought she'd have to go home to the US but couldn't even afford the flights.'

'My parents would've paid for her.'

'She said. But I think she didn't want that. She wanted to prove she could make it on her own. Anyway, one day we were really desperate because we'd run out of food and money. Had no luck in job market and Alice had just had another rejection for a job she thought she was going to get so we thought we may as well call the number.'

'And?'

'The guy, Jeremy, told us where to meet him. Told us about the club. When we got there he was very upfront about what the job entailed. We liked his honesty. He wasn't trying to pretend it was anything that it wasn't. But the whole thing was done tastefully. I know you probably are picturing something else but it was classy.'

'So you just became strippers, just like that?'

'Don't judge us unless you've been where we've been. And no, we talked it over for a while but then realised we didn't have much choice. We both said we'd just do it for a while and that we'd keep applying for other jobs and would quit when we found something. But we never did.'

'And what was it like, working there?'

'It was fine. At first anyway. It never felt like a job and I was never made to feel disrespected. Some of the men just wanted to talk to a beautiful girl for a couple of hours. You might've put two and two together by now but that is how your sister and Ethan met.'

I'd always wondered how my sister had ended up crossing paths with someone like Ethan.

'Ethan was a regular client. Jeremy told me that Ethan came in a lot but that we had to be discreet because he was married and famous. We had to sign NDAs for all sorts of people that came in – politicians, reality TV stars and singers. They were basically all married. Jeremy told us it was hard for famous people to have affairs so that was where the club came into play. Ethan was different though. Most of the men were interesting but most of them were older. Ethan was young and hot. All the girls wanted to dance for him. He wanted Alice though.'

'Right. And so she danced for him and then they became involved?'

'Pretty much. It's not as sleazy as it sounds. Sometimes she'd dance for him but a lot of time they'd talk and have drinks together. After a while they basically just had dates in the club. It was perfect because Ethan could hide out from the paparazzi there and so nobody knew about their relationship.'

It's like she's trying to justify things but it still sounds seedy to me.

'Okay, so you worked at this club. If it was such a classy relationship like you said, how did Ethan use that to blackmail you? It sounds like he had a lot more to lose than you did.'

She sighs. 'It wasn't just the club. I got addicted to the money and the lifestyle. Some of the members of the club started asking to see me outside of it. At first it was just for company. We'd go on dates where they'd take me for lavish meals at places I'd never even dreamed of. We'd go on shopping trips at Selfridges and Harrods and they'd let me pick out whatever I wanted. It was a lifestyle I never thought I'd have.'

There's more to this.

'But it changed. I wanted more and more. I got addicted to the money, the lifestyle. One of my clients, a regular, he was some sort of politician and earnt a lot of money. I knew he was married, with kids. But he wanted to go further.'

'Further?'

'He offered me money if I slept with him.'

'You didn't?'

'I did. I wasn't going to at first but the more I thought about it the more it seemed like it wasn't so bad. I knew the guy and people sleep with people they've just met all the time, right? And they do it for free. He was a nice guy so I did it and it wasn't so bad. So then I kept doing it. And then I just started doing it with other people.'

'And that's what Ethan had on you.'

'Yes. He said he had proof of what I'd been doing it and would send it to my family if I told the police about his relationship with Alice.'

'And my sister,' I gulp, 'did she also…'

'Not that I'm aware of. But he told me that he had enough on her to ruin her reputation too. Either way, it was enough to silence me. And I'm sorry because I realise now that I may have hidden crucial information about your sister's disappearance. At the time I thought it wasn't that big a deal. I honestly believed that he just didn't want his wife finding out about his affair and that's all there was to it. Especially with all that speculation about a serial killer in London. I never thought he had something to do with it. Looking back now I was so naïve. So when I found out he had been arrested for murdering Tori … I realised he could've murdered your sister.'

'I know.' I put my head in my hands. 'Was he ever violent with her?'

'No. She never said anything like that.'

'I suppose that's something.'

'If I had any suspicion he was actually involved you have to know I'd have gone to the police. But I was scared about the evidence Ethan had going to my family. And I was scared of him in general. When he blackmailed me it wasn't just what he was saying but the way he was acting. I got the impression that he wouldn't let me talk no matter what.'

'But even then, you didn't think he was involved in what happened to my sister?'

'No. I never thought he'd hurt Alice. He adored her. It was only when he got arrested I knew what a mistake I'd made. I regret what I did. If I'd told the police about Ethan maybe he would've been put away and Tori would still be alive now.'

She sniffs and I'm not sure if she's on the verge of tears or has a cold. Why did it take something happening to Tori for her to finally speak up?

'Anyway, I'd best be going. If you want me to go the police I will. I'll go on the record. I can't make up for what I didn't do back then, for my cowardice. But I can try and get justice for you now.'

'Wait.' I jump up. 'Before you go, can you tell me where this club was? I'd at least like to check it out.'

'I'll message you the address. Just look for the poker chips.'

'Thanks.'

'Why are you planning to go there?'

'I just want to see where my sister spent so much of my time. I'd like to know more about her and Ethan so I figured I'd go ask.'

'Maybe not the best idea … they really value their privacy there. I'm not sure it's safe to go snooping about.'

'Well, I'd still like to go. Look around a bit. Maybe I'll find something that can help with the investigation into my sister.'

She leans in close. 'If you want to take a look around I'd go during the day. It's empty. Owner is basically nocturnal so doesn't open up before 6pm.' She takes a card out of her purse and slides it towards me. 'I don't know if it still works but that might get you access. Jeremy kept files on all his customers in his office. He always had dirt on them just in case he needed to use it.'

'You don't work there anymore?'

She shakes her head. 'Alice's disappearance was a wake up call me for me. I didn't want to be put in that position again where someone can use what they know about me to force me to compromise my integrity.'

'Well, thank you, but won't you get in trouble for giving me this?'

'Consider it my apology for failing you and your sister. I hope you get some answers. If you find out what happened to Alice, can you please tell me? I still think about her.'

Chapter Thirty-Five

VICTORIA 'TORI' SIMMONS

Chapter Thirty-Six

ETHAN SIMMONS

All there is to do now is wait. I wish I could watch the hands of a clock as time passes, the digits on a watch as the numbers change. There's something comforting about watching time pass. But no, instead I have to stare at this same wall. What annoys me most is that there is a crack in the corner of the wall that somebody has clearly tried to paint over but has used a slightly darker shade of white and it sticks out. When there's nothing else to do, it's the small things you notice.

I don't know how long is left. All I know is that in a few hours either I will be walking out of here or I'll be charged and locked up until the trial. Ellen said that even if they release me it's likely they'd still be investigating me so I wouldn't even be free, not really.

My ears are alert for the sound of any footsteps outside my door. When I hear them, I'm sure it'll mean that my fate has been sealed. If I'm charged that means I have to go through another trial. I could be found not guilty. Just because they charge me doesn't mean it is the end of everything for me but I still have to go to jail while we wait. All this time it's felt like somebody is working against me. Somebody who videoed me threatening Tori. Somebody who planted her blouse in my hotel room. It doesn't seem like just a coincidence. I would have said it was Tori but it can't be her. If that blouse really is covered in her blood, then she's gone. I can't imagine a world without her in it.

I hear footsteps and I brace myself. This is it. The guard opens the door.

'Your solicitor is here to see you. Follow me.'

The moment that I have been waiting for these past few hours – or however long it has been. Whatever Ellen is about to tell me could change everything.

I'm shown back into the same room. Well, actually it could be a different room but it looks exactly the same. Windowless, soulless. Ellen is already there writing something in her notebook. I take my seat opposite and try to work out the news from her expression but the woman has a great poker face.

'So? Am I being charged or not?'

'I wish I could tell you. They've made an application to extend another twenty-four hours.'

'What? No. How is that okay?' I slam my hands against the table in rage but wince as my palm collides with the edge of the table. I run my hand through my greasy hair. I can't deal with this uncertainty. The unknown.

'Because you are suspected of murder, they can hold you for up to ninety-six hours.'

'It feels like it's been for ever. I need to get out of here.'

I haven't showered since I arrived and can smell my own body odour. Once they take me back I should ask the guard about showering.

'And so are they going to hold me for another twenty-four hours then?'

'I don't know yet but it's likely the permission will be

granted. I heard through my colleagues that the DNA testing is being held up at the moment. Apparently there was some sort of fire at one of the main testing facilities overnight and they are still trying to work out what was damaged and they've lost valuable equipment.'

'So they might have lost my DNA samples?' I try not to sound too hopeful.

'We don't know yet as they've not assessed what has been lost but it doesn't really matter if they have because they can take it again while you're here. It would make a difference if the blouse of Tori's was damaged because they wouldn't be able to compare any DNA on that with the swabs taken from you.'

'I see. So it's likely that I'm not going anywhere soon…'

Is it a coincidence that the lab might have lost DNA samples relating to my case? Or maybe the Alice case? Either way, I'm not worried about the evidence they have that they found in my hotel room because there is no chance there is any of my DNA on that. Not unless somebody made it that way.

'I'm sorry not to be able to tell you more. I was down here visiting another client and thought I'd update you. I find the part my clients struggle with is not knowing.' She gives me a brief smile. 'I know you probably think I don't know what you're going through but I've had enough clients and listened to their stories to know how hard it is.'

'Thanks. I guess.'

There's a knock at the door.

'That's probably them letting us know if the application to extend was granted,' she says to me. 'Come in.'

'Mr Simmons, you're free to go,' DC Hayes says.

'Go? As in back to my room?'

'You're free to leave.'

'What?' both myself and Ellen chime in unison.

'There is no longer a case against you for the murder of Tori Simmons. You're free to leave. If you follow me you can collect your belongings and we will process you for release.'

'What is going on?' Ellen asks.

'You'll see. It's better you see for yourself.'

It's a cryptic message but I can't hide my joy that I get to leave this place. I had been preparing myself to spend at least another twenty-four hours in custody but now I get to leave and it sounds like they aren't even investigating me anymore for Tori's murder. I wonder what happened. Maybe the DNA evidence came back and proved that I didn't have anything to do with it. Does this mean I'm also no longer a suspect in Alice's disappearance? I want to ask but I'd rather not bring it up and remind them. I'll have to ask Ellen.

We get to the desk for processing. I feel human again as I'm given my clothes to change back into and my personal belongings. I nip into the toilets and although I feel dirty from the lack of a shower, at least I look more like myself. My watch back on my wrist. I rub my chin and notice dark brown stubble poking out. I need a shave but it's nothing I can't fix once I get to a proper bathroom. I haven't looked at my reflection since I was arrested and the bathroom mirror shows my skin is dull, grey. The bags under my eyes make me look like a ghoul.

It isn't enough to dampen my spirits though, as I head towards the exit, excited to taste the fresh air. 'Mr Simmons. Your bag.'

One of the women behind the desk hands it to me. I'd almost forgotten that I had an overnight bag with me because I was going to our Cotswolds home. It's probably best I head there now but maybe I'll take a taxi the entire way to avoid the fanfare. Thankfully I know a taxi driver that can be discreet. I should have used him in the first place. I'll have to offer him an incentive to take me so far.

Ellen is standing waiting for me.

'Did they tell you why I was let go? Am I really free? That's it – it's over?'

'Yes. They no longer think you had anything to do with the murder of Tori Simmons.'

'Well, that's what I was telling them. So I can leave? They aren't going to come after me again?'

'Not for this, no.'

'What about … the other thing?'

She shrugs. 'It seems they aren't arresting you for that at the moment, which is all I can say.'

I feel like I need to thank her in some way so shake her hand. 'Hopefully I don't see you again anytime soon, no offence.'

'None taken.'

I turn and walk towards the entrance, beaming. I can finally get my life back on track but then I stop suddenly when I see my worst nightmare has come true.

'Hello, Ethan, missed me?'

I wish I was still locked up.

The Aftermath

'In revenge and in love, woman is more barbarous than man.'

Friedrich Nietzsche

Chapter Thirty-Seven

@THETRUTHISGREY

My meeting with Catrin has given me answers but also left me with so many questions. I have to go to Backdoor and see if I can learn more about my sister. I can't believe there is this whole world that she was part of that I never knew anything about. I just hope it's not some sort of seedy place that will tarnish my memory of her.

I want to talk to this guy that recruited her. Catrin said his name was Jeremy and he's the one that introduced them to the club and got them working there. If he knew my sister and he knew Ethan I bet he knows about their relationship. And she said he has lots of dirt on his customers. Another person who had important information that might have been instrumental in my sister's case that never came forward. My guess is that he didn't want the cops investigating his business.

I hadn't even been paying attention to my phone while I was speaking to Catrin, I was so engrossed in what she was saying and trying to process the implications of the secrets she was revealing. I check my phone and immediately see more unread messages and notifications than I can remember ever having. And it doesn't take me long to work out why.

App Notification:

The London News
Breaking news: Disgraced actor Ethan Simmons released as his wife Tori is found alive and well.

Ethan has been released and is no longer a suspect in the disappearance of Tori Simmons. That, on its own, would be a big enough headline that would pique my attention and have my mind racing. Catrin only told me what she told me because she felt safe with Ethan in custody. She must have been sure he was about to be charged and put on trial. But with Ethan back out, it could change things – she might not feel comfortable telling the cops what she knows. Does this mean his DNA wasn't a match for Alice's jacket? Is he innocent?

But Ethan being released isn't even the biggest headline. The major piece of news is the reason that Ethan has been released: his wife, disappeared and presumed dead – well, actually presumed murdered by her husband – seemingly strolled into the station alive and well. Ethan can't have killed Tori because she isn't dead. Ding dong the bitch is alive.

Well, that is the shocker that nobody was expecting. Tori had been 'missing' for three days now. Nobody had seen or heard from her and she's a celebrity who has just been involved in one of the most talked about trials in recent history. I stand in the busy London street, glued to my phone. I read every article that I find. I have to jump out of the way as guy riding a bike on the pavement nearly sends me flying. The details are scant but Tori claims she visited a wellness retreat because she was struggling with the stress of the trial.

Supposedly she got a pre-booked cab there and surrendered her phone – the retreat was one of those that is cut off from the rest of the world in order to allow participants to detox from the hectic social media lifestyle.

It sounds exactly like the sort of retreats that all the celebs are doing these days. I did a video for TikTok last year about an actress that went to a similar retreat after she was arrested for a DUI. She came back and said it had changed her and that she had a different outlook on life. And then she went and got arrested four months later for another DUI and ended up behind bars that time. There was also a politician's daughter that did the same. She was from England so maybe it was even the same place.

They aren't saying anything explicitly but I can tell from the news coverage that nobody is really buying that Tori was on some sort of holistic retreat this whole time. For a start, why did she run out mid-trial? It doesn't make any sense – can't you be arrested for running out of a trial? And why wouldn't she tell anybody where she was going? Surely she should have at least told her parents so they weren't so worried – they did a plea on the news last night. And how did the retreat's staff not see the news coverage and tell anyone what was going on? Instead Tori has managed to waste all the nation's resources and attention by making people think she was in trouble.

I think the reason that I'm so annoyed at Tori's lies is because my sister really did go missing and if she had half the resources invested in finding her as Tori had for her stunt then maybe she'd have been found long ago.

If Tori was alive this whole time, the anonymous TikTok count still could have been her. I wrote it off as a possibility because I thought she was dead.

@thetruthisgrey

Tori? Was it you this whole time?

@thetruthisblackandwhite2011

I told you I'm not Tori but she does know
who I am.

@thetruthisgrey

Ethan has been released. Are the police
even testing his DNA against Alice's
jacket? What if he disappears?

@thetruthisblackandwhite2011

Ethan is being dealt with. Trust me. He
won't be getting away with anything.

Ethan will surely disappear now. If he is guilty of being involved with Alice's disappearance, which I'm sure he is, he must know that his DNA will be matched to her clothing eventually. His clock is ticking. I'm building up a picture of evidence for the police. I need enough that they can't keep dismissing me and I think the final piece of the puzzle will be found by going to Backdoor. If Ethan is smart he will get on a plane before he's rearrested. But I can't have that happen.

Ethan may not have hurt his wife but it doesn't change my view that he probably killed my sister.

My phone pings again.

@thetruthisblackandwhite2011

If you want to know the truth, you know
where to find it.

Another cryptic message as always but this time I know what they mean. It reaffirms my decision to go Backdoor right away to find out the truth. I duck into the closest underground station and head there.

Chapter Thirty-Eight

VICTORIA 'TORI' SIMMONS

I would say it all started with Alice but actually Alice was only the final straw. The nightmare that is my marriage with Ethan started long before he'd even met her.

When I first met Ethan, he was unlike anyone I'd ever met. Of course he was effortlessly handsome and had the body of someone who spent hours in the gym each day – because he did exactly that. But it was never his looks that attracted me to him because being handsome isn't special in celebrity circles. Most people have won the genetic lottery or have enough money to make it look like they have. What I liked about Ethan was his charm. He knew exactly what to say to me to make me laugh. He had a carefree nature that I loved. He was so new to being famous and I saw the sparkle in his eyes. I had the same when I was recruited for Lipstick Lasses and our first single came out and we knew that we were going to be something.

He was a bit younger than me but as soon as I met him we clicked. I don't know how to describe it but I knew immediately I wanted to spend all of my time with him and he felt the same about me. I knew he was *my person*. And I was his.

And I thought it was true love. When he proposed to me I was unbelievably happy. My parents had never warmed to Ethan much but that didn't bother me because they'd never actually liked any of my boyfriends before. I think they wanted me to date somebody outside of the celeb world – they had this idea that everybody famous was vapid and self-obsessed. But I'm famous too, so what do they think of me?

But our marriage was a lie. On his part at least. I really did love Ethan. I felt things for him that I've never felt for anybody else. Probably things I will never feel for anybody else. The truth is that Ethan Simmons is an incredibly good actor. And I'm not talking about his lead role in the *Aces & Diamonds* films or that small role he had on that crime investigation TV show for five episodes. No, the best role that Ethan has ever played is off screen and that is the role of being a loving husband.

Things were good when we first met. He swept me off my feet. It was once we got married that things really started to change. I always knew that Hollywood relationships are rife with unfaithfulness but I naïvely thought it wouldn't happen to us. Once we married, Ethan started staying out late a lot more; sometimes he wouldn't come home until the next morning. One time he came in and he smelt of perfume. He always had an excuse.

I had to go back to the UK not long after we got married. My mother was getting more unwell with dementia and my family needed help with her care. I wanted to be there for her. So Ethan and I had to go long distance. There were lots of rumours about him and his co-star Nikki swirling but I tried to brush it off. But one night I flew over as a surprise after I knew he'd been having a hard time at work because the director was being tough on him.

So I got his agent to tell me where he was staying and give me a key so I could let myself in and surprise him. I never expected to open the door to find him and Nikki on the sofa going at it.

He promised he'd change. He flew over to England with me to try and make things work, flying back and forth as much as he could while he was filming.

Luckily the rumours about Nikki stayed as that – rumours. No evidence ever surfaced and we convinced the public we were strong.

I thought that once he didn't have as much temptation he wouldn't stray but I was wrong. If anything it got worse, far worse. It seems that Ethan likes himself an English rose – he clearly has a type. I was going to leave him and expose him but then he found out about Blair. I realised I no longer had a choice but to stay with him, otherwise he'd drag me through the mud with him.

Blair Priest. She was my big secret. I can't sing. I never could sing. I was recruited to be part of Lipstick Lasses because of my looks. I don't want to brag but especially when I was younger I was always being complimented on my looks. I saw an open casting for a record company looking to form a new girl group. I went along because I've always wanted to be a singer even though I knew I didn't have the talent. There were so many girls there who were more talented than me, but I was picked.

I kidded myself that it was because I was talented but it was a lie. Once we started recording I was only allowed to sing in the chorus. When we went to perform at *Top of the Pops* they switched off my microphone – only mine – and told me to lip sync. They'd always dress me in much more revealing outfits than the others. When I confronted the record label they told me my role in the girl band wasn't as a singer but as part of the overall image. I was several years older when I finally accepted my role.

So when the band broke up and people went their separate ways I tried to find a normal job but I craved the lifestyle of being in a girl band. It's addictive. Fame is like a drug. I had money but the thing is that money doesn't last very long when you're used to a certain lifestyle. I decided I wanted to try a career as a solo artist like some of my ex-bandmates were trying. My old record label didn't want to sign me so I took singing lessons and managed to find a label that signed me based on my fame rather than my talent.

I recorded an entire album with them. But it flopped. Barely charted and the label didn't make any return on the money they'd invested. I was distraught. I moaned to Jessika and she told me that nobody was interested in my album because the auto-tune was so obvious and people were saying online that I couldn't sing. She said she'd spoken to my label and they were willing to let me record another album but only on one condition. That I didn't sing.

Obviously I looked at her like she was crazy. How could I record an album without singing? But she said they would hire someone who would pretend to be me. She said it was very common in the industry and most people lip synced when they did live performances. She said my brand was being a good performer. I really wasn't sure at first. I didn't want to lie to my (very few) fans and it didn't feel worth it. But then shortly after that I walked in on Ethan and Nikki and felt worthless. I was at a low point and I wanted the success of a chart-topping album to make him want me again.

When I first met Blair it was at my home studio. I wanted her to record at my house rather than in the label's main studio because it felt less connected that way, less dirty. I didn't tell Ethan because I was ashamed. But he walked in on us once.

Ironic, almost, us walking in on each other and the problems it's caused.

I lied to him about why she was there but I think he knew then. She was in the recording booth when he came in while I was scrolling on Instagram. Later I ended up admitting the truth to him. I suppose I could've kept him in the dark but I really believed that him moving over to London would be a new start for us and I didn't want to lie to him.

And I really thought it was a whole new beginning. But how wrong was I?

Chapter Thirty-Nine

ETHAN SIMMONS

My wife is alive. In fact, she's not just alive but she looks better than she did before she absconded. I can't explain how my heart dropped when I saw her standing there, decked out in designer looking like she'd just sauntered off the pages of *Vogue* – not the images I'd conjured up of her lately. How can a dead woman be so beautiful? She looks so unbothered; not like she's been the subject of a nationwide police search.

'Tori? You're ... you're alive.'

'Well, obviously. I'm here, aren't I? Were you expecting something else?'

'But, how? We all thought you were dead.' *I was arrested for your murder!*

She cackles. 'Funny, isn't it. I had *no* idea about the shitstorm that had been created. I just popped off to a little wellness retreat. I was terribly stressed about the trial and I just needed a break from everything. You know how frazzled I get sometimes. Anyway, it was a spur of the moment decision so I didn't tell anyone and the rules of the retreat are no contact with the outside world. Which *obviously* I was in favour of because I was sick of people slating me in the press and circulating those ... those photos.' She scrunches up her nose as if she's just smelt something rotten. 'I only just finished my break and I ordered an Uber and the guy looked at me like he'd seen a ghost. I thought he'd just never met a celebrity before but it turns out he's never met a dead celebrity.' She giggles and waves her hands about like it's all one big joke. I've been trapped in a cell with no shower and having to eat mush because she decided to have a digital detox and not tell anyone? Angry is an understatement.

'So, you were safe all this time?'

'Not just safe, I feel rejuvenated.'

'And you really had no contact with the outside world?'

'No. I got my phone back and you should've seen the number of notifications. Think I might've smashed the world record for the most social media notifications at any one time. I've barely been through them.'

Do I believe my wife? How does a celebrity go missing for three days and nobody finds out that she's been at a wellness retreat? Are the cops really that inept in this country? And I don't understand about the supposed evidence in my hotel room. If Tori was on a wellness retreat, how did the clothing she was wearing that night end up in my hotel room? Covered in blood? This story is covered with holes but I don't even know what to think right now. My head is scrambled. My dead wife is very much alive.

None of it makes sense.

'Darling, shall we get out of here and talk? I had a lot of time to think at the retreat, especially without the distraction of the trial and the media. And I thought a lot about our relationship and I really want to get back to what we were. Remember when we first met and how good things were? I miss that. I miss us. We just need a break, a chance to spend some time together.'

Is she being genuine? After everything?

'Yeah, sure.' I'm not sure what else to say but there are so many eyes on us at the moment and even more waiting outside the door. Going somewhere private sounds ideal. 'Let's speak somewhere a little less public.' I know what people are like. Somebody will be secretly recording and our entire conversation will end up online for people to dissect.

But also, I don't just want to get out of here. I want to get out of London, out of this country. I'm sure that somebody is trying to take me down and I won't stick around to watch them try again. Somebody already went to extreme lengths trying to frame me for Tori's murder: filming us fighting and sending it to the media and then planting that shirt somehow in my hotel room without my knowledge. Somebody wants me behind bars and will do anything they can to make that happen. Even if it means framing me for a crime I didn't commit. That nobody committed, it turns out. It's only a matter of time before the police start to figure out what happened to Alice and my and Tori's involvement in it. And that is a crime that definitely happened.

'I know just the place for us to go to. Somewhere super private. I promise you, nobody will know where to find us.'

She reaches out to take my hand. I slide it in hers, feeling the sharp tips of her acrylics press against my palm. I should be glad. I'm leaving the police station without being charged; I have my freedom back. And of course, I have my wife back. My wife has come back from the dead, so why do I feel scared?

'I have a car.'

I expect her to mean she's ordered a taxi but as we get closer to the vehicle I realise there's no driver. We have to fight our way through the crowd of spectators that have already formed. Tori jumps into the driver's seat as we reach the car.

'You're driving?'

I've seen Tori drive only a few times and this isn't her car because she leaves it at the Cotswolds home. This must be a rental. Tori hates driving in London so I'm surprised.

'Well, it's not like you can drive. You'll end up driving on the wrong side again. You nearly hit that poor woman that one time. And that other time you nearly crashed into that family on the motorway, remember?'

I hang my head in shame as I remember the time I drove on the wrong side of the road and almost hit an ongoing car. Thankfully neither of us were going quickly and both stopped in time, but sometimes I think of how different things could have been if that hadn't happened. If one of us had been distracted. Life is full of near misses that could change everything.

'This is a new start for us, Ethan. Things are going to change after today. I promise you that.' She pecks me on the cheek and then turns the key in the ignition.

I should be over the moon, so why do I feel like I'm walking into a lion's den by leaving with her?

Chapter Forty

@THETRUTHISGREY

I take the underground to Oxford Circus. Unsurprisingly, Backdoor isn't listed on Google Maps, just as Catrin warned me, but luckily she told me the street name or I'd have been wandering the streets attracting attention. Catrin told me the building was plain except for the image of two poker chips. I pace along the street, eagle-eyed, looking for anything that could be Backdoor. I don't want to miss it so inspect each building closely. I didn't think this would be so hard.

I'm almost at the end of the street when I finally spot the building. The poker chips are at the top of the building and I almost miss them because they're small. I have to use the zoom function on my phone to double check it's not just graffiti. They look like they are meant to light up but because it's daytime it's harder to see. It makes sense – Catrin said nobody would be there during the day and I have to bank on that or I'll be in a world of trouble. Hopefully just a slap on the wrist but maybe arrested. Maybe worse if the people running this place are dangerous. I could get Catrin in trouble if they realise she gave me her card, which, even after her lies, isn't something I'd want to happen.

I slide my hand in my pocket and wrap my fingers around the entry card. I'm not very optimistic that this is going to work. I can't remember if Catrin said how long it's been since she last worked here but surely they've deactivated it by now, especially given how seriously they seem to take security. It's a long shot but it's also probably my last shot.

My phone lights up. It's a blast from one of the news websites I've been following to keep up to date with Tori and Ethan news. Apparently Tori and Ethan were spotted driving away from the police station and heading west. Witnesses apparently overheard the pair discussing heading to the airport. They must be on their way to Heathrow already. Ethan's so close to boarding a flight and the trail's going cold once more.

I walk towards what I think is the entrance for Backdoor.

A noise behind startles me and I quickly walk past the entrance before anybody sees me near the building. Is it the owner? Luckily the building is on a corner so I dip behind it and hide. A car has pulled up outside Backdoor. A coincidence or an early punter? Or Jeremy?

But the voices I hear prove that it's neither of those things. It's Tori and Ethan.

What are they doing here?

Chapter Forty-One

VICTORIA 'TORI' SIMMONS

Backdoor. This place hasn't changed since the last time I was here – the day that set this whole thing in motion. I swipe Ethan's access card to enter and the doors open. The club is in darkness. I flick the light switch and the dancefloor is illuminated, although not by much; it's still pretty dark but I can make out the shapes of the booths and luxurious leather sofas. The bar is deserted yet still stocked full of bottles, ready for the eager punters that will arrive later.

'Why did you want to come here?' Ethan says. 'Of all the places...'

'I'm sorry, I thought this was your favourite place?'

He scowls. 'That isn't funny.'

'Sorry, I'm a singer not a comedian.'

I walk around the club, running my hand along the tops of the sofas. I remember the last time that I was here vividly. It may as well have been yesterday.

'Tori, I need answers. What are we doing here? Why would you bring me back here? You said you wanted to talk?

I thought this was about saving our relationship so why would you bring me somewhere that destroyed it?'

Ethan has a habit of acting like a stroppy teenager at times. He folds his arms across his chest and sticks out his bottom lip.

'Do you ever miss her?'

'Miss who?'

'You know, Alice.'

'Seriously, Tori, are you really going to go there? We agreed not to talk about it again and I don't understand what you thought you were doing bringing her up at trial. Do you know how risky that was? The cops have been sniffing around.'

I shrug. 'As far as I'm aware they've only been questioning you.'

'Yeah, because they thought you were dead!'

I walk over to the booth where I know Ethan always used to sit. 'This place must remind you of her.'

He stares down at the ground. 'Of course it does.' I think I can detect a note of sadness in his voice. 'I thought we were going to get out of London. People will be here later so we need to leave.'

'You don't understand?'

'I thought we had a deal not to speak about Alice. It was better that way for both of us.'

'I know. But you know what also wasn't part of any deal we had? Asking Blair to testify at the trial? Thank goodness she pulled out. Were you going to get her to say she recorded my latest album?'

'It was Owen's idea.' How convenient.

'Well, how would Owen get the idea unless you told him? You could have destroyed me. My entire career.'

'Well, she didn't testify in the end, did she? Pulled out last minute so no harm done.'

'Yes, because my team fixed it. Reminded her of the NDA

my label had got her to sign and scared her that if she testified she'd end up prosecuted.' He has no response. 'And what about leaking those photographs? Where did you get those from? They're fakes. Whoever is behind them clearly did a great job to fool everyone else but I know the truth.'

'Again, it was Owen's idea.' Typical Ethan. He never owns up to his own mistakes. It's much easier for him to pass the blame to Owen. Owen, his clueless agent who is always chasing the next big thing instead of dealing with his own clients. I'd have more respect for Ethan if he could just admit that he's a dick who has tried to ruin my life. That's the thing with people like Ethan, they always want to be winners, no matter who they hurt in the process.

'I never even wanted to do this defamation trial. I entertained it at first and we planned things out but I changed my mind. I didn't want to be associated with it. But your agent was so obsessed with the idea and when I refused you went ahead and brought the action anyway!'

'We gave you a choice. It's not my fault you didn't want to go along with it. And with you bailing we changed the script a bit in my favour – and considering your big mouth is the entire reason the trial got brought, it felt only right you were punished.'

'But the photos, Ethan? The photos?'

He grins, a horrible, twisted grin that makes me sick to the stomach.

'Have you seen what they've been writing about me online? My label has dropped me.'

'Now you know how it feels to have your career taken away from you.'

'Like you, you mean? I should have a grotty hideaway strip club for any extra-marital behaviour? Although you weren't always careful. Remember how I found you and Nikki that time – that wasn't very well hidden, was it?'

He rolls his eyes. 'This place was never grotty. And don't compare Alice to Nikki. Nikki was just a fling, you know that. She was just hot and you know I found the long-distance thing difficult. I have needs, you know? Needs you couldn't fulfil from all the way here in London.'

'Are you trying to justify cheating on me with Nikki because I wasn't able to have sex with you? Because I had to go to London to take care of my sick mother?'

'You're twisting my words. I'm just saying I was going through a hard time and she was there for me.'

'Okay, but how do you explain Alice?

'Why do we have to talk about Alice so much? Besides, you got rid of that problem, didn't you? So why does it matter?'

'I only did what I had to do.'

'You really like to make out that you're Queen Tori and you are such a victim sometimes. When those photographs came out I thought it would show people what a liar you really are, but somehow you even managed to turn that around and had people feeling sorry for you.'

'Because those photos weren't real! I never had an affair or so much as looked at another man. Unlike you who slept with half of Hollywood.'

'Maybe the photographs weren't exactly the truth but the things you've done are much worse than that, aren't they, Tori? Cheating is one thing, but murder. Murder is the worst sin of them all.'

'Shut up.'

'You know the police are looking into her disappearance again? They questioned me about it and I so easily could have ratted on you to save my own skin. But I didn't. I stuck to what we agreed but I'm starting to think that was a mistake. I should go back to the station right now and tell them the truth about what you did.'

'You can't do that.'

'Actually I can, I'm going to go there right now and tell them that you killed Alice Grey. You know they have the jacket she was last seen wearing? I don't know how they got it but they are going to put the pieces together sooner or later. I'm sure your DNA will be all over it.'

'You can't do that.'

'I have the texts, you know? The ones you sent me when you were disposing of her body?'

'We agreed to destroy our phones. You swore to me you'd done that.'

He grins. 'I did say that and I wasn't lying. But I had everything backed up onto a device I keep hidden. You should never have trusted me.'

Chapter Forty-Two

@THETRUTHISGREY

They didn't hear me coming, didn't notice me listening in to their conversation. How could I have got it so wrong? Tori killed my sister? She 'disposed' of her body like she was a piece of trash. I've been so wrapped up in Ethan that I never thought about the jealous wife. Of course she would be angry if she found out Ethan was having an affair and of course it's always the woman that gets blamed. All this time I thought Ethan blackmailed Catrin to protect himself but what if he was protecting Tori instead? What if he was scared of her?

'That phone implicates you just as much as me, you know that,' Tori says.

'That's what you think.' Ethan seems to be enjoying this.

'You wouldn't take yourself down with me. You're too narcissistic for that.'

'You're right. Maybe I'll need to find another way to make sure you can't cause any more problems.'

'You mean, like you tried already?'

'I don't know what you're talking about.'

'It's okay. I shouldn't have been surprised that history was repeating itself.'

I need to get to them. I need to know everything right now. I also need to make sure they don't leave. I crouch down on the floor of the bar. I try not to think about the sticky substances under my feet. I can still hear the voices arguing behind me. I stumble over and accidentally knock into a chair which scrapes against the floor, making a high-pitched squeal.

Tori turns to look where the sound came from and we lock eyes.

'Who the fuck are you? What are you doing here?'

I don't know what to say. I don't know how to act in this moment. I want to run but my feet stay planted to the floor.

'I'm going to ask again, who the fuck are you?'

'My name is Riley. Riley Grey.'

'Grey?' Tori says and I see her searching my face for the resemblance.

'Yes.'

'Wait, I know you. You were the one questioning me outside my hotel,' Ethan says as he comes closer. 'Are you … are you Alice's sister?'

'Yes. And you killed her, didn't you?' I say to Tori.

The tears rain down my face involuntarily. I don't know whether to launch myself at Tori or throw up.

'Let me tell you what happened to your sister.'

NOVEMBER 2024

'When love is in excess, it brings a man no honour, no worthiness.'

Euripides

Chapter Forty-Three

ETHAN SIMMONS

When I was with her, all my senses were on fire, electricity circulating through my veins, sparks every time I touched her skin. She was all I would think about. When I wasn't with her, I was thinking about when I could next see her.

London was in greyscale but she was a neon sign. She was the only good thing in that miserable city.

My phone pinged.

Alice [17:21]
Hey handsome, what are you up to?

I smirked. A text from her always brightened my day. Who needed sunshine when you had someone like Alice Grey in your life? I snapped a picture of my shirtless body and sent it to her.

Ethan [17:21]
Wish you were here…

Ethan [17:21]
Am I seeing you tonight?

I'd been seeing Alice for a few weeks and barely a day had passed where we hadn't seen each other. She was the highlight of the prison sentence that was living in England. I never wanted to come to London but after Tori gave me an ultimatum I didn't have a choice. And yes, I did not stay faithful once we moved to London but Tori was so focused on her singing career and I felt like she barely had any time for me. It was all harmless fun, even though some of the girls got too emotionally involved. I did tell them I wasn't looking for anything serious but they never listened to me. I had to get Owen to deal with them as they tried to threaten me with exposure. But Alice was different. She reminded me of Tori when I first met her, so free-spirited.

I thought the idea of coming to London as much as I could would rekindle our relationship, but Tori was constantly at the Cotswolds house in that recording studio of hers attempting to sing. She barely spent time in the London house and I refused to be stuck in the countryside with nothing to do. She ignored me and when we did spend time together she acted like she hated me. I didn't get why she dragged me out here if she hated spending time with me so much. I challenged her on it and she said it was because our relationship was in the 'healing' stage. I didn't know what that meant but it sounded like psychobabble bullshit to me. I was due back in Canada for filming soon anyway.

Alice [17:40]
I'll be in the club from 9pm tonight
to 1am

Ethan [17:41]
Perfect. I'll be there. I have a surprise for
you too.

I counted down the hours until I could leave the house. I vaguely heard Tori come back home as I was putting on my jacket. She was actually spending time in London that week because she was at her label's studio. Sometimes I'd think she was the one having an affair, with the amount of time she spent alone in the Cotswolds house – she could be doing anything and anyone, I'd be none the wiser.

'How was the studio?' I asked.

'Fine,' she responded.

'Just fine?'

'Well, you know. Had a productive day. Made good progress.'

It was difficult to try to have a conversation with my wife. I resented having to make all the effort.

'What are you doing tonight? We could go out to eat?'

I raised an eyebrow. 'As in, to a restaurant? In public?'

It sounded like a silly question but we hadn't been seen in public for so long. Every time I'd suggested doing anything she shot me down.

She nodded. 'It's about time. Besides, you've probably seen the rumours…'

I had. Although our agents had collectively managed to keep any rumours of my infidelity out of the media, since I came to London, there had been several articles about how little time we had spent together as a couple and a lot of speculation about trouble at home. The rumours weren't wrong but the thing about Tori was that appearance was everything to her. She wanted the world to think everything was fine even when it wasn't.

'Did this come from Jessika?' I knew this would have been her agent's idea. Jessika was always getting her to do things she didn't want to, just to improve her image. Sometimes I was glad that Owen was a pretty terrible agent and didn't care about me enough to suggest things like that.

She didn't answer but gave a half-hearted shrug that I knew was her way of saying yes.

'Well, I can't. I'm going out tonight.'

'Again?'

I shrugged. 'You haven't cared before now. I didn't know you wanted to go out tonight. We can do another night this week before I leave. Maybe I can book that Italian place you really like.'

'Sure. If you can make time for me, that is.'

Her tone was harsh. Part of me thought she was trying to pick a fight with me. It would be easier for her to convince herself that she hated me for what I did than to admit to herself that she still loved me and wanted this to work. She tried to push me away when every part of her wanted me to stay.

I moved towards her and took her hands in mine. 'One day, you'll forgive me for everything.' I leant in to kiss her cheek, feeling her turn her head and brush me away as I did it.

'One day isn't just yet though.' She dropped my hands. 'Enjoy whatever it is you're doing tonight.'

Could she know where I was going? Who I was seeing? Surely not, I had been so careful. The club was such a private place and I only went there at night so it wasn't like somebody would see me. I always used discreet taxi services to get there and even turned the location tracking on my phone off. But something about the way her voice broke made me think perhaps she could.

She'd already walked out of the room and I was going to be late if I didn't leave. I ordered a taxi on my phone. I grabbed a baseball cap as usual and my sunglasses – just in case.

When I got to the club I scanned my membership card to

get inside. I was met by security who gave me a once-over. They knew me but they didn't bend the rules for anyone. I didn't mind; the place was exclusive and they didn't let just anyone in, and that was how I liked it. Even though you could only get in here with a card, you couldn't rule out unscrupulous individuals getting their hands on one.

I spotted Alice's housemate, Catrin, in the corner. I gave her a wave. She seemed to notice me but didn't acknowledge me. I had the impression that she didn't like me. I didn't know what I'd ever done to her but I could tell she didn't approve of my relationship with Alice. It was none of her business. I was just glad she hadn't tried to sell a story about me for her fifteen minutes of fame. She didn't need the money though; I knew from Alice that the tips were more than generous.

Alice was in the centre of the dancefloor as always. She was the most skilled dancer. This wasn't some sleazy strip club. The girls were actual dancers and the entire thing was more of a show. It was performance art and the girls were never fully nude. It was better when you couldn't see everything, you know?

I took my place in my usual booth. Jeremy strolled over to greet me.

'The usual?' he asked.

'Yes, thanks,' I said, not really paying him much attention.

I heard him chuckle. 'You can never take your eyes off her. Not even for a second. Can't say I blame you, mate. She's certainly striking. I'll be back with your drink. Alice is going on break in thirty minutes.'

He disappeared and Alice caught my eye and smiled. She always looked so serene when she danced; I'd never seen anybody move in the way that she did. It was what made me want to get to know her. Of course she was very good-looking, but that's not what made her unique.

After a few more songs, Alice finished dancing and came to join me. I asked Jeremy for a glass of champagne for Alice – her favourite.

'How are you?' she said, planting a kiss on my lips before taking a seat.

'I'm fine. Had a bit of an argument with Tori before I came out so I'm much happier now I get to see you.'

'Oh, right.' She didn't like it when I spoke about my wife. 'You said something about a surprise?' she said, deliberately changing the subject.

'I spoke to Jeremy. He said we can have the club to ourselves for a romantic dinner tomorrow before I fly back to Canada.'

'And then who knows when I'll see you next,' Alice murmured, her voice almost too quiet to hear.

She wasn't usually like this. She was always so upbeat and positive but that day she had more in common with Tori's sourness. I wondered if something had happened to cause it.

'I know. I know it's not ideal and I promise you I'm going to work things out so we can be together properly. But I have to think about Tori and also—' I stopped abruptly.

'Say it,' she said.

I swallowed the lump in my throat. We'd often skirted over this subject without really talking about it. 'But also, I'm about to go back to Canada for filming, for a longer period this time. I'll get a break at Christmas though.'

'Canada isn't close,' she said, staring into the distance.

'It's not, but you could visit me.'

'But could I actually come with you? Or would we need to find another secret location to hang out in because you don't want people knowing about me?'

'Alice…' I reached out towards her but she slapped my hand away. 'Don't be like that. It's just Tori…'

'Tori what? You say you want to be with me, not her, but every time we speak about it you make excuses for why you need to stay married to her. Do you actually intend to leave her?'

I didn't answer.

'Your silence tells me everything I need to know.'

She got up and left, walking back towards the dancefloor. Her drink untouched.

Alice didn't talk to me all night. She barely glanced in my direction. I wanted to stay after she finished but she disappeared straightaway. I didn't understand what I had done to provoke this sort of reaction. I tried calling her all of the following morning, messaging her, but she wasn't answering my texts. There was only one thing for it. I decided to visit her flat, which I rarely did because I was worried somebody would spot me.

Her house was inconspicuous. It was one of those Victorian townhouses that had been converted into flats. I gently knocked on the door and it swung open. Catrin stood in the doorway.

'She doesn't want to see you, Ethan. You shouldn't have come here.'

'Is she in? Come on, Catrin, I need to talk to her.' I glanced behind me. 'At least let me in before anyone sees me.'

She snorted with derision but stepped aside to allow me in. 'Typical Ethan Simmons, only caring about what everyone else thinks.'

'What does that mean?'

'Exactly what you think it means. This whole mess is

because you're too much of a coward to end your marriage so you string both women along instead.'

Was that what Alice had been saying to Catrin?

'Look, I don't know what Alice has said—'

'Alice hasn't said anything because she thinks the world of you. You can do no wrong in her eyes and she's moping in her room like a lovesick puppy instead of going out and meeting people, finding someone who is actually proud to be with her instead of only seeing her in a dark room.'

'She's in her room?'

'Shit. I didn't mean to say that. You need to go. Let her go. She's wasted too much time pining after you. Besides, you're going back to Canada soon enough. It's easier to cut this thing off now.'

'Whatever, Catrin. You don't know what you're talking about.'

I walked past her in the direction of Alice's room. Catrin didn't try to stop me. I grabbed the knob and turned it but the door didn't give way. It was locked. I knocked.

'Alice, it's me, Ethan. Can I come in, please?'

There was no answer.

'Please, can we just talk? I don't understand what I did to upset you but whatever it was I can make it right. We can have a real discussion about our future. You were right about everything you said last night and I haven't been fair to you. I want a future with you. You need to know that.'

I knew she was there; I could hear her moving about. I thought I'd said enough for her to unlock the door but she didn't and I heard her footsteps retreat.

'Look. I'm going to go to the club tonight. Remember, I said that we could have the space for that romantic dinner. I was hoping to make it special, a proper date night before I leave.

I'm going to go there and I really hope you'll join me. I'll be there from 8pm.'

I waited just in case Alice decided to talk to me but it did no good so I left.

'Goodbye, Ethan,' Catrin called from behind me.

———

I didn't know if Alice was going to show up but I'd made an effort. She was upset about us not feeling like a real couple so I'd rearranged the club to look like a restaurant. I'd ordered steak which would be arriving in the next few minutes and even brought the fancy plates and cutlery from home so I could plate it all up. I'd also swiped a few candles that Tori wouldn't notice were missing so I could use them in the centre of the table. I found the largest bouquet of roses in my local flower shop for Alice.

I wanted tonight to be special but I knew there was a chance she wouldn't turn up. I heard a knock at the door and my heart fluttered but it was only the food. At least I could get it ready for when she arrived. I stared the time on my phone. It was already 8.30pm. Maybe she wasn't coming.

But then the door opened so I knew it was someone with a keycard. The club wasn't open and Jeremy insisted I could have it tonight for a fee so I would be furious if anyone else was there. But it was Alice. She looked just as beautiful as always. She was in a tight-fitted dress, her long blonde hair spilling over her shoulders.

I stood. 'Alice, I'm so glad you came.'

'I thought about not coming,' she said, 'but I think we need to talk.'

'That's what I've been trying to tell you, we need to speak

about things. We can work it out but you just need to talk to me. I've been thinking a lot about what you had to say and I hope this evening shows you that I'm listening to you.'

I gestured towards the table where I'd laid out dinner. It should have still been warm. She took a seat.

'Wine? The guy in the wine shop recommended this to me.' I poured her a glass before she answered.

She didn't even pick up the glass; instead she stared at it, her head clearly somewhere else.

I frowned. 'Do you not like red wine? Sorry, I just assumed … it goes best with steak, you see. Well, I can run out and get something else. I know you like prosecco so I could go get that? Or something else? Anything you want?' I realised I was nervous and couldn't stop blabbering.

'No, I like red wine. It's not that I don't want to drink it, I *can't* drink it. I can't drink any alcohol.'

'Wait. Are you saying…?'

'That I'm pregnant? Yes.'

'And it's mine?'

'Of course it's yours! How dare you ask me that? I'm not sleeping around, am I? I would never cheat on you. We are exclusive, right? Well, except your wife but you said you don't sleep together anymore.'

'Yes, of course we are. Sorry, I don't know why I asked that.'

'I've been trying to work out how to tell you. That's why I started ignoring you. I just thought if I did that I could pretend it wasn't happening. I wasn't planning on this. I must have forgotten to take my pill or something.'

'How long have you known?'

'Only a couple of days. When you came to the house though and started talking about how we could be a real couple, it made me realise that I didn't need to be scared to tell you because we can be a real family. We can move to Canada together and get a house. We can be together. The three of us.'

She looked down and cradled her stomach, even though it was as flat as a pancake. This wasn't how I expected tonight to go. I was not even sure if I wanted kids – I still felt so young. Tori and I had briefly discussed having children but both agreed we weren't in the right mindset. Well, we agreed that I wasn't. But Alice ... Alice and I hadn't been together that long and now it felt like this had all been thrust upon me. Suddenly the sight of the steak on the plate was making me feel nauseous.

I needed to get out of there. I stood up abruptly, knocking over my wine glass so it splashed red wine all over the floor.

'Where are you going?' Alice asked.

'Anywhere but here.'

'Wait, no. We need to talk about this. I thought you'd be excited about our child. You told me you loved me and wanted a future with me. Is this not enough for you to finally leave Tori?'

'This was all a mistake. How do I know you're even telling the truth? I bet this is a lie to try and trap me but I won't fall for it.'

'You really are a piece of work. I thought you loved me.'

'That was before you tried to keep me here with this fake news.'

I walked towards the exit, intending to leave Alice behind for good. I never should have gotten involved with her. This baby is her way of trapping me, using me to get her fifteen minutes of fame – if it's even real. Milking me for my income. I should have been more careful; I'd read stories about exactly this type of thing happening.

'I'm sure the papers will listen to me if you won't, or even better, Tori.'

I stop still. 'You wouldn't.'

'Try me.'

'You can't. You can't tell anyone.'

'Why? Are you worried Tori will find out? Newsflash, you've spent nearly every night out here for the last few weeks, I think she knows.'

'It's not just Tori.' It was everything. My reputation, my career. There was no way out. Unless…

'You know what? I'm sorry. Look, if it's money you want, I've got plenty, okay? I can send you money so long as you keep quiet, about everything. That's the deal.'

'You can't buy me.'

'Then what do you want?'

'You were never going to leave Tori, were you?'

I didn't say anything.

Which was a mistake.

She grabbed the bottle of wine and smashed it on the floor. There were shards of glass and wine everywhere. Jeremy was going to kill me. I bent down to pick it up, careful not to cut myself on the glass. I picked up a larger piece and felt the jagged edge cut my skin. I dropped it.

'You are crazy, you know.'

'Crazy? You lied to me and manipulated me and I'm the crazy one? You know, I'm going to call Tori right now and tell her everything.'

I chuckled. 'Nice try but you don't have her number.'

'No, but you do.'

I glanced up and noticed she was holding my phone in her hand. I couldn't let her tell Tori. She'd forgiven me for Nikki but if she found out about Alice then our marriage would never recover. I jumped up, lunging for the phone, and attempted to prise it from Alice's grip. She wouldn't let go but I overpowered her and she fell to the floor. We struggled, and in the commotion accidentally knocked against the dining table.

And then a scream pierced my ears.

Chapter Forty-Four

VICTORIA 'TORI' SIMMONS

As soon as Ethan said he was going out, turned down my dinner invitation, I knew he was going to see *her*. He was so egotistical that he genuinely believed I had no idea that he was out every night seeing her. Like I wouldn't notice he never spent a night in. And I knew he wasn't seeing what few friends he had in London because they're also famous and their antics would be splashed over the papers. I didn't know what it is about men – do they think they are super smart and good at covering their tracks or do they think we are all stupid?

They have a tell, you know, people who cheat. I didn't notice it when Ethan was in Canada because, well, I physically wasn't with him. But I still knew something was going on by the way he'd talk to me, especially on the phone. People who cheat often overcompensate. They seem to be more loving, more eager, more willing to please. I didn't know if it was conscious or if they were trying to mask their betrayal but I had seen it when I'd been cheated on in the past. And I saw it with Ethan.

Of course, it was never a surprise to discover Ethan

cheating on me again. They say, *Once a cheater, always a cheater. A leopard never changes his spots. Ethan Simmons can't keep it in his pants.* When that cheater lived with you, the tells were even more obvious. He started to smell better – not of a woman's perfume, because even he wasn't that stupid, but he'd wear heavy aftershave to cover up any indication he'd been hanging out with a woman. He was always in the gym, more so than usual. He was buying new clothes. He was always, *always* on his phone.

I should have ended it after Nikki. That is what any sensible person would have done. If it had been one of my friends, Shelley for example, I would have been screaming at her to leave the man. I would have dragged her away myself if I had to. But no, I did what I always said I would never do and I forgave him.

I wondered if they'd done it in the house. In our bed. It was a stomach-churning thought but it was all I could think of. I tried not to but my mind couldn't help but picture them on the cotton sheets, rolling around and entwined with one another. I didn't spend as much time in the London house those days. My family was much closer to our Cotswolds house. But Ethan pretty much drew the line at living in the Cotswolds. He found the UK bad enough so I had to at least let him have London. But he'd basically lived the life of a single bachelor while I'd been gone.

I hoped he at least washed the sheets.

I knew exactly where Ethan was that night. Another reason Ethan was careless was that he used the same car service as me. They were very discreet, of course, but I'd found one or two were more amenable when you offered large sums of money. All I had to do was start talking about Ethan and I'd know if they knew anything about what he'd been up to by how much their eyes widened, how much they hung their head and tried to avoid answering.

But Ethan's real downfall was that one of his drivers recently discovered his wife of twenty-five years was cheating on him with a man half his age. And he was devastated. So when I started crying about suspecting Ethan was cheating on me, he told me everything. He told me where he was taking Ethan. He told me how long he was spending there. And then he told me who he was *with*. People are surprisingly lax about what they talk about in a taxi. Apparently Ethan would regularly talk about how he was going to leave me.

I'd had enough of Ethan's lies. He kept pushing the knife in over and over, twisting it each time just to make sure it cut even deeper. I'd had enough of being walked over and of him making a fool of me, thinking me to be the naïve wife sat at home alone while he shagged his mistress. I called up the driver service, asking for the same driver that filled me in on Ethan's dirty secrets and then asking him to drive me to Backdoor.

I'd been to this building before. Not inside, obviously, but I'd walked past it in daylight, staring at it, wondering how Ethan ended up in this place. There was nothing about it online. It seemed to be one of those places you hear of through a friend. I asked my agent about it, because they always know about their clients' illicit activities; after all, they need to fix it if things get leaked. I could tell she didn't want to tell me but she also didn't want me investigating myself so coughed up the details.

She said it was an exotic dance club. I asked her if that was code for a strip club but she said it wasn't quite that. She said it was something classier, more burlesque and theatre rather than women taking off their clothes and rubbing themselves on punters for money. She said it was also meant to be a private space for people of influence to get away from the crowds. She had other clients that went there, and yes, mostly it was because they were cheating on their partners. It's harder to be a cheater when you're famous, it seems. How my heart bled for those people.

I'd followed Ethan to the door of the club before. I hadn't gone in, but I'd watched out of sight as he entered. I hadn't plucked up the courage to follow him inside but that day was different because I'd heard him on the phone earlier. He always thought he was being so quiet but what he didn't realise is that I put a recording device in the bedroom. I had to get proof of what he was doing. It was mostly because I wanted to see if he was bedding her in our bedroom as I couldn't sleep on the sheets if he had, but an added benefit that I didn't think about was that it picked up his phone conversations.

I was curious and checked the recording. I found the phone call I needed. I didn't know who he was on the phone to but he mentioned Backdoor and 'wanting exclusive use of the space' for tonight for what he described as 'the date of all dates'. I knew it was with her. Tonight seemed like the best time to confront them, find the two of them together. I could record it and send it to the newspapers. Ruin his career. I'd tell them all about what Ethan Simmons is really like. I knew he had a morality clause in his contract. I bet if I told the director all about that he'd lose his starring role in his film series.

I just needed to hope that I could get into the club. I swiped Ethan's access card a few weeks ago. I found it sticking out of his jeans that he'd left crumpled on the bedroom floor while he was showering. I couldn't help myself. I hoped that if I took his access card away he'd stop going to see her and he'd come back to me. It was entertaining watching him frantically searching for it that day. Of course he couldn't ask me if I'd seen it, which made it all the funnier. I wondered if that would really be the end. But he went out again that night, and I followed him and he seemed to still be let inside so he must have gotten a replacement. But I held onto the card.

During the journey to the club I crafted a script for what I was going to say when I confronted them. Would they be in the middle of a date? Or would they be in the middle of having sex? I had no idea what I was going to walk into and I didn't know what would be harder to take. Part of me thought that watching Ethan lovingly gaze into the eyes of another woman would be far worse than anything sexual.

'Mrs, we've reached the destination,' the taxi driver announced. He had to be wondering why I was sitting here, unable to move. 'Are you alright?'

'Yes, I'm fine,' I said and took a deep breath in. I opened the door and swung my legs to step out of the car. I couldn't back out now but I couldn't fight the feeling that it would be less upsetting to stay living in ignorance, to pretend that what I knew was happening wasn't actually happening. So many people did it, especially in my industry. Image was everything to people like us, and nobody wanted to reveal their husband was cheating on them. Especially for the young starlets – they need to be seen as desirable for some stupid reason and having their partner want someone else was seen as the worst possible thing for their career.

I had to resist the urge to immediately find another car to take me back home and forget about everything. I slid my hand into my pocket, clamping my fingers around the thin plastic. *I can do this. Only a few more seconds and then it will all be over.* I needed to know the truth and I needed to confront Ethan. I needed to see his deceit with my own eyes if I was ever going to move on. It was just so hard admitting that I made a mistake, that I chose to join my life with the wrong man, the wrong person. It made me feel like a failure for entwining my life so much with someone who could be so callous and manipulative. I saw a future with this man. I wanted his children. I'd have to start again.

I reached the door. I'd watched Ethan enter there so many times and I was standing in the same spot. The access card might not even work, which would be the end of things. I placed the card on the reader and the red light turned to green. I heard the sound of a door unlocking. I placed my palms on the front door and leant into it, the door gently opening under my weight. I was in.

I'd seen the outside of the building so much but I'd never given much thought to what the inside would look like – I didn't let my mind go there. It looked like any normal swanky cocktail bar or high-end nightclub. It was eerily similar to a late-night haunt in Mayfair where I'd spent too much money on overpriced cocktails. I couldn't hear much at all. For some reason I expected to hear Ethan's voice as soon I entered but it was silent. Maybe they'd already left. Or maybe they were hidden away in a back room.

The hallway I was in eventually led to a bar area. I knew immediately that something wasn't right. It was too quiet. The place was set up for a romantic evening, a table laid out but the table was a mess. Cutlery, plates. I walked closer and saw Ethan. And her.

'Oh my god' were the only words I could muster. Of all the things I expected to see, that was not it. Ethan turned to face me, his eyes wide and his white shirt stained with blood. He was kneeling over the woman on the floor. And she had a knife protruding from her stomach.

'Is she…' I asked.

'I don't know.'

'What happened?'

'She did it to herself,' he said. 'We were fighting. She's … she's pregnant and she wanted to run away together. I didn't want to. I said I have my life with you and that she was only meant to be a fling. You have to understand, Tori, I just had a moment of weakness but it was nothing serious. And she was trying to trap me into this life I didn't want. She was hysterical, grabbed the knife and said she was going to kill herself if I didn't want her. It all happened so fast…'

'We need to call an ambulance,' I said, grabbing my phone. At that moment I didn't care about whether to believe him or the confirmation of his cheating. All I cared about was the young girl in front of me bleeding out.

'No, no.' Ethan stood quickly, grabbing my wrist. 'We can't do that.'

'Why not? She might still be alive. They could save her.'

'I'll end up being blamed for this. Nobody will believe me when I say it was self-inflicted. She used the knife I had already touched when cutting the steak so they'll say I did it. And she's pregnant with my baby.' He broke eye contact as he said it. 'So they'll say I have a motive. Don't you get it, they'll put me away for this. If the ambulance come so will the police.'

'We can't let her die.'

'She's basically already dead. We can't let her ruin everything for us.'

'For us?' I didn't understand what any of it had to do with me.

'You have more motive than me, you're the angry partner who has just discovered this girl is pregnant with your husband's baby. I'm sure they'll find a way to implicate us both. It's easier for us both if this just goes away.'

He spoke about this woman like she meant nothing to him. All he cared about was saving himself.

'I'm not going to do that, Ethan. We need to do the right thing.'

'No. We don't. You need to help me get rid of her body.'

'Why would I do that? I'm not doing that.'

'Because if you don't, I'll go the newspapers about Blair Priest.'

I winced. 'You wouldn't. You know what that would do to me.'

'Well, now you know you have as much to lose as I do. Do this thing for me and we can go back to our lives. I promise, I won't cheat again.'

He pulled me closer to him in a tight embrace. 'I love you, Tori, always have and always will.' He pulled away and I realised my blouse was now coated in blood from his shirt. 'Jeremy keeps some spare clothes round here for accidents. I'm going to find a new shirt. I can't leave here looking like this. I'll be right back.'

I noticed that he wasn't concerned about my clothes, that I would have to leave with blood on me.

I should never have come, then I wouldn't be in this situation. I waited for Ethan to come back but it was quiet, too quiet. I called out but Ethan didn't answer. I followed the direction he left in but as I got closer I realised that there was only one direction to go from there, and that was through the exit leading to the streets.

No. He couldn't have. But I already knew the answer. I rushed around, opening every door I could find but it was hopeless. Ethan was gone. He'd left me to deal with his mess while he no doubt found himself an alibi.

I heard a groan coming from the direction of the body. I hurried back.

'Please.'

She was alive.

322

NOW

Chapter Forty-Five

@THETRUTHISGREY

'So you're telling me that when you left my sister, she was alive?'

Ethan nods. 'So Tori must have finished her off.'

'You left my sister to die instead of calling the ambulance?' I can't believe what I'm hearing. Ethan isn't exactly innocent in this.

'Well, I thought she was dead. So I didn't exactly leave her to die because I thought she was already dead. There was no point calling the ambulance. The harm was already done,' Ethan says.

'Did you even check her pulse?'

'I can't remember. I must have done but maybe in the panic I couldn't find one.'

'So when did you realise my sister was alive?'

'When Tori started calling me. I didn't pick up so she texted me saying that Alice was alive. She sent me lots of texts, actually.'

'So what did you do when you found out my sister was still alive?'

He bows his head. 'Nothing. I ignored the messages.'

'Why?'

'I didn't want to deal with it. Tori's better at dealing with difficult situations than me anyway.'

'He didn't want to ruin his alibi,' Tori interjects. 'He made his way to an event he'd been invited to that he was planning to miss. Very public. He was clearly doing it so that if he was questioned about her he could say he where he was and hopefully nobody would remark on the fact he was late,' Tori says.

'Seriously?' I ask Ethan.

He shrugs. 'Look, you're focusing on the wrong thing here. The important thing is that your sister was *alive* when I left her which means I didn't kill her.'

If an ambulance had been called, the cops would have been too. But that can't have been the case because my sister was never seen again. Tori must have killed her. Maybe it was because she was a jealous wife. Or perhaps she was worried about Ethan's blackmail coming out. Or she just panicked and didn't know what else to do.

I see red and all I can think about is hurting Tori.

'Riley, you need to listen to me, okay? It's true Ethan didn't kill your sister. But I didn't either. I need you to trust me and let me tell you the rest of the story. There's a pretty important part that Ethan has conveniently left out.'

I don't know who to believe. If Tori killed Alice then she could be dangerous, and now that I'm on to her, she could kill me to make sure that the truth doesn't come out. I'm paralysed by indecision.

'I have been lying to you, Riley. I've been lying to everyone but it's for a good reason. All of it, all of this, has been to try and get Ethan to face justice for what he's done, for what he did to your sister. He's got away with so much, so much more than I ever knew, and we wanted him to have his entire life ruined just like he did to us. Everything from the moment I found Alice has been set up to culminate in this moment. The moment we destroy Ethan Simmons. This was our plan.'

'Our?' Ethan and I both ask at the same time.

'I couldn't have done all of this by myself.' Tori turns to the corner behind her. It's dark, but I can make out the shape of the back of someone's head. 'I think it's time to tell her the truth now.'

The figure stands up and walks towards me. It takes a while for my eyes to adjust but my heart stops.

'Hi, Riley.'

'Alice … You're … you're here?'

She nods. 'I never left.'

NOVEMBER 2024

Chapter Forty-Six

VICTORIA 'TORI' SIMMONS

She was alive. For a moment I hesitated over whether that was a good thing or not, before I reminded myself that of course I was glad she was alive. I didn't want her dead, even if she was having an affair with my husband.

'I'm calling an ambulance for you right away,' I said to her, not sure if she could hear me. I lied to her though; I called Jessika first and asked for her to be discreet rather than going via the emergency services route. I told her I needed an ambulance but that I didn't want it driving to the NHS hospitals, I wanted a private wing in a private hospital. Celebs did it all the time so it was not an unreasonable ask although it was usually for cosmetic procedures such as a nose job or face lift. This was a slightly different situation.

Jessika arranged it all. The ambulance arrived quickly which was lucky as Alice was unresponsive. I watched as they loaded her in and said I'd meet her at the hospital even though she probably couldn't hear me. I called Ethan straightaway to tell him she was alive but he ignored it, either sending it to voicemail or having turned his phone off. He left me to clean up his mess and didn't care that I needed help.

I caught a taxi directly to the hospital but they didn't let me see her for hours as she was in surgery. The doctors and nurses kept asking me for her identity but I couldn't help. I didn't even know her full name at that point.

It was over twenty-four hours until I was allowed to see her. The doctors assumed I was her family and if I'm honest I could see the similarities. They let me see her when she woke. There were no family members there but they didn't even have a name to work off.

Luckily they left me alone with her or things might have turned out very differently.

'Let us know if you need anything,' the nurse said before she left.

'Tori?' she said. 'What ... what's going on?' Her speech was laboured, a struggle as if she was winded after a long run. Her accent was clearly American, which was unexpected.

'Do you remember what happened? Ethan said you tried to hurt yourself.'

She attempted to move but winced in pain and gave up after several feeble attempts. Her makeup from the night before had crusted in her eyes, mascara on her upper lids and foundation settled in the corner of her nose.

'No ... Ethan ... no.'

'Try not to move. They said you need to rest.'

'No, Ethan. He ... he did this.'

'Wait,' I say, 'what did you say?'

'He tried ... to kill me. Wanted me ... gone. I'd become ... a problem.'

I needed to know more. I wanted to know what she meant. Ethan said she hurt herself, called the girl hysterical, but she was saying the opposite. I knew only one of them was telling the truth.

'That's not what he told me.'

She shook her head.

'Ethan told me that you stabbed yourself. That you were hysterical.'

'Did you … believe…?'

I didn't know what to believe. I knew my husband had a dark side. But every time he showed me his dark, monstrous side, his charismatic side would come out and make me forget about the evil.

I knew that Ethan was a monster but I never thought he'd go so far as to kill his girlfriend. She could be lying, of course. Should I trust Ethan instead? Ethan who abandoned me to leave me with his dead girlfriend. All he cared about was protecting himself.

'He's going to get what is coming to him. You have to go to the police, report the attack. I'll be a witness, ' I said.

'No.'

'Why wouldn't you tell them about Ethan?' At first I thought it was because she still loved him but when I looked closer I recognised the expression on her face and it wasn't love. It was hate.

She pointed to her bag which I'd brought to the hospital and left on the chair in the corner. I brought it over but she was too weak to properly look inside, so I picked things out until I found what she was looking for. Eventually she nodded but the object raised more questions than answers.

'Who is Tilly?'

NOW

Chapter Forty-Seven

@THETRUTHISGREY

I can't stop staring at my sister. She looks the same but in so many ways completely different. She looks hardened, her skin slightly rough, her bones more angled. Thinner. She was always slim but she's lost weight. Significantly older, even though it's not even been a year since I last saw her. Still beautiful but somehow haunted.

I don't know whether to be hurt or happy. 'You let me think you were missing all this time?' I say. 'You let our parents grieve for you! They convinced themselves you were dead. I was the only one that didn't give up hope!'

Alice hangs her head. 'I know. That part has been so difficult but I had to stay away for our plan to work.'

'Plan?' I ask.

She glances at Tori. 'I was never honest with Ethan about who I am. The truth is, I never fell in love with Ethan. I was investigating him.'

'Investigating him? You're not a cop, Alice.'

'No, I'm not. I'm a dancer, a dancer at a place full of

influential people. Influential people who have money, contacts.'

'I don't understand,' I say.

'It wasn't a coincidence that I ended up in a relationship with Ethan. I planned for it, engineered it. Spent time studying what he likes, reading everything about Tori and why he liked her. Spent ages on internet gossip sites about his rumoured affairs. I needed to get close to him.'

'And getting pregnant? Having his child? What happened to the baby?' I say. Is it possible that I have a niece or nephew all this time and I've never known?

'I was never pregnant. It was all part of the plan,' she responds.

'Alice was paid by somebody else who uses this club, somebody very prominent in the UK political system. Ethan had been having an affair with his daughter and then she went missing and they knew Ethan was a member of Backdoor. This guy had used the traditional routes to try and find out what happened to her but nothing had been done. So he got chatting to Alice one day and she offered to get close to Ethan to see if she could find out what happened,' Tori says.

'Poor guy just wanted closure. I didn't ask for money but he insisted,' my sister adds.

'What the fuck?' Ethan says. I forgot he was still here. 'You were investigating me? I don't know what you're talking about but I have nothing to do with a missing girl.'

'Her name was Matilda Green. Her father's surname is Wright,' Tori adds. 'A very senior member of the government who needed discretion. He couldn't have anybody knowing about his connection to Backdoor.'

'I don't know anyone with that name,' Ethan says but I spot the recognition in his eyes.

'She went missing last year,' Alice says. 'And her father

always thought Ethan had something to do with it but couldn't prove it.'

'Why didn't her father tell the police about Ethan?' I ask.

'He did but there was no evidence he was involved. I'm not even sure they formally interviewed him. He was never considered a suspect. Her body wasn't found and so the trail went cold. But her father was convinced. So I offered to see if I could get him to slip up and admit what he'd done.'

'You're such a bitch,' Ethan spits. 'I'm out of here.'

'Wait, I remember the Matilda Green case. The police thought she could be connected to your case but they didn't do much with that theory,' I say. 'But her body just turned up … with your passport on it?'

Ethan heads towards the door.

'You're not going anywhere. I want to hear them finish,' I say, grabbing his hand and digging my nails in.

'Of course you're also a psycho, clearly runs in the family.'

'When I was investigating Ethan, I couldn't get him to slip up about Matilda. And then he was going back to Canada for filming and I knew the trail was about to go cold. So I tried to get him to stay. I know it's a terrible thing to do to pretend to be pregnant but you have to understand we were worried if he went back to Canada I'd never find out what happened to Matilda. But obviously it backfired as Ethan was willing to get rid of me,' Alice says.

'It was after Ethan attacked her that I turned up hoping to confront them about their cheating and found Alice. I helped Alice when I realised she was alive and she told me everything at the hospital. She told me how Ethan was suspected of having something to do with Matilda's disappearance and I agreed that we would work together to take Ethan down. I wanted my revenge for how badly he's treated me and I wanted justice for the people he's hurt. He'd tried to kill Alice so there was no doubt in my mind he was capable of murder,' Tori says.

'I kept tabs on Ethan, followed him. Tried to see if he'd slip up. And for months he didn't. But then just before the trial started, he got sloppy,' Alice says.

'This is some kind of joke. None of this is true. It's all lies.'

Chapter Forty-Eight

VICTORIA 'TORI' SIMMONS

'Did you plant Alice's passport on Matilda's body? They thought she was you, Alice,' Riley says.

'Once we found the body, we planted the passport on her as another way of getting the police to link her to me. And then Tori called the police telling them about the body anonymously.'

'How do you know he killed her?' Riley asks.

'I had my PI follow him for weeks and eventually he led us to the body. He knew where it was, as if he'd visited plenty of times before. He killed her, tried to kill me and tried to kill Tori. If he'd succeeded, we would both be dead,' Alice says.

'He tried to kill Tori?' Riley asks.

'Ethan hired someone to have me killed,' I say.

'Lies,' Ethan calls. I keep forgetting he's still here.

'The only reason I'm alive is because of your sister. I had a suspicion that Ethan would be furious about me mentioning Alice at the trial, basically threatening him. I was pushing him, hoping he'd do something stupid that we could send to the police. You see, I don't think Matilda is the only person he's killed. I think Ethan has left a long line of bodies and has managed to get away with it because he hires somebody else to do his dirty work.'

'We've had a private investigator watching Ethan for some time, reporting back to us both. He told me he saw Ethan heading to Tori's house, which is where I've been living.'

'I suggested she wait outside and film him in case he incriminated himself,' I say.

'We didn't know what he would say but we knew we could use it to show people how Ethan could really be. People love a video. We were going to post it online and hope it went viral,' Alice says. 'That was the original plan and I was waiting for Ethan to be well clear before I came out of my hiding space, but then someone else came. It was a male figure, dressed all in black. I knew there was something off with him and then I watched him use a key and walk straight in. I called Tori straightaway to warn her and followed behind him.'

'I was able to get to the kitchen. Switch all the lights on and arm myself. He had a knife in his hand. A balaclava pulled over his head. Maybe the intention was to make it look like a robbery gone wrong – I don't know. But before I could think Alice appeared behind and smacked him with a plant pot she'd found near the front door. It startled him enough to make him drop the knife. He was unconscious so we tied him up. It's a good job there were two of us as we'd never have managed it otherwise. He was a big guy.'

'Tori wanted to call the police but I realised we could get creative with things. The hitman told us that Ethan had hired him and paid him £200,000 to kill Tori. Ethan gave him the keys to the house. He actually came by to the house to check she was alone.'

'Alice's idea was to pay the hitman off. It wasn't cheap, believe me. But we told him to report to Ethan that I was dead.

But then I had to disappear because we wanted Ethan to believe that he'd solved the problem. I wanted to get him arrested so the police could take his DNA. We were sure his DNA would be on Matilda or even connected to another unsolved case. There's a hidden room in the London house where Alice has been staying for the last few months. I've been hiding out there.'

'Ethan's a good actor, isn't he? You saw his reaction when Tori didn't turn up to court. I think finding out he can act was the biggest shock of all this.'

'Alice also planted the clothes I was wearing in Ethan's hotel room and then tipped them off. It was pigs' blood but it was enough to convince the police – for a while at least. They'll realise eventually.'

'We knew we could never get Ethan convicted for my murder because I wasn't actually dead, even though we knew Ethan would be sweating because he thought I was, although he knew he couldn't be linked to it as he'd hired someone to do it for him. We couldn't actually get him for Alice's disappearance either because she was alive. But there's a reason I came back today.'

'You bitch.' Ethan says. 'You realise what you've put me through? Well, what are you going to do now, huh? Clearly Alice is alive and well. God, Tori, you can't even do revenge right.' He laughs, a deep, foul laugh that makes the hair on my arms stand up.

'He's kinda right … what's your plan now? If it was to frame Ethan for murder you've done a pretty poor job,' Riley says, 'Sorry.'

'Like I said, the plan was always to get Ethan arrested so the police could get his DNA in the system but we knew there was a chance that Matilda was a contract kill and Ethan couldn't be traced to her. And then there was a fire at the DNA testing laboratory – we saw it in the news. We don't know if Ethan was behind that or if it was a lucky escape or even if Matilda's DNA was affected. But we came up with a contingency plan which we think is a better idea.'

'And what's that?' Riley asks.

'We want you to do what you do best, Riley. Let's make a video about Ethan Simmons. It's time people knew the truth.'

Riley smirks and pulls out her phone from her front pocket.

'It's a good thing that I've been livestreaming this entire time then.'

A FEW MONTHS LATER

Chapter Forty-Nine

VICTORIA 'TORI' SIMMONS

It's been a few months since Riley went live on TikTok. Ethan was arrested, this time for the murder of Matilda Green. Apparently the DNA results also came back which showed DNA matching Ethan's on Matilda's body. His DNA also matched evidence recovered in several other missing persons cases in the UK.

It turned out, after all that, Matilda died of a drug overdose. A lethal dose of heroin. The papers reported she had a problem with drugs so it was assumed the case was open and shut. Alice doesn't agree though; she thinks Ethan was still behind it, injected her himself. I don't know what to think.

Ethan has been 'cancelled' according to social media. Everything worked just like it was supposed to. Ethan is no longer celebrated and looked up to as some sort of idol. He's a pariah. Thanks to Riley's large following the news went viral pretty quickly.

Unfortunately Ethan never ended up getting charged in relation to any of the disappearances. Apparently all of the evidence was too circumstantial but everybody knows what we always suspected – that Ethan was involved in these disappearances. I did tell the police about the attempted murder of me, but with the hitman unable to be located, there's nothing to prove that Ethan paid somebody to kill me. I did get briefly arrested for cleaning up Alice's crime scene and obstruction of justice for hiding her while she was a missing person. Thankfully they dropped the charge.

Ethan has left the country, as far as I know. He was getting hounded. I think somebody actually threw eggs at him at one point. He was getting death threats and I'm sure he knew it was only a matter of time before the police gathered enough evidence to put him away for good. I don't know where he's gone. There are constant rumours and reports but nothing concrete. It makes me angry that he's managed to get away with everything. The only thing he's lost is his fame. The worst part is that he is free to carry on hurting people.

Riley's livestream led to other women coming forward who had met Ethan and fallen under his spell. It turns out he'd cheated on me even more than I could have ever imagined. I don't think Ethan ever stopped living the life of a single man; it didn't matter that he married me. Vows meant nothing to him, clearly. And he blackmailed all of them into staying silent. He had different methods of doing it, apparently. Now I hope that no woman will go near him ever again. But I can't help but think about what he did to the ones that couldn't be blackmailed.

We couldn't have done it without Riley's help. Our anonymous TikTok account was created with the sole aim of getting her to England to help with our fight. I feel bad she had to be kept in the dark for so long about Alice, but it seemed like the only way. We couldn't tell her everything until we were ready.

Faye tells me that the case Ethan brought against me has

officially been dropped so I don't need to worry about being carted back to court. I'll be happy to never see the inside of a courtroom again.

Alice and Riley have gone back to America. They said there are too many bad memories here and I don't blame them. They keep in touch regularly though and I know they are working on trying to locate Ethan. They're also interviewing anyone that Ethan blackmailed to try and build up a dossier of evidence. I know they won't stop. It becomes personal when somebody tries to kill you.

We're getting a divorce and I'm free to start again. Ethan isn't around to fill in the paperwork but my legal team is exploring ways of getting the divorce through. Maybe I can finally find someone who is happy with being only with me. Maybe I can be enough for someone? It doesn't help that my name has been in the press for so long that I worry nobody will go near me. But maybe, eventually, I can go back to being a noughties pop star and the only time people will mention my name is in connection with their favourite pop hit. My label offered to re-sign me but I declined. I don't want to do something I never had any talent for. I told them to sign Blair instead and she's been doing incredibly. I heard her first single last week and I can tell it's going to top the charts.

Maybe one day Ethan will face justice, but for now, I'm just glad he's out of my life.

Chapter Fifty

ETHAN SIMMONS

Moving to Australia has been good for me. I'm trying to put my previous life behind me. I have a bit more anonymity here. I've really leant into the culture. I've taken up surfing, had my hair coloured, managed to get a tan.

I'm enjoying not having the media chasing me around constantly. I'm enjoying this anonymous life. I sometimes miss the fame and adoring fans but I can't go back to that now. At one point I thought I was going to jail. I've managed to dodge that bullet twice but I don't want another brush with the law. As long as nobody knows who I am, I hope to live out my life in peace. I'm working at a local bar at the moment to earn enough money to live on. I've not been accessing my bank accounts, so as to keep my life offline. I don't want anybody knowing where I am. There's something gloriously normal and mundane about having a job that gives me a thrill.

Sometimes I check up on Tori online. I say 'sometimes'; it's the first thing I do when I wake up. But I resist messaging her. Even after everything she did to me, it still hurts to let her go. She's the only woman I've ever truly loved.

I pull on some shorts and slip into a white polo. The evening sun is already burning through the window of my rented flat. The landlord lets me pay in cash and doesn't ask too many questions, which suits me fine. I grab my backpack and head to the bar. I'm the first one to arrive other than the manager. She tells me to start unloading today's delivery while she deals with some admin in her office. I pour myself a glass of whiskey as I always do to start the evening. I leave it on the bar as I kneel down and start opening the boxes stacked on the ground to see what stock we have in.

The door swings open.

'We're closed,' I call, not looking up from the inventory I'm trying to sort.

'I'm looking for someone.'

I freeze. I recognise that voice.

'His name is Ethan Simmons.' The voice gets closer. I glance up and notice her face peering down at me from the bar. 'Do you know where I might find him?' She grins.

'Alice. What are you doing here? How did you find me?'

Even if she worked out I was in Australia, how did she find this suburb? How did she find this bar?

'You were in the background of a photo the bar put on its Instagram. Someone sent it to my sister and asked her to report on your whereabouts on her channel. I wanted to come check if it was really you.'

I take a swig of my glass of whiskey, my throat suddenly like sandpaper.

I forgot that Alice's sister is a TikTok celebrity. I did watch the videos she made about me, out of curiosity. After the TikTok went viral, Riley's account blew up. She had over two million followers last time that I checked. That's the thing with being famous, people will do anything to have a slice of your fame, and if it means sending in tips and photos just to feel like they're part of your world, people will latch onto anything they can. I should have known I wasn't safe.

'But why? You need to leave me alone.' I can't stay here now she knows where I am. Alice will seemingly stop at nothing until I'm behind bars. Alice started this when she agreed to investigate me. And I know that it was her and Tori behind all the evidence they used to frame me but it must have been Alice at the forefront. It was Alice's phone, Alice's jacket and Alice's passport. My wife is not a mastermind but I always knew Alice is smarter than she looks.

I glance towards the door where I know my manager's office is located. She always wears headphones when she does admin so I doubt she could hear if I called out. Alice has tracked me down and every part of me knows it isn't for anything positive. The look in her eyes scares me. I back into the bar, my hands searching for a weapon in case I need to use it.

'I wanted to talk to you.'

'What about?'

'About what you did to me.'

'What I did to you?'

'Yes.'

'I'm sorry, okay, but I never tried to kill you. It was an accident, we knocked into the table and that knife just fell into your stomach. I panicked and didn't know what to do. I don't know why you told Tori that I tried to kill you.'

'What you did to me was as bad as killing me. You left me for dead. And I'm sure you did the same to Matilda and other girls.'

'Matilda died of a drug overdose, you know this.'

'I'm sure you, or someone you paid, administered it. Did she lie dying and you ran away like you always do?'

I run my hands down my face. 'I can be a dickhead

sometimes but I'm not a killer. Yes, I cheated a lot. Yes, I used a lot of women and blackmailed them into staying quiet. But I never hurt any of them. I didn't hire a killer to kill Tori either. Threatened her, yes, but I didn't want her dead.'

Alice smirks. 'You didn't hire anyone. But that's not what I paid him to tell Tori. She was starting to question what we were doing so I needed to put her back on the right track with a bit of motivation. You might not be a killer but you're still a bad person. You'll find another woman here and break her heart or threaten her or maybe even worse.'

'No. I won't. I'm trying to turn over a new leaf. Things are different now. Is that why you've come here? Are you on some crusade to stop men screwing over women?'

'You don't get it, Ethan. You're not going to stop. You're never going to stop hurting women because it's who you are. It's part of you. You are a bad guy.'

I shrug. 'Okay. I'm a bad guy. Now, if you'll excuse me, I have to go back to work.' I take another sip of my drink.

'You should really watch your drink. That's what they tell us girls. Make sure you never let your drink out of your sight in case somebody spikes it. Wouldn't it be a shame if someone took advantage of you for once?'

'You are actually insane.'

And then she leaves. And I'm left to wonder if she put something in my drink or if it's another game of hers. I pour the whiskey out, inspecting the glass, looking for a telltale sign that she put something in it. I would have known, right? I'd know if she tampered with my drink. But now I can't think straight and my head feels like it's on fire. Everything is becoming blurry and I feel faint. I fall to the ground on my knees, my hands covered in the whiskey I tipped out. I lie down waiting for something to happen but it doesn't. I'm fine.

It was just a false alarm. And then my phone flashes with a photo she's airdropped me. It's a black screen with text.

One wrong move and next time I'll finish the job.

Acknowledgments

Writing a book is hard, but sometimes I think writing acknowledgements is even harder. It's a real task to remember everyone I want to thank. I want to start off by thanking you, the reader: anyone that read my first book, *The Clique*, and is now here because they enjoyed it; anybody that championed my first book and anybody who has just discovered me as an author. I've always thought of myself as a reader first and a writer second. I love nothing more than reading, and it makes my day when people tell me they love my writing. A big thank you to every single book blogger who has spread the word about my books – you mean the world to me.

I have to thank my incredible agent, Rachel Neely at Mushens Entertainment. She always knows the right thing to say and is my greatest support.

Thanks also to my editor, Jennie Rothwell at One More Chapter. As soon as I pitched this idea to Jennie, she was on board with it. Trying to combine a celebrity defamation trial with a thriller was not the easiest of tasks but I think we pulled it off.

I'd also like to thank the entire One More Chapter team for their help producing the book, and a special shout out to Kara Daniel for deciphering my handwriting.

I am so grateful to all the authors that helped support my first book, and all the authors that have supported me since. I need to give a special mention to G D Wright who I was honoured to share a publication day with last year and who has been the biggest support. I am also eternally thankful to Lauren North for her constant help.

Thank you to all my friends who bought my first book and continue to support my writing. A special thank you to Maria for buying five copies of my first book, and to Sohail for getting me to sign my first book and treating it like his most prized possession.

As I write this, I'm about to marry my fiancé Tom. Thank you to my almost husband for always reading my books, especially when they are the only books you read. Thank you for understanding when I can't spend time with you because I'm always writing.

The author and One More Chapter would like to thank everyone who contributed to the publication of this story...

Analytics
Abigail Fryer

Audio
Fionnuala Barrett
Ciara Briggs

Contracts
Laura Amos
Inigo Vyvyan

Design
Lucy Bennett
Fiona Greenway
Liane Payne
Dean Russell

Digital Sales
Laura Daley
Lydia Grainge
Hannah Lismore

eCommerce
Laura Carpenter
Madeline ODonovan
Charlotte Stevens
Christina Storey
Jo Surman
Rachel Ward

Editorial
Kara Daniel
Charlotte Ledger
Federica Leonardis
Jennie Rothwell
Tony Russell
Sofia Salazar Studer
Helen Williams

Harper360
Emily Gerbner
Ariana Juarez
Jean Marie Kelly
emma sullivan
Sophia Wilhelm

International Sales
Peter Borcsok
Ruth Burrow
Colleen Simpson
Ben Wright

Inventory
Sarah Callaghan
Kirsty Norman

Marketing & Publicity
Chloe Cummings
Grace Edwards

Operations
Melissa Okusanya
Hannah Stamp

Production
Denis Manson
Simon Moore
Francesca Tuzzeo

Rights
Ashton Mucha
Alisah Saghir
Zoe Shine
Aisling Smyth
Lucy Vanderbilt

Trade Marketing
Ben Hurd
Eleanor Slater

The HarperCollins Distribution Team

The HarperCollins Finance & Royalties Team

The HarperCollins Legal Team

The HarperCollins Technology Team

UK Sales
Isabel Coburn
Jay Cochrane
Sabina Lewis
Holly Martin
Harriet Williams
Leah Woods

And every other essential link in the chain from delivery drivers to booksellers to librarians and beyond!

Don't miss *The Clique* by Rhiannon Barnsley, an intoxicating psychological thriller with unexpected twists

There's only one way to join their society. If someone leaves, or dies…

High-flying lawyer Sara O'Neil had it all; the career, the money, the prestige.

And then she jumped to her death.

Cassandra Harlow never expected to see her friend fall from their office rooftop. Someone knows what really happened. But the only people who might know the truth are a secret women-only society, Inside, whose promise is to fast-track your career.

But if Sara was part of it and they helped facilitate her rise to the top, could they also be the reason she came crashing down to earth?

Available now in paperback, ebook and audio!

ONE MORE CHAPTER

One More Chapter is an
award-winning global
division of HarperCollins.

Subscribe to our newsletter to get our
latest eBook deals and stay up to date
with all our new releases!

signup.harpercollins.co.uk/
join/signup-omc

Meet the team at
www.onemorechapter.com

Follow us!
 @OneMoreChapter_
 @onemorechapterhc
 @onemorechapterhc
 @onemorechapterhc

Do you write unputdownable fiction?
We love to hear from new voices.
Find out how to submit your novel at
www.onemorechapter.com/submissions